Freeman Wills Crofts w... died in 1957. He worked... company as an engineer... detective fiction.

His plots reveal his mathematical training and he specialised in the seemingly unbreakable alibi and the intricacies of railway timetables. He also loved ships and trains and they feature in many of his stories.

Crofts' best-known character is Inspector Joseph French. French appears for the first time in *Inspector French's Greatest Case*. He is a detective who achieves his results through dogged persistence.

Raymond Chandler praised Crofts' plots, calling him 'the soundest builder of them all'.

BY THE SAME AUTHOR
ALL PUBLISHED BY HOUSE OF STRATUS

FREEMAN WILLS CROFTS

Sudden Death

1932

HOUSE OF
STRATUS

This edition published in 2000 by House of Stratus, an imprint of Stratus Holdings plc, 24c Old Burlington Street, London, W1X 1RL, UK.

www.houseofstratus.com

Typeset, printed and bound by House of Stratus.

A catalogue record for this book is available from the British Library.

ISBN 1-84232-414-4

CONTENTS

PART 1

As Anne Day Saw It

SATISFACTION

No one would have thought from Anne Day's appearance, as she sat with closed eyes in the corner of her third-class carriage, that her mind was seething with a delicious excitement. But seething was a mild description of the turmoil that was in process therein. For this commonplace little journey which she was making down into Kent was one of the great events of her life. It was the opening, so she fondly allowed herself to hope, of a new and happier chapter in her fortunes, a turn for the better long, very long, overdue.

For life had not recently smiled on Anne Day. Alone, out of work, and with her little balance dwindling at an appalling rate, she had for eleven weary months fought a losing battle with the devils of panic and despair.

Anne was an only child and an orphan. Her mother died when she was twelve, and from then till his death ten years later she had kept house for her father in the old Gloucester parsonage. The Reverend Latimer Day was a scholar and a recluse, a brilliant thinker, but out of touch with the world, and therefore out of touch with its material rewards. At his death Anne had found herself homeless and with an income of barely thirty pounds a year. Her friends in the parish had been kind, but she could not stay with them forever, and three weeks after the funeral, with seventy pounds, the proceeds of the auction, she had left the district to try her fortunes in London.

Fate at first had been kind to her. After only a fortnight's search she had found a job as companion to an old lady. Mrs Hume was kind and soon treated Anne like a daughter, but she was poor, and could not pay enough to enable Anne to save. For six years Anne had remained there, happy indeed in a way, but in spite of all her efforts, unable to better her position. Then Mrs Hume had died, and at eight-and-twenty Anne had found herself once more on the world.

She had no special qualifications. Though she had acted as secretary to her father in his research for a critical work on the Pentateuch, she had not the necessary training for a business career. Nor had she any degrees or diplomas which might have helped her to get a post as a teacher.

Life, indeed, became very hard for her. For eleven terrible months she had haunted registry offices and searched the files of papers in the public libraries, while shoes and gloves, and latterly even food and lodging had grown more and more hideously insistent problems. In spite of it all she could hear of few suitable jobs, and such as did materialise were snapped up by young women with better clothes or qualifications. For many weeks she had had her name down for domestic service, but none of the mistresses she could easily have served would take her without previous references, and those who overlooked this formality were of a type with which she vowed only hunger itself would force her in contact.

And then, just as she had decided to take a position as scullery maid in a large house, this job had turned up, this job to which she was now travelling. When on her weary round she had for the hundredth time asked at the desk at

Mrs Allsopp's registry office the question from which hope had well-nigh departed, the marvel had happened. Instead of the shake of the head and the perfunctory, "Nothing yet, I'm afraid, Miss Day," to which she had grown so sadly accustomed, she had been told to wait. Ten minutes later she had been called into Mrs Allsopp's room, and there the marvel had become a miracle.

A tall, well-built, well-dressed man with strong features sat facing Mrs Allsopp. Anne was presented, or rather indicated. Mr Grinsmead was polite. He got up, smiled, and held out his hand as if Anne really was a human being and not the piece of furniture Mrs Allsopp so evidently considered her. Then briefly he stated his business. He wanted a housekeeper. His wife was a semi-invalid and the strain of running things had become too much for her. He wanted someone to relieve her of it. But a mere house-keeper was not enough. He wanted a lady of tact who, while competent to manage everything on her own responsibility, would yet defer to his wife and carry out any directions she might choose to give.

"I wish her to be pleased and humoured," he said. "If her desires run counter to what you consider the best way of doing things, you must give way, or at least make her believe you do. I don't want anyone who will take up the position, 'Well, I'm responsible for this and I must do it my way or not at all.' You follow me, Miss Day? The actual efficiency of the household management is of less importance than the pleasing of Mrs Grinsmead."

Anne agreed eagerly. Mr Grinsmead nodded slowly and went on.

"Now the question is whether you could manage the work. Mrs Allsopp tells me that you kept house for many years for your father, but it is possible that we may, for instance, do more entertaining than your father. Perhaps you would tell me something about your experience in that way."

Equally eagerly Anne explained. There had been clerical lunches, church functions involving entertainment at the parsonage, visits of professors and others interested in the early books of the Bible. She was sure she could do what was required.

Again Grinsmead nodded. His household consisted of his wife, two small children, the governess, two servants, and the gardener-chauffeur. She thought she could do it?

She was sure of it.

Very well. So far as he could see, she would suit admirably. But he couldn't definitely offer her the position. Would she come down on a month's probation?

Would she go down? Anne laughed to herself at the question. Did this clever, successful-looking man know that her worldly assets amounted to just four pounds, seventeen shillings and threepence halfpenny? Yes, she would go down; as soon as he wanted her; and she hoped his wife would find her suitable. At all events she would do her very best to please. She did not try to bargain. She did not even ask the salary. Things had gone too far for that. Her voice was sharply eager as she asked where she was to go, and when.

She had almost been overcome by what followed. For a moment the man had looked at her fixedly, then he had taken notes for five pounds from his pocket and handed them over.

"An advance on your salary," he had said. "You may want to get a few things. Besides, there is the fare down. I live near Ashbridge. Will you come down tomorrow by the train leaving Victoria at 3.45? The car will meet you and take you out to Frayle."

She had bought the few things and caught her train by a margin of nearly an hour.

A job! Surely with a month's opportunity to show what she could do, she would be certain to retain it? A congenial job, moreover, with congenial people! She could not bring herself to conceive of them as otherwise. For Mr Grinsmead – he had given his name as Severus Grinsmead – had said that she was to live with them as one of the family. And with a good salary; one hundred and twenty pounds a year and all found: twice, more than twice, what she would thankfully have accepted! As she compared her present outlook with that of only yesterday morning, she felt overwhelmed with thankfulness and joy.

Yet it remained true that had she known all that awaited her at Ashbridge, she might well have drawn back in dismay, preferring the known humiliations of the scullery maid's job to the agonies of fear and horror and suspense which she was fated to endure with the Grinsmeads.

No one could have called Anne beautiful. She was small with a rather squat figure, an undoubted snub nose and a mouth of generous proportions. But truth and honesty shone in her grey eyes and her firm chin showed courage and determination. No fool, Anne looked, but a capable and reliable young woman, a good friend and an ally worth having in a tight corner.

As the brakes grated on the wheels she opened her eyes and looked around. This surely must be Ashbridge. Her heart beat a little quicker as she stood up to collect her meagre belongings, the cheap cloak bought among other things out of the nine pounds seventeen shillings and three pence halfpenny to which Mr Grinsmead's advance had raised her capital, the old-fashioned solid leather port-manteau which had been her father's, the five-shilling umbrella which she had so long coveted. A poor collection, yet in spite of it and of her dumpy figure and thumping heart, she had an air which made the chauffeur who presently came up to her as she was standing on the platform, touch his hat respectfully.

"For Mr Grinsmead's, miss?" He was a youngish man, pleasant enough looking, dressed in a neat dark blue uniform, and with a soft intonation suggestive of the West Country. Anne at once took to him. She felt suddenly com-forted. This pleasant beginning to her job was surely a good omen.

"It's about two miles out, miss," the man went on as he picked up the portmanteau. "Very nice country."

"It looks lovely, as far as I could see from the train," Anne agreed. "I've never been here before."

"No, miss? I'm sure you'll like it." He held open the door of a large blue car, shut Anne carefully in, and mounted the front seat. The car rolled smoothly off.

Anne was too much excited to observe her surroundings in any detail. Dimly she was conscious of passing through a pleasant looking Town with good shops, and out into undulating, well-wooded country. The contrast between yesterday's weary, hopeless trail through the pitiless London streets and being borne thus luxuriously through this beautiful country, filled her mind too poignantly for observation. What a change in her fortunes! Oh, that she might not fail, was the burden of her thought! That she might please these Grinsmeads and be kept on! She clenched her hands in the intensity of her desire.

The two miles passed before she was well aware that they had left the Town, and slackening speed, the car swung through an ornate gateway. A little plate, fixed to the gate, bore in ornamental letters the name "Frayle." The drive curved past masses of rhododendrons to a fair-sized house. This was evidently quite modern, being built like thousands of others with the lower storey of brownish purple bricks, and the upper storey and roof covered with "antique" reddish brown tiles, and with long, low, lead-lighted windows. Behind were trees, some fine beeches and sycamores. Anne glimpsed a brightly coloured garden at one side of the house and a tennis court at the other as she passed from the car to the porch.

The door was opened by a slightly unpleasant looking maid, who took Anne's portmanteau from the chauffeur. "I'm Gladys, miss," she said civilly enough. "I'll show you your room, and when you are ready Mrs Grinsmead would like you to have tea with her."

"Thank you," Anne smiled, as she followed the girl into the hall. "What a delightful country this is. I've never been here before, and after London it looks heavenly."

Gladys admitted briefly that the country was "naice" and led the way upstairs. The house, from the glimpses Anne had got so far, was well but plainly furnished, the house of a successful though not exactly wealthy man. It seemed of comfortable size, neither cramped not yet in any sense a mansion. Gladys threw open a door not far from the head of the stairs and led the way in.

Anne could scarcely refrain from a cry of delight as she saw what was to be her room. It was not large, but it was delightfully arranged as a bed-sitting room. A luxurious looking divan was evidently the disguised bed, while a kind of davenport became, when the lid was lifted, a basin with running hot and cold water. There were comfortable armchairs, a couple of little tables, two large built-in wardrobes, a cheery wallpaper and pretty curtains and furnishings. But the glory of the room was its window, a large square bow with an enclosed window seat. Anne hurried across the room and gazed out.

The outlook seemed to be west: it was at the side of the house overlooking the garden and the sun was shining on the angle between it and the front. Anne experienced another little thrill of delight as she saw the garden. She was passionately fond of flowers, and here were flowers in gorgeous profusion. Immediately below, along the side of the house, was a narrow plot of well-kept grass. Then came some herbaceous borders, masses of red and yellow and blue. Behind was a rose pergola, a blaze of colour, with at one side a small pool and rock garden. Beyond, towards the back of the garden were the beeches, while in front were open views over the rolling, well-wooded country.

"How lovely!" Anne cried.

"Very naice view, miss," Gladys answered. "If you'll please ring when you're ready, I'll show you the drawing-room."

She withdrew silently, and Anne, brought back to earth, hastened to make her toilet. She wondered if she was the first housekeeper to occupy this charming room, or whether she was just one of a succession. She felt almost frightened as she thought of her luck. The large salary, this delightful room, the respectful air of the servants, the life as a member of the family, the pleasant master of the house: was it not too much? Anne's experience of life had been that such perfection simply did not exist. Against it all must there not be some horrid crab?

Perhaps, she imagined, the drawback might be Mrs Grinsmead's personality. And when a few minutes later she was ushered into the drawing-room, she felt that this might indeed prove to be the truth.

The drawing-room occupied the front corner of the house on the opposite side to Anne's room. It was a good-sized, but rather badly proportioned room, with two bow windows. The furniture was expensive, but with the exception of the carpet, not quite to Anne's taste. Anne at once lost her heart to the carpet, a gorgeous carpet, thick and soft to the feet, and bearing conventional Chinese flowers in dead gold on the most vivid of blue backgrounds. But the other things she thought were pretentious rather than comfortable. She noticed with pleasure, however, that there were books in plenty both on shelves and lying about, and, being musical, she thrilled at the sight of the superb grand piano.

In the smaller of the two bow windows sat the mistress of the house. Sybil Grinsmead was tall and fair and washed-out looking. Her hair was light without being golden, her eyes a watery blue, and her features aristocratic, though slightly indeterminate. She was thin and unhealthily pallid, languid and evidently wanting in grip. Her dress was expensive looking, but a little untidy, as if she lacked the energy necessary for the small finishing touches which make the difference between being well and indifferently gowned. She was lying back in an easy-chair, a novel on her knee, and beside her a tea tray on which an electric kettle sang lustily. She rose as Anne entered and came forward with a faint smile.

"How d'you do?" she said apathetically, holding out a flabby hand. "Won't you sit down? You're ready for tea after your journey?"

Judging from what she had heard from others in positions similar to her own, Anne had reason to be pleased with her reception. And yet, though Mrs Grinsmead's manner was perfectly courteous, it left Anne vaguely dissatisfied. There was no pretence of even ordinary cordiality behind the words, such as had been shown by the other members of the household with whom she had come in contact. Of course in a way Anne could not expect cordiality, but there was not even that quality of manner which passes for cordiality in the ordinary relations of life. Mrs Grinsmead seemed absolutely uninterested in Anne's arrival; as if it were just the same to her whether Anne came or stayed away. Anne, of course, expected no interest for her own sake, but as the woman's future deputy in the control of the household, she was surprised at being taken so casually.

During tea Mrs Grinsmead talked carelessly on a variety of subjects, all of which Anne noticed with some bewilderment had one peculiarity in common. With the exception of a perfunctory reference to Anne's journey, every remark that the lady made was impersonal. Politics, travel, art, the country: yes. Anne Day, Sybil Grinsmead, or Sybil Grinsmead's household: no. She did not then, nor did she till a long time after, ask Anne anything about herself; not even about her previous experience. Strangers they met, strangers they remained.

It is true that after the tea things had been removed she did turn to business.

"Mr Grinsmead no doubt told you that you would have full charge and control of the household," she began. "I don't know if he gave you any details?"

"He said I should have to take charge under your instructions. Beyond mentioning what the household consisted of, he told me nothing."

"Quite so." An ordinary reply, and yet Anne felt vaguely disquieted with it. Mrs Grinsmead's voice had a sort of mocking intonation, a dry scepticism which with a little more energy would have been sardonic. There was a slight pause, then the lady continued: "I shan't interfere much. If you can satisfy Mr Grinsmead, you'll probably satisfy me. I shall give you full control, you do what you think is best, and if either of us don't like the result you'll hear about it." A slight smile robbed the words of any harshness. "Did Mr Grinsmead tell you I should want you to give me a little personal help as well?"

Anne shook her head. "He didn't actually say so, but of course I shall be only too glad to do anything I can."

Mrs Grinsmead looked at her keenly. "It's very little," she said, "just to write a few letters occasionally. Invitations when we have people and that sort of thing."

"That's nothing, Mrs Grinsmead. Of course I'll do it. I did all my late father's secretarial work, and though I'm not a trained secretary, I know a good deal about it."

Mrs Grinsmead did not ask what kind of work the late Mr Day had required. She repeated, "Quite so" rather coldly and went on with her exposition.

"You will have the whole of your time to yourself, consistent with seeing that household matters are properly conducted. If you are a golfer there is no reason why you shouldn't join the club. You will be expected to have your meals with us, and I should like you to sit with me here in the evenings. Of course if on any special occasion you want to go out or to sit in your room, you are free to do so. Subject, as I say, to obliging me occasionally on special points and under special circumstances, you can do as you like."

Anne was really grateful, and said so.

"I hope you are a bridge player," Mrs Grinsmead continued. "I get tired in the evenings, and when we have people in I should be glad if you could take my place so that I could go to bed without breaking up the game."

"I play," said Anne, "but I'm afraid I'm not very good."

"Like Miss Cheame. Miss Cheame is the governess. She also plays, but is not very good. Perhaps a little practice may help you. She doesn't seem able to improve."

There was a pause and then Anne said with a little hesitation how much she liked her room and how beautiful she thought the garden.

"You're fond of gardening?"

Anne was intensely fond of gardening.

"Well, make friends with Hersey and go and work there as much as you like. It's supposed to be our garden, but it's really Hersey's. That's the worst of these professional gardeners. They think the whole place belongs to them, and sooner or later it does."

"Is Hersey also the chauffeur?"

"Yes. He's supposed to be a good all-round man, but he's a better gardener than a chauffeur, I should say. Now you had better see the servants. Just ring the bell, will you, please?"

Gladys answered and was sent for Meakin, the cook. Both were then formally introduced to Anne, who greeted them pleasantly, shaking hands. On a second inspection Gladys seemed less objectionable than Anne had first thought her. She was a young woman, probably in the late twenties, with a rather sulky, bad-tempered expression, but her face was honest and dependable. Not attractive, but one whose bark would be worse than her bite, Anne thought. To Mrs Meakin, on the other hand, Anne took instinctively. She seemed about fifty, and looked a woman who, after passing through deep waters, had reached peace and a certain quiet happiness. Kindliness, sympathy, decency in the best sense and a quiet strength radiated from her, and Anne could have sworn that she was neither incompetent nor in any sense a fool. A woman who, no matter in what station of life, would be worth having as a friend.

Mrs Grinsmead's voice broke into Anne's reverie.

"I wanted to tell you both that Miss Day will act for me, and you will take her instructions as you would mine. I shall expect you both to help her in every way you can. You would like to see the house, wouldn't you, Miss Day? Meakin will show you the kitchen and then Gladys will take you through the rooms. I'll see you again later about the household books."

When Anne had completed her tour of inspection she found herself more pleased with the house than she had expected. Downstairs the accommodation – service rooms, dining-room, study and morning-room – was ordinary, though good of its kind. Upstairs there was more approach to luxury. There were two spare rooms, each with bathroom attached. Mr and Mrs Grinsmead occupied separate bed-rooms, each again with its private bathroom. In the other rooms, her own, Miss Cheame's, the night nursery, and the servants' rooms, there was running water. The day nursery was a delightful room, not very large, but light and airy and full of toys. Anne was struck by the decoration. It was all very light in colour, particularly upstairs. The bedrooms were papered in light shades, while the landing was done in pale cream, with white enamelled doors and woodwork.

Anne made it a point to talk pleasantly to Gladys while she was being taken round, and the girl thawed somewhat. Altogether Anne thought that if she had had her pick of all the jobs she had ever heard of, she could not have chosen one which would have more exactly suited her.

She went out to the garden, revelling in the flowers, until it was time to dress for the seven-thirty dinner.

2

DOUBT

The governess and children were out when Anne was going over the house, so she had not seen them. But when she came down to the drawing-room shortly before half-past seven, Miss Cheame was there alone.

Edith Cheame was a rather ordinary looking young woman, occupying what might be called the middle range in attributes. She was neither tall nor short, stout nor thin, fair nor dark. Nor could she be described as either beautiful or ugly. In fact, she was of an average type, not unlike hundreds of thousands of other young women of the same age and station. But she looked intelligent and she had an air of leisurely competence calculated to induce reliance on her ability to handle any situation with which she might be confronted. Her expression was neither pleasant nor unpleasant, but she smiled as she rose and came forward to Anne.

"Miss Day, isn't it?" she said in a deep contralto voice. "I am Miss Cheame, the governess. Have you just arrived?"

"A couple of hours ago, and already I've fallen in love with the country and the garden, but particularly the garden."

"I did just the same. It seemed such a marvellous change from London. I'd been living there for some time."

"So have I been," Anne said ruefully, "for nearly seven years. Ever since I left home near Gloucester."

They talked of the West Country. Edith Cheame had been at Cheltenham and Evesham, and had loved it.

Presently the door opened and Mr Grinsmead entered.

He was one of those men, Anne thought instantly, who does not look his best in evening dress. He somehow seemed too big, too forceful, not to say too brutal for fine clothes. Tweeds and plus fours would better have fitted his personality. He had a trick of poking forward his head as if he were preparing to drive his great shoulders on through all obstacles. He came forward to Anne, hand extended, and smiling pleasantly enough.

"Well, Miss Day, so you've got here all right? That's good. And how do you like the country?"

"Lovely! A lovely country and such a garden! I was just saying to Miss Cheame how much I admired the garden."

"Very glad if you'll take an interest in it. Mrs Grinsmead doesn't care for anything but the finished product and I haven't time to worry with it."

"Oh, Mr Grinsmead, how kind of you! I'd love to work in it."

Mr Grinsmead began a reply, then broke off abruptly and rose to his feet. Mrs Grinsmead had swept into the room. She looked well in evening dress, better and brighter than in the afternoon.

"Dinner's ready," she announced. "I met Gladys coming to tell us. Will you come in?"

She led the way to a second door in the back wall of the room. As she reached it it was opened by Gladys, and she passed through, followed by the others.

For some time they continued to discuss gardening, then the talk turned to local personalities, and Anne perforce sat silent. Occasionally Mrs Grinsmead made a perfunctory but unsuccessful effort to include her in the conversation. Anne sat listening with a good deal of interest. She was surprised to discover how much one of the family Miss Cheame seemed to be. She had evidently been with the Grinsmeads for a considerable time. She seemed to know all their friends, and discussed them as if they were her own. Mr Grinsmead in particular spoke to her as if she were a relation. Mrs Grinsmead, however, was not so cordial.

Mrs Grinsmead's manner, indeed, caused Anne a growing surprise. At first she had thought that between her three companions the best of good fellowship obtained. As the meal progressed she became less certain. She found herself wondering if all was quite so happy and light-hearted as she had imagined. Instinctively she began to sense an undercurrent of strain in the atmosphere, and for this she became increasingly sure Mrs Grinsmead was responsible. But it was all very vague; she was unable to put her finger on any definite word or action to which exception could be taken.

"What about some bridge?" Mrs Grinsmead suggested when dessert was over. "Are you too tired, Miss Day?"

Anne was not the least tired, but she said again that she was not much of a player.

"I expect what you want is practice. Let us have a rubber. We may go now; the coffee will come to the drawing-room."

If Anne did not acquit herself with glory, she at least did not cover herself with shame. They played three rubbers, and then Mrs Grinsmead said she was tired and would go to bed.

"After breakfast tomorrow if you'll come to my room I'll show you the household books and then you can take over," she said to Anne; "till then don't trouble about anything. Good night. Good night, Miss Cheame."

She disappeared, and as she did so Anne felt the strain go out of the atmosphere. So then it was Mrs Grinsmead. Whatever of unrest or anxiety there was in her mind came out, probably quite involuntarily, but quite unmistakably. Anne wondered what could be wrong.

Mrs Grinsmead's retirement broke up the party. With an apology that he had some work to attend to Grinsmead betook himself to his study. Edith Cheame chatted for a moment, then in a marked way took up and opened a novel. Whereupon Anne said she would like to get her unpacking done and excused herself.

Anne was too much excited to sleep for some time after she got into bed. Her mind was full of the most profound thankfulness for the change which had come over her fortunes.

A pleasant household, this, she had entered. And yet she could not but feel that there was something wrong. She reviewed her evening, wondering just what had given her that feeling of strain. As she did so, one rather interesting fact gradually emerged. She could not remember a single occasion on which Grinsmead, or Mrs Grinsmead, had spoken directly to one another. Nor had she seen them exchange glances or show any of the little signs of intimacy so usual between married persons. Their communications had been strictly impersonal, and had invariably been made through one or other of their employees, for so she and Miss Cheame were. And now that she came to think of it, Mrs Grinsmead had bidden her and the governess good-night, but she had not spoken to her husband. At the time

Anne had thought nothing of this, assuming that they would meet again later, but now she remembered they occupied separate rooms and might not.

Was this marriage one of those unhappy failures which seem so common nowadays? Anne wondered.

She wondered also what part in the establishment Miss Cheame really bore. That the lady was familiar with both husband and wife was evident. Did she know and ignore what Anne suspected?

As her interest in the situation grew, Anne warned herself to be careful. Her employers' relations were nothing to her. What she had to do was to mind her own business and concentrate on her work.

Suddenly it occurred to her that she mustn't do too well in her work. If Mrs Grinsmead had been making a hash of it, she mustn't pull it straight too quickly. The lady wouldn't appreciate too glaring a commentary on her own administration. No, Anne would have to walk warily and not be in a hurry to make changes.

However, next morning she saw that she might have saved herself anxiety on this point. When after breakfast she went to Mrs Grinsmead's room to be shown the books, she found that things were competently enough managed.

The mistress of the house was in bed. She seldom got up, it appeared, before midday. But she was not altogether idle. Some letters and several books littered the bed and a fountain pen and blotting pad were on the table at its head.

At once Anne sensed the same coldness in her employer's manner. Mrs Grinsmead was polite, but unapproachable. She made a few perfunctory remarks before turning to business, but these were the same as on the previous afternoon, quite impersonal.

Her system of household books Anne found easy to grasp. Moreover, it was efficient, and Anne felt she could not do better than continue it.

The financial side of things dealt with, Mrs Grinsmead went on to explain her methods of running the house, ending up: "If anything is not clear to you, come and speak to me about it. Otherwise, as long as things go well I don't want to be bothered. Now hadn't you better go and see Meakin about today's meals?"

Anne spent a busy morning trying to master the details of her new job. Surprisingly easy she found it. The maids had been well trained and carried out their work efficiently. Mrs Meakin was helpful with suggestions about meals, and Gladys willingly gave any information she was asked for.

Anne was much pleased and not a little surprised that neither of the maids seemed to resent her coming. Indeed she fancied they rather welcomed her. She had spoken nicely to them when they met, but Anne felt it was more than this. Could it, she wondered, be relief at being brought less directly in contact with their mistress?

At lunch she met the children, who dined with the three women of the establishment. Grinsmead did not come home in the middle of the day. There were two children, a boy and a girl. Anthony, the elder, was just turned six, while his sister, Christina, was four. Charming children, Anne thought them, but rather serious and with too grown-up a manner. Whatever love might or might not be lost between their mother and father, there was no doubt that they and their mother were passionately attached. When speaking to them Mrs Grinsmead's whole manner changed, and Anne could not mistake the look of intense affection in her eyes. This feeling the children evidently returned. Miss Cheame they seemed merely to tolerate, though there was no sign of active dislike. Anne, who was very fond of children, determined that if she could do so without seeming to interfere, she would make friends with the pair.

That afternoon she had a walk with Edith Cheame. "Mrs Grinsmead likes to have the children from lunch till tea," the governess explained, "and I usually go out. Would you care to come and explore?"

Anne, who had finished her own work for the time being, was delighted. She wanted to see the country, but much more she wanted to be on intimate terms with this woman who seemed so much at home in the household.

She found it less easy than she had hoped. Edith was friendly enough, but she was reserved. She would discuss Anne's affairs without hesitation, but not her own. Anne, however, could not object to this. She did not, indeed, care for people who were ready too easily to unburden their private affairs. Nor did the two women speak much about their employers. Only one remark the governess made which gave Anne to think.

"I'm afraid, you know," she said, speaking of Mrs Grinsmead, "she's rather ill. She's certainly worse than one would imagine at first sight. I have been here over a year now, and she's not getting any better. Indeed I'm afraid she's worse. I think Mr Grinsmead was wise to get you, though she wasn't very keen on it. She wants rest from every form of excitement."

"Then these bridge parties that I've heard of surely can't be good for her? Though she did say she goes to bed before they're over."

"They're not good for her at all. She can't sleep after them. I don't think Mr Grinsmead likes to have them, but she herself insists on it."

Anne hesitated, then took the plunge. "What is it that you think is wrong?" she asked.

"I don't know exactly," Edith Cheame said slowly. "She seems to have something on her mind, but I can't imagine what it may be. I've often thought that a psychoanalyst might help her, but, of course, I don't know."

Anne was interested, but she wondered how far the governess was giving her real opinion. Was it not that Mrs Grinsmead was simply unhappy, because she had made an unhappy marriage? This, at all events, was a theory Miss Cheame was unlikely to put forward, at least to a stranger.

"She's better when we're alone," went on the governess. "We've had a fair number of visitors staying in the house, and they always seem to upset her. Particularly old Mrs Grinsmead; that's Mr Grinsmead's mother, you know. She was here for three or four days a few weeks ago. She's not altogether easy to pull with, and she rubbed our Mrs Grinsmead up the wrong way."

"Very old, is she?"

"No, she doesn't look more than sixty, if that. And as hale and hearty as you please. A clever woman and strong-minded. She's one of those who sees only black and white: no greys anywhere. Efficient, but heavy on one's nerves."

Anne knew the type. "Does she come here much?" she asked.

"Not a great deal. She's been here twice in my time; for ten days last winter, and then this three or four days a few weeks ago. I understand she's due again shortly."

"Then if they keep me on, I'll see her," Anne smiled, and the talk drifted to other channels.

That second evening passed much as had the first. Anne changed early and went down to the kitchen to see that everything was right for dinner, then after dinner they had three rubbers of bridge. At about ten Mrs Grinsmead went to bed, Grinsmead disappeared to his study, and Anne was left in the drawing-room with Edith Cheame. Mindful of the hint that she had received on the previous evening, Anne had provided herself with a book. But Edith did not seem anxious to read, and for an hour they chatted over the fire. Then the governess yawned and said she would turn in, and Anne, after going round the house to see that it was locked up for the night, followed her example.

Anne was surprised to find with what ease and speed she fell into the ways of the house. A week had flown before, as she put it to herself, she had well started. The more she saw of the place and the job, the more she liked it. She found the work easy. It was infinitely less of a strain than housekeeping in her father's house had been. There the great and ever-present difficulty had been money; how to live with reasonable comfort and entertain even to the limited extent that was necessary, on a ridiculously inadequate stipend. Here there was plenty of money for everything. She saw, indeed, that she would be able to maintain the Grinsmeads' standard of living on con-siderably less than Mrs Grinsmead had been spending.

The end of this first week found her on increasingly good terms with the other members of the household. As she had imagined, she found the cook, Mrs Meakin, a real friend. She wondered what the woman's history could have been. That she had a history, Anne was sure. Her husband, Anne supposed. She wondered if he were alive or dead. Mrs Meakin, however, was reticent, and Anne did not like to fish for information.

Gladys also seemed to have taken to Anne. Though she still looked sulky, she smiled when Anne spoke to her, and always did with great willingness any little thing Anne asked her. So also did Hersey. With him she had been careful to pretend to no knowledge of gardening. She had asked him to let her help him to transplant some seedlings at which she found him at work. He speedily found she did it as well as he could himself, and with uncanny readiness handed over the job to her. She smiled inwardly, but persevered till it was finished. Thereafter she found she could do what she liked. Indeed on one occasion Hersey had asked her opinion as to the best position for some new tulip beds for next season. This she justly considered a triumph.

Edith Cheame had thawed considerably and had told Anne something of her life. Her history was surprisingly like Anne's own. As a girl she also had assisted her father, a mechanical engineer and inventor. Then it had been realised that this work would not bring her in a livelihood, and she had begun to train as a nurse. But only four months later her father had died, leaving practically nothing. Like Anne, she had a terrible struggle, and then had come this job as governess. To her it had seemed like passing into heaven. She had held it now, as she had already mentioned, for over a year, and during the whole of that time she had never had a word from either of the Grinsmeads which was not kind and pleasant. Partly because of that, though, she admitted, principally to keep her job, she had done her very best for the children, and though she feared that she had never entirely gained their confidence, they seemed to like her sufficiently well, and were growing up as their parents wished.

Of Grinsmead Anne saw but little. On two other evenings he had come to the drawing-room and they had played bridge, but on other occasions he had withdrawn to his study after dinner. On the first morning at breakfast Anne had found him and Edith Cheame with newspapers propped up before their plates, and he had pointedly offered a third to Anne with a joking remark about their mutual rudeness at that time of the day. Breakfast therefore was a silent meal. Occasionally they talked a little if there was startling news, but on several mornings not a word except good morning had passed. Then Grinsmead went off to Ashbridge, where he practised as a solicitor, and the strings of the others' tongues were unloosed.

But though Anne thus liked and was liked by her fellow employees, and when not ignored, appeared to be liked by the master of the house, she found she could make no progress whatever with Mrs Grinsmead. Indeed quite the reverse. The lady's manner had got shorter and colder in spite of all that Anne could do to propitiate her. More than once Anne quickly raised her eyes to find the other's gaze fixed on her with a kind of intent inquiry, tinged with suspicion; and when Mrs Grinsmead had found that her look was observed, her expression had turned to actual hostility. Anne could not understand it. She was quite sure she had done nothing to invoke her employer's displeasure, and she found it intensely hurtful to be subjected to this suspicion and dislike.

Towards the end of the week, however, she made a discovery which, while it did not explain the puzzle, at least made it more tolerable for her. She found that Mrs Grinsmead comported herself in precisely the same way both to her husband and to Edith Cheame. Both she seemed to distrust, and to both at times she seemed definitely hostile. But she never said anything. To all three of them she was cold and distant, apparently continually on the defensive.

Had she not been otherwise so very normal, Anne would have suspected her mind was affected. Indeed when she remembered what Edith had said about Mrs Grinsmead's sleeplessness and the possible advisability of psycho-analysis, she felt that this might indeed be the solution.

Another thing that Anne discovered gave her a slightly unpleasant sensation. She wanted something in her room, and chanced to follow her employer upstairs as the latter was going to bed. Anne was just approaching Mrs Grinsmead's door when it closed. To her surprise, she heard a bolt being shot.

Many people bolt their room doors at night, but to Anne there seemed something sinister in that dull sound. Was it, she wondered, against Grinsmead that his wife bolted it, or was it merely a part of her general suspicion? Anne wondered if she had always bolted it, and if not, what had occurred to make her begin.

Next day she learned some more about it. She was talking to Gladys about Mrs Grinsmead's early tea, and she asked the girl who unfastened the door. She wondered if Mrs Grinsmead got up to do so. Gladys explained that the bolt was an electric one, and was worked from the bed by a couple of pushes. Her mistress could therefore bolt and unbolt it without disturbing herself. Later Anne went into the room and experimented with the arrangement herself.

Rather suggestive, Anne thought, but energetically she reminded herself that it was not her business. She believed it would not be difficult to turn Mrs Grinsmead against her to such an extent that she would have to go. A little curiosity might easily do it. The less said, indeed the less seen, the soonest mended.

3

PERPLEXITY

It was on the ninth day after Anne's arrival that an incident happened, trifling in itself, but which left an unpleasant impression on her mind.

During dinner that evening Mrs Grinsmead seemed to be labouring under a good deal of excitement, for which Anne could see no cause. However, something had evidently occurred to upset her. She was restless and nervy and quite sharp in some of her remarks. Her behaviour gave an uncomfortable air of strain to the meal and Anne was glad when it was over and they returned to the drawing-room.

It was one of the evenings on which they played bridge, and after they had settled down round the table and Anne was making the first deal, the trouble came out. Mrs Grinsmead had a nasty headache. Grinsmead at once suggested that they should postpone their game till another evening and that his wife should lie down. But she said lying down would not help her, that she always felt better sitting up.

"What about a couple of aspirins, Mrs Grinsmead?" Edith suggested. "If you would care for them I could get them in a moment."

Mrs Grinsmead looked undecided. "Perhaps they might do me good," she said doubtfully. "As a rule, I don't care to take them, but they might quiet me."

Edith rose from the table, but she had not pushed aside her chair when Grinsmead called her back.

"Don't trouble, Miss Cheame," he said. "It happens that I was not feeling too well myself today, and I got a bottle in Ashbridge. I have it here."

He drew from his pocket a little bottle and handed it across.

As he did so Anne happened to catch sight of his wife's face. It bore a dreadful expression, an expression of fear and horror. She looked as if she had seen something in the distance beyond the party, though what it could have been Anne could not imagine. Anne was startled and was about to cry out and ask what was wrong, but Mrs Grinsmead, with what was evidently a tremendous effort, composed her features. So far as Anne could see, neither her husband nor Edith Cheame had noticed anything.

"Thanks so much," said Mrs Grinsmead in a rather breathless voice, "but on second thoughts I think I won't mind. Aspirin does upset me, you know. For a moment I thought it might be worthwhile, but I think I was wrong."

"Oh, don't you think you will?" Edith remonstrated. "You know you've often taken it and it has always done you more good than harm."

Once again a flicker of almost desperation showed in the lady's eyes.

"No," she said a little wildly, "I won't take it. I won't take it." She paused a little, then added unsteadily, "I don't feel that it would do me good."

"Don't press her if she doesn't want it," Grinsmead said quietly, holding out his hand for the bottle and the incident ended.

All the remainder of the evening the mistress of the house remained nervy and upset, and when a little earlier than usual she betook herself to bed, everyone breathed a hidden sigh of relief.

It happened that that night Edith Cheame also went early to her room, leaving Anne alone with her book in the drawing-room. Just as she was thinking of following the others' example and turning in, the door opened and Grinsmead entered.

"Ah, Miss Day; not gone up yet?" he said pleasantly. "I think I left my cigar case here." He moved over to the chimney piece, picked up the case, carefully selected a cigar, and put the case in his pocket.

"Well," he went on, standing with his back to the fire, "and how are you liking Frayle?"

"Oh, Mr Grinsmead," Anne answered earnestly, "I just can't say how much. I love it. I only hope I am managing to carry on to your and Mrs Grinsmead's satisfaction."

He smiled. "You could easily do it to mine," he said, "for I don't know what's going on half time. And I haven't heard Mrs Grinsmead complain about you, which, if you only knew it, is high praise."

"I should like to help her all I could," said Anne, thinking of that fleeting expression of dread which she had so recently witnessed.

Grinsmead grew more serious. "She needs it, Miss Day. She is far from well. I don't know what it is. She has seen doctor after doctor. All say the same thing: she has something on her mind. But neither they nor I can find out what

31

it is. It's really serious, I'm afraid; not now exactly, but it may grow into something serious if it's not stopped."

Anne did not reply and he went on. "You notice how she treats all of us. I dare say she treats you in the same way. She holds us all at arms' length and won't be friendly and natural; or can't, I suppose I should say."

"Yes," said Anne, "I've noticed that."

"I think myself," Grinsmead spoke more confidentially, "that she has got a slight persecution complex. The doctors think the same. But none of them seem to be able to do anything about it."

"Have you thought of psychoanalysis?"

"It has been suggested, but she won't hear of it. She won't really do anything that's suggested." He sighed. "That, of course, is one of the symptoms."

He seemed to feel the matter very deeply, and Anne suddenly conceived a new view of him. Though he had been outwardly friendly and pleasant, she realised that she had never really liked him. Now she felt a wave of sympathy for him. He was evidently deeply attached to his wife and upset by this terrible fear that all might not be well with her mind.

"I am so very sorry about it," Anne said softly.

"I'm sure you are, Miss Day. You must be surprised to hear me speaking to you, a comparative stranger, in this confidential way. But I felt that you were sympathetic. I wanted just to ask you to be as much of a friend to her as you can."

"Oh, but of course, Mr Grinsmead. I should have done that in any case."

"I'm sure you would. I'd like you to understand also that if she does not seem as friendly to you as she might, that it is her health and not anything that you have done."

"Of course I understand, and thank you so much for saying all this. You may rest assured that anything I can do to help will be done."

"Just what I should have expected you to say. Well, Miss Day, I mustn't keep you up, or rather I must go and attend to my own work. Good night, and thank you for your sympathetic attitude."

When he had gone Anne sat on before the dying fire, considering the interview. She felt at once that Grinsmead was correct in his diagnosis. A persecution complex was a serious matter, she knew; not in itself perhaps, but it was usually symptomatic of deeper trouble. She wondered about the psychoanalysis. She had never herself known a case of persecution mania being cured by it, but she had not enough experience to say whether or not such a cure was possible.

Then suddenly a rather terrible explanation of the aspirin incident occurred to her. Surely it *couldn't* be possible that the woman was afraid to take what she was offered? It couldn't be possible; no, it couldn't! And yet – There was that look of fear and horror. *Could Sybil Grinsmead have feared poison?*

Anne dismissed the idea from her mind, but it returned obstinately. It might, indeed, she saw, be the truth. A fear for her life, absurd though it might be, would account for her whole attitude and manner. And after all it was only a rather more advanced form of the persecution complex. Anne shivered. Poor, poor woman! If this were true, what a hell her life must be! Anne instantly made up her mind that so far as in her lay she would help the unhappy lady to fight her terrible disease.

Next day, however, Mrs Grinsmead's special upset seemed to have passed over, and things settled down as before.

A few nights after the episode of the aspirin the Grinsmead's had some people to dinner. There were six guests, three men and three women: a Mr and Mrs Bolsover, a Mr and Mrs Alcock, a Mrs Holt-Lancing and a Mr Merrow. The affair was a source of some anxiety to Anne, who felt that she was more or less on trial and wanted everything to go off well.

She had the weight of the entire arrangements on her shoulders. First she had to write the invitations, then arrange the menu and other details, and finally see that her plans were properly carried out. Mrs Grinsmead would give no help. When Anne asked how she would like things done she replied that Anne was to do what she thought best, and that it would probably be all right. The servants, however, remembered what had been done on previous occasions, and Anne was thus able to keep to the desired standard. She took a lot of trouble, superintending every detail herself, and she had the satisfaction after it was over of being complimented both by Grinsmead himself and Edith Cheame.

The dinner, at which both Anne and Edith were present, passed off uneventfully. With two exceptions the guests struck Anne as being very ordinary, and not particularly attractive at that. They were pushing people of the world, inclined to loudness and self-assertion. They were carelessly polite to Anne, but she vaguely felt that they did not consider her as belonging to their world, in which, indeed, they were quite correct.

The exceptions were both women. One struck her pleasantly and the other the reverse. Mrs Alcock was a homely, natural sort of woman of about fifty. She was not good looking, but she had a kind, dependable face and her manner suggested tolerant common sense. Before the evening was over Anne found herself telling her the story of her troubles and her delight at finding herself in so pleasant a post.

The other woman was Mrs Holt-Lancing, a grass widow, Anne afterwards learned, living in a small house close by. Her husband, who seemed to be known and liked by everyone, was the captain of a liner running to the Far East, and was at present at sea. Mrs Holt-Lancing was a contrast to Mrs Alcock in almost every respect. Of medium height and build, she was possessed of extraordinarily small and delicate features, with a perfect complexion, the pallor of which was intensified by her dark eyes, dark lashes and dark hair. She wore a somewhat attenuated dress of some golden material, relieved with bands of dull black and enlivened with quite an array of jewellery. Her manner was vivacious. She was not actually impolite to Anne, but practically she ignored her. A hard woman with an eye to the main chance, thought Anne, or, as she put it to herself, on the deadly make every time.

Mrs Grinsmead's appearance Anne did not at all like. She was at the end of the table with Mr Bolsover on her right and Mr Alcock on her left. Bolsover was a stout old bore, with a *penchant* for endless tales of encounters with shadowy individuals and what they said to him and what he said to them and how he downed them over it. Mr Alcock was dry and thin-lipped, and had "law" stamped on his features. He rarely spoke, allowing Bolsover every opportunity to recount the discomfiture of his friends. To these stories Mrs Grinsmead listened with polite attention, but there were angry spots of colour on her cheeks and her eyes looked wild and over-excited. Not at all good for her, Anne thought, as she remembered that Edith had said that after these parties the lady seldom slept.

Anne found it hard to join in the conversation, which was principally about people of whom she had never heard. Indeed only one subject was discussed which she could entirely follow: burglaries. The remarks in themselves were commonplace, at the same time the conversation after- wards recurred to Anne as being the first of the outstanding landmarks in the terrible drama which was to follow.

It was Mr Alcock who introduced the subject. It seemed that there had recently been no less than three burglaries in the neighbourhood, of which the last had taken place on the previous night at a house not half a mile away. In all three cases the burglars had got away with a pretty considerable haul.

"They're working in an unusually clever way," Mr Alcock remarked in his prim elderly accents. "In fact – er – were I myself a burglar I believe I should adopt the same tactics."

"I can see you catting it up a water pipe," drawled Merrow. "That's their scheme, isn't it?"

"It was not to that precise phase of it that I alluded," Alcock returned dryly.

"Oh, do tell us, Mr Alcock," cried Mrs Bolsover with heavy humour. "It might be so useful in case we ever wanted to take up the profession. How would you do it?"

"I should confine my operations to one locality. It is a recognised principle in police work that if a gang cracks a crib at one place today their next operations will be carried out as far away as possible from that locality. Therefore they will not be looked for near the original place."

"All rot, Alcock," Bolsover asserted. "If your next-door neighbour is burgled tonight, you'll see that your door is fast and your pistol loaded tomorrow night. What do you say, Grinsmead?"

"It's human nature, I think," Grinsmead said smoothly. "All the same, I agree with Alcock that a number of outrages in the same locality is not usual."

"But surely people don't keep pistols in these days, do they?" Mrs Holt-Lancing asked. "Do you keep a pistol, Mr Grinsmead?" She flashed her eyes at her host.

Grinsmead smiled. "As a matter of fact, Mrs Holt-Lancing, there's an automatic pistol in the drawer of my desk at the present moment. I've had it since the war, and keep it on the pretence of target practice."

"Ah," Merrow drawled, "you make me feel defenceless. I have neither pistol, revolver, cannon, mortar, bow and arrow, or poisoned dart blow-pipe in my entire establishment. I trust you won't make use of that information, Mrs Bolsover."

Mrs Bolsover said she would remember it next time she felt a yearning for Mrs Merrow's diamond necklace, and the subject dropped.

Dinner came uneventfully and somewhat tediously to an end. The men went with the women to the drawing-room and the inevitable bridge tables were got out. The Grinsmeads and their guests made up two fours, leaving Anne and Edith out. The latter was considered, and freely admitted herself, not good enough for these serious players, and Anne, whose play had turned out to be quite fair, was to take Mrs Grinsmead's place when she retired.

About ten, each table had played two rubbers, and they knocked off for drinks. Mrs Grinsmead then disappeared and there was a reshuffle of the players. Anne's partner was Merrow, against Grinsmead and Mrs Holt-Lancing, while the Bolsovers and the Alcocks took each other on at the second table.

The play was good, but not beyond Anne's standard. For a while she concentrated all her energies on it, but when she found she was the equal of her companions, she allowed herself to take more notice of her surroundings.

Merrow had been opposite to her at dinner and she had then formed the opinion that he was a rather stupid youth, so full of himself and his own affairs as to be unable to think seriously about anything else. Now he seemed lost in the play or in some matter known only to his own inner consciousness.

The result was that the attention of both Anne and Merrow had remained concentrated on the table. To this it was probably due that on Anne's happening to glance suddenly up, she saw something that she was not intended to see.

Mrs Holt-Lancing and Grinsmead were looking at one another. In this alone there was nothing to interest Anne or anybody else. But there was that in their look which revealed their secret. There was question, there was understanding, there was agony. There was love!

Anne dropped her eyes. She did not think her indiscreet glance had been observed. She felt suddenly battered as if she had received a material shock. Was this the secret of this unhappy house? Was this the explanation of Sybil Grinsmead's cold distance? Was – ?

Anne came violently to her senses. This would not do at all. In the nick of time she had caught herself about to revoke. The Grinsmeads' love affairs were not her business. She must concentrate on the play. Whether the others suspected anything or not, they became more discreet; at least she saw no more injudicious glances. Grinsmead was himself when the guests left about midnight, congratulating Anne on her arrangements in his pleasant, but not quite enthusiastic way. Anne went to bed with a good deal to think about.

If Grinsmead and Mrs Holt-Lancing were in love, and Sybil Grinsmead knew it, it would certainly account for Sybil's manner. The manner was obviously not natural to Sybil, as the extraordinary change which came over her when she was with her children showed. Probably it was due to her pride, which would not allow her to show how much she was being hurt.

An affair between Grinsmead and Mrs Holt-Lancing would also explain the very unusual conditions on which Anne herself had been engaged. Anne did not believe she was really wanted. She had learned that she was the first housekeeper, and that until she came Sybil had carried on, so the servants seemed to think, with perfect ease. No, Anne could have sworn that she was wanted for another purpose, to act with Edith in preventing a *tête-à-tête* between husband and wife. That was why so much was made of her living with the family and being present at meals. These two unfortunate people could not bear each other. The company of strangers was necessary for them if they were to carry on ordinary intercourse.

So Anne thought. It was not till later that a more sinister explanation of the affair entered her head.

She was profoundly distressed about the whole thing. She had the type of mind which rejoices in the happiness of others as well as sorrows for their miseries. But apart from that, the affair touched her personally. When the inevitable burst up came, she would be no longer wanted. Then the London registry offices would claim her once more.

However, there was nothing to be done about it. At worst, this job would be a pleasant interlude in her grey months, a restful holiday to strengthen her for the ensuing battle.

Next morning Anne found her fears had largely departed. Life recovered its sweetness. The novelty of her position passed away. The house practically ran itself and she began to devote more and more time to the garden. Hersey thought the world and all of her, and received her lightest suggestions as immutable law. Sybil still held her aloof attitude, but seemed to have grown accustomed to Anne and to accept her as a necessary part of her environment. With the children also Anne had made friends. At first they had suffered rather than encouraged her advances, but now they greeted her enthusiastically when they saw her, running to her and clamouring for stories. And with this familiarity neither Sybil nor Edith Cheame had seemed other than pleased.

But until the month of probation was up Anne was not wholly content. With anxiety she had noted the dawning of the day, and as its hours sped she had waited more and more anxiously to learn her fate. To her surprise no one took the slightest notice of it. She was tempted to say nothing about it and to take an absence of notice as confirmation in her job. But her uncompromising honesty forced her to speak of it to Sybil when the latter was about to retire.

"Was that the arrangement?" Sybil returned negligently. "I had forgotten. I shouldn't raise the question, if I were you."

Anne was delighted. "Oh, thank you, Mrs Grinsmead," she cried. "That means you are keeping me on? "

"Oh, I think so. You've done what you said you would do, haven't you?"

"I've tried to."

Sybil nodded and went on to bed. Though Anne was profoundly thankful for the decision, she could not help wondering at the way in which it had been given. "I don't care whether you go or whether you don't go, but for goodness sake don't bother me about it." That was Sybil's manner, polite, but distant, and cold as ice. Anne sighed, then she told herself that this was illness, not ill-feeling, and to some extent was comforted.

Gradually the days drew in. Summer had gone and autumn was already well advanced. Then occurred, one after another, certain incidents which reawakened all Anne's fears and seemed to bring the household to the verge of tragedy.

– 4 –

FEAR

The first of these incidents developed out of a chance remark of Edith Cheame's.

She and Anne had by this time become good, though not very close friends. Edith was reserved by nature, and though she obviously fought against it, this reserve tended to prevent too great intimacy. But she seemed to like Anne, and Anne was grateful for it and met her more than half way.

Partly because of this reserve and partly because of her own natural caution, Anne had never breathed a word of her suspicions as to the cause of Sybil's fears or the relations which she believed existed between Grinsmead and Mrs Holt-Lancing. Nor had Edith ever said anything to indicate that she might share such beliefs.

Occasionally, however, they did speak of Sybil's health, and it was during one of these conversations that Edith made her chance remark.

It was the day after one of the usual dinner and bridge parties, and the two women were discussing the effect this had had on the mistress of the house.

"She never sleeps after them," Edith declared. "You can tell by her appearance next morning; heavy and black under her eyes and all that. I always think that what she wants is an occasional sleeping draught; taken with discretion of course. I had an aunt once – she's dead now – who had the same trouble. The doctor ordered her draughts, and they did her a lot of good."

Anne was impressed. "That seems rather an idea," she said slowly. "Have you ever mentioned it to her?"

Edith Cheame smiled mockingly. "Do you think it's the sort of suggestion that she would be likely to accept?"

"I don't," Anne returned bluntly. "At the same time, if they would really do her good I think one shouldn't funk a possible rebuff."

"My dear creature, it's not a question of funking a possible rebuff, as you know perfectly well. It's a question of turning her completely against the idea. You know the way to prevent her doing anything is to suggest that she should."

Anne knew that it was the truth. All the same, if it would help the poor woman …

"Have you ever mentioned the idea to Mr Grinsmead?" she asked.

"No, and I'm not going to. And if you take my advice you won't either. He won't thank you. In this house it's your place and mine to mind our own business."

Anne was not convinced, though she let the subject drop. But that night after she got into bed it returned to her mind and after consideration she decided she would mention it to Grinsmead. If he considered it an impertinence she couldn't help it. But she did not believe he would.

With Anne, performance usually followed close on the heels of decision. The very next evening Grinsmead came into the drawing-room while she was waiting alone for dinner. For a few moments they talked generalities, then fearful that one of the others would come in, Anne hesitatingly made her suggestion.

She was a trifle surprised, indeed dismayed, at the way he took it. For a perceptible time he did not reply, but stood looking at her with a somewhat curious expression. Then hearing sounds in the hall he said quickly: "Don't say anything about this. I'll speak to you later."

He wasn't in any hurry to do so. Indeed it was not till the third evening that Anne saw him alone. That evening, as she was following Sybil and Edith to bed, he appeared in the hall and beckoned her silently into his study.

"I've been thinking over what you said, Miss Day," he said, after he had settled her in an armchair, "and I'm not sure that it's not a good idea. I may tell you that I have often thought of it, but I have hesitated to put it forward for certain reasons." He paused and began to pace the room, an anxious frown on his face. "First of all, I don't know how Mrs Grinsmead would take the suggestion. There's no use in mincing matters. You've been here long enough to know – er – well, I'm afraid we must admit that her mind is not perfectly normal. She might – I'm speaking in confidence to you, Miss Day, and if I may be allowed to say so, it is only because of your conduct since you came here that I am venturing to do so – she might, I'm afraid, misunderstand my motive in suggesting it."

He looked keenly at Anne. For a moment she was puzzled, then his terrible meaning occurred to her. Did he think, as she had done, that his wife feared for her life? She gave a little gasp of horror.

"I see you know what I mean," he said gently. "God knows it's a terrible admission to have to make, but if she has fears of that kind in her mind I couldn't bring myself to do anything to give them substance. But," he went on after a little pause, "there's more than that in it." He lowered his voice and looked steadily into the fire. "Is there not a real fear of putting the means of suicide within her reach?"

Anne gave a cry. "Oh, Mr Grinsmead, not suicide! She would never – "

"She would never, if she were normal. But unhappily she's not normal, and there's nothing to be gained by shutting one's eyes to the fact."

"I couldn't believe it."

He shrugged. There was silence, then he went on:

"All the same I believe your idea's a good one, and I'll tell you what we'll do. You have a talk with the doctor. If he thinks well of it you could sound my wife; unhappily for me, she would take it better from you than from me. If she agrees, so much the better; if she objects, we are none the worse off."

Anne believed this was true. She said she would do her best, and got up, but he raised his hand.

"Whatever the outcome of this," he said, "I want to thank you for your kindly thought. I'm glad you're here, Miss Day. Your coming was a lucky thing for us. I'm perfectly aware that money doesn't enter into your motives, but I want to say that from the first of next month I'm raising your salary. All the household arrangements are running admirably and you need have no hesitation about taking it."

Anne was taken aback, and in one way not altogether pleased. She would, of course, be glad of the money, but she wished it had come in some other connection. Either Grinsmead was tactless and wanting in delicacy, or else he was conveying a deliberate snub, reminding her that she was a paid servant who should mind her own business and let the affairs of her employers alone. She wished now that she had said nothing about the sleeping draught. But she had done so and she could not now back out.

Accordingly, on his next visit, she put the idea up to the doctor.

Dr Roome hemmed and hawed. He wasn't very keen on sleeping draughts, except in cases of absolute necessity.

"Who would decide when one was to be given?" he asked.

"I don't know," said Anne. "I suppose Mrs Grinsmead herself."

Dr Roome shook his head decisively. "Under no circumstances," he declared. "The only condition under which I would give them would be if you, Miss Day, undertook to administer them. They're not exactly dangerous things, but their continual use is excessively injurious."

"But, Dr Roome, Mr Grinsmead did not suggest that you should give them unless you thought they would be beneficial."

The doctor hesitated. "It'll do her no harm to try the experiment," he said at last. "I'll send you a few and we'll see what effect they have on her."

"I've not asked her yet whether she'd like them."

"Well, do so and let me know. Now, Miss Day, you must only give them," and he went on to mention the circumstances. "I'll write all that to Mr Grinsmead. I think also you should always consult him before giving one."

Once again Anne was sorry she hadn't let the thing alone. She should have known, she now told herself, that if they had been required, Dr Roome would himself have ordered them.

She was sorrier still when, at a suitable opportunity that evening, she raised the question with Sybil. In fact for a moment she was dismayed to the extent of speechlessness. For Sybil's face slowly took on the same expression of horror and dread which it had worn on the evening on which Grinsmead had offered her the aspirin.

"Oh, Mrs Grinsmead, what is the matter?" Anne gasped. "If you don't like the idea we'll not say anything more about it. It was only that I thought an occasional draught might help you."

Sybil stared fixedly into her eyes. "Is this your own idea?" she asked presently.

"Partly," Anne answered. "As a matter of fact Miss Cheame told me of a relative of her own who was greatly helped by sleeping draughts, and we both wondered whether they might not help you too."

"Did you mention your idea to Mr Grinsmead?"

"Yes, I did."

"And what did he say?"

"He was not greatly taken with the idea, but he told me to ask the doctor."

"And did you?"

"Yes. Dr Roome said that a very occasional draught could do you no harm, though he was emphatic that they should not be taken often. He told me to ask you what you thought, and if you liked the idea he would send some on."

Once again Sybil Grinsmead looked Anne fixedly in the eyes.

"Is all that true?" she asked tensely.

Anne felt as if she had been hit in the face.

"Really, Mrs Grinsmead," she exclaimed, "I do think that's rather uncalled for. When have I ever told you an untruth or given you any reason to treat me as you do? You can't think how hurtful it is always to be treated as an enemy when I'm trying all the time to do everything I can for you. Yes, it's true. Every word of it is true. You're the only person I've ever met who has consistently doubted my word."

A faintly eager look had come into Sybil's eyes. She made a little gesture as if sweeping away everything that had happened. "Don't mind me," she said quickly, "I'm not really quite well. Tell me something about yourself. How did Mr Grinsmead find you?"

Anne was surprised at this sudden reversal of outlook. "Why, at Mrs Allsopp's registry office," she answered readily, going on to give Sybil an account of her engagement.

"He didn't ask you to do special things for himself for extra pay?" she asked.

"Never," Anne said a trifle indignantly. "Nothing of the kind."

"Nor has he asked you since you came here?"

Anne reassured her. She was becoming more and more astonished at the change in Sybil's manner.

"Very well," Sybil continued. "Now tell me about yourself. Who are you and where have you lived?"

Sybil now seemed not only interested in Anne's replies, but almost excited. She asked innumerable questions as to Anne's upbringing, her life with her father in the Gloucestershire parsonage, and her experiences job-hunting in London. Finally she said in a much more friendly way than she had yet spoken: "Well, I'm glad to know all that. I often wondered about you, but I didn't like to ask. You may get those sleeping draughts. Often I would have given anything to have one."

As a result of this permission Dr Roome sent the draughts with instructions to Anne that she must keep them under lock and key and only give them to Sybil under certain conditions and after consultation with Mr Grinsmead. But with that Sybil began to sleep better, and it was a considerable time before Anne used the first.

Some days later, however, the incident had an unexpected sequel. Anne went to consult Sybil about the arrangements to be made for a guest who was coming to spend a few days at Frayle, when Sybil asked her to shut the door and sit down. There was an eager look on her face, surprisingly in contrast to her usual expression.

"I think, Miss Day," she began in a low voice, "I have been doing you an injustice and I owe you an apology. You are not really against me?"

"Against you, Mrs Grinsmead? How can you think such a thing? Of course I'm not against you. I only want to help you in any way I can."

"Yes, I believe you. I do believe you. I must tell you though. When you told me something about yourself the other day, I wrote to an old friend who lives in Gloucester, asking him to make some inquiries about you. He did so, and I have just heard from him. From what he tells me I feel I may trust you. But you came here a stranger and how was I to know? I do apologise."

Anne was first amazed, then angry, then relieved, and finally delighted. "Dear Mrs Grinsmead," she exclaimed, "I'm so glad you feel that way. I knew, of course, you were suspicious, but indeed I don't think you had any reason to be. I'm sure you're making a mistake."

"About you, yes. I will trust you now. I can't possibly tell you what a relief it will be to have someone I can talk to."

"But surely," Anne returned, and then hesitated. "It's not my business, of course, but I can't help saying it: surely there is no reason to distrust anyone? Everyone feels as I do towards you."

Sybil Grinsmead's face grew hard.

"No, don't talk about that. Don't spoil my little pleasure. Don't let's think of anything but the present."

Anne thought rapidly. This fear was an obsession. The only thing for it was to drag it out into the light of day. Put it into words to another person, and it would be robbed of half its terrors.

"But I must speak of it," she said earnestly. "I know that things like that have only to be put into words to show that they have no foundation. Tell me, once and for all, what it is you fear."

In some apparent alarm Sybil again looked very searchingly at Anne. She seemed to be reassured, then turned away her head.

"Don't you know?" she asked in a low voice.

"I know what's wrong," Anne declared stoutly. "You mustn't mind my saying it. You've got a very common, but very trying, complaint: a persecution complex. You've bottled it all in and it has grown worse. You want to talk about it and it will get better."

Sybil was not offended by this plain speaking. "My dear girl," she said, "don't be an ass. I know. And so would you if you weren't obsessed by your good heart that won't believe evil of anyone." The old miserable expression came back into her eyes, as she repeated in a low intense voice: "I tell you, I know!"

Anne, at a loss what to say, did not reply, and Sybil went on in fierce undertones.

"I shouldn't say anything, particularly about my own husband. But I must, I must! For nearly three years I have kept it to myself, till I have felt that I was going mad. I am going mad, I think. I can't keep silence any longer. I must get the relief of speech. You mentioned it yourself. You were right. I must speak. Haven't you seen what's going on? Do you mean to tell me you don't know? Oh, I thought every one in the world must know!"

Anne, more at a loss than ever, still remained silent. But the sympathy she felt for this unhappy woman must have shown in her face, for Sybil went on with scarcely a pause.

"Don't you know that all he wants is that woman?" she cried passionately. "Don't you know that all she wants is him? Don't you know that they want me dead? *Dead!* They're waiting their opportunity, biding their time! There'll be an accident or it may look like suicide. But it'll do what they want! *I'll be dead!*" Her voice rose hysterically.

Anne was inexpressibly shocked. This poor, poor woman! What a hell life must be for her, living with her mind full of these terrible thoughts! Pure imagination, of course. These things didn't happen; not among the people that one knew.

And yet – Anne very vividly remembered the look she had surprised between the two. There was no mistaking that look. It was as if the cover of their minds had been raised and she had seen right down into their very souls. No mistake about what was there! There was anguished, despairing love, primitive and overwhelming. That part of it was true; absolutely, utterly, fundamentally true.

But it was one thing that they should be in love and quite another that they should contemplate murder. After a moment Anne's commonsense reasserted itself.

"I did think they were fond of each other," she admitted in a low troubled tone. "But the other; oh, no, it's too dreadful! They couldn't possibly think of such a thing. Oh, no, Mrs Grinsmead! Put it out of your mind. It's wrong; it's wrong; it's not true!"

Sybil had quieted down. Her excitement subsided. For a moment she looked mournfully at Anne and then burst into a storm of tears.

Anne slipped to the door and turned the key. Then she went back and put an arm round the other woman. She said nothing, but waited with a silent sympathy.

It was terrible to her to witness Sybil's distress. But she felt that the breakdown would prove an unmixed blessing. For far too long Sybil's awful suspicions had been bottled up within her own breast, festering there and growing more and more hurtful. Confession in this, as in other matters, was good for the soul. The outbreak would be like the opening of an inflamed abscess. The wound would remain sore, but the sharp pain would be gone.

For ages the long anguished sobs racked Sybil's light frame, but at last her passion spent itself and she grew calmer from sheer exhaustion. Anne helped her to bed; then she went down and made her some tea.

When after a heavy sleep Sybil woke, Anne was still beside her. Sybil seemed pitifully tired and fragile, and Anne urged her to sleep again. But instead Sybil insisted on taking up the conversation at the point at which it had been dropped.

"The question I cannot solve," she said wearily, "is what I should do. I've thought and thought and thought, and I can get no light on it. I feel that I must do something or it will be too late, but wherever I turn I seem to be faced by an impassable wall. If you were in my place, Anne – I must call you Anne, and you must call me Sybil – if you were in my place, what would you do?" She gazed at Anne half eagerly, as if hoping against hope for the solution whose existence she had come to doubt.

"Oh, dear Sybil," Anne exclaimed, "it's so good of you letting me call you Sybil – you don't mind me speaking very directly? I feel sure, quite certain, that you are wrong in these terrible suspicions. Mr Grinsmead and Mrs Holt-Lancing are fond of each other; yes, I have seen that. But not for a moment do I believe there is anything more in it. You don't know the kind way he has spoken of you, and not once, but again and again."

Sybil shook her head. "He's clever, that's all," she said dully. "He has taken you in as he took me in – at first. No; they want me out of the way, and what am I to do?"

It was a cry of despair and it affected Anne strongly.

"If you really are convinced in your own mind," she said presently, "why not go away? That doesn't mean that I think you're right; I don't. But if it would ease your mind, why not leave Mr Grinsmead, at least temporarily?"

Sybil made a hopeless gesture. "How could I?" she returned. "You don't understand. I have nowhere to go. My people are dead, and I have no money of my own. I could not support myself and he wouldn't support me under the circumstances, even if I could bring myself to take it."

"What about a divorce or a judicial separation?"

"No proof, no evidence of any kind. They're too clever for that. If I could get a divorce wouldn't I jump at it! But he would never allow a divorce because it would ruin his business, and he has no money either except what he makes."

"Well, is there no one in whom you could confide? No man of the world who would advise you? There must surely be someone. Would you think of speaking to Major Oliver, the chief constable? You know him, don't you?"

"My dear Anne, if you who I believe are sympathetic to me, if you won't believe me, what chance have I of getting a stranger to do so? And I couldn't go to the police without proof. Besides," she shook her head miserably, "think of what anything like that would mean for the children."

For some moments silence reigned, then Sybil said more brightly: "But there, I mustn't spoil your life, too. I feel better for this talk. There is nothing we can do. But we must just look out and try to recognise danger before it comes. I am used to it by this time. I can carry on."

"Dear Sybil! You may count on me to the utmost!"

"I feel I may, and things won't be so bad now when I feel I have you by my side. The worst thing after the actual fear, was the terrible feeling of loneliness. I had no one to speak to, no one with whom I could relax. Now that will be ended. Oh, Anne, no matter how this finishes up, I'm thankful you came here!" And sitting up in bed, Sybil threw her arms round Anne's neck and kissed her hungrily.

5

DANGER

It was about this time that Edith Cheame went up to Town to see a sister who had come over from Canada with her husband on a visit to his people. Anne volunteered to take her place for the day, to the by no means secret delight of the children. Charming youngsters, Anne thought them, and their fondness for her had obviously increased. Indeed they were much more at home with her than with Edith herself.

She took them out for a walk during the morning, during which they prattled freely about their home, so that Anne obtained a pretty clear idea of their reactions to everyone in it. Edith, Gladys and Hersey they disinterestedly tolerated, evidently finding them neither agreeable nor obnoxious. Mrs Meakin and Anne herself they liked. Their mother they idolised, but they seemed a little uncertain about their father. This surprised Anne, because she thought Grinsmead was extraordinarily good to them, and entered wonderfully into their childish ideas and pursuits. Sybil's influence, she thought, either conscious or unconscious.

But it was about their grandmother, old Mrs Grinsmead, that they really waxed eloquent. "Grannie" in their view was a terrible person. From their disjointed remarks Anne painted her as a hard, stern, tyrannical old woman with white hair and a long chin, dressed in black, everlastingly looking out for offences and with a *penchant* for improving the opportunity to the children. They did not seem to be afraid of her, but they clearly detested her, and Anthony's assertion that his mummie had said she was shortly coming to stay, was received almost with tears by Christina.

From the day of Sybil's outburst about Grinsmead and Mrs Holt-Lancing, Anne's relations with her took on an entirely new character. Gone were Sybil's coldness and distance, her apparent self-centredness, her assumed carelessness about others. Whether her belief that she was surrounded by enemies had been well or ill-founded, it was evident that she was starving for human sympathy and friendship. This, to the best of her ability, Anne supplied, and Sybil reacted by displaying a confidence and esteem which quickly ripened into a real friendship.

Anne, on her part, had been greatly touched by the whole incident. While in her own mind she ridiculed the idea that her employer was in physical danger, she had no doubt as to the reality of her mental anguish. Earnestly she set herself to help to carry the load, and the slight but measurable improvement which showed in Sybil's health and spirits assured her that her efforts had not been wasted.

But less than a fortnight of these changed conditions had elapsed when a further incident occurred which burst the bubble of Anne's complacency and left her in the same state of doubt and horror in which Sybil herself was submerged.

It was one of those gorgeous autumn days which make one feel that summer not only has not gone, but has no intention of going. There was real heat in the afternoon sun, so that sitting out of doors was a delight. Rain on the previous night had freshened everything up, and a pleasant aromatic smell came from the earth and from such flowers as still remained. The sky was clear blue, but there was a slight haze in the distance.

It was Sunday afternoon, and Frayle was wrapped in something more than a Sunday quiet. Sybil, Edith and the children had gone out in the car, with Hersey at the wheel. Grinsmead was playing golf. It was Gladys' afternoon out, and very carefully made up, she had vanished an hour since, leaving Mrs Meakin in charge. Anne was recovering from a sick headache, a complaint to which she seldom fell a victim. Sybil had suggested her going out with them, on the grounds that the air would be good for her, but Anne had felt that the only thing she wanted was to get her head down on the pillow of her bed. That was an hour ago, and since then Anne had had a little sleep.

She woke a good deal better, sat up, and found she could move about without making her head throb or bringing on those horrible sick qualms. The room felt close, and she thought Sybil had been right about the fresh air; it would do her good. She therefore wrapped herself in a cloak and went down to the garden.

Though so much better, she found that the walking was knocking her up again, and she looked round for a seat. The garden chairs did not appeal to her; she wanted shade from the sun as well as shelter from the slightly chilly breeze. But she knew where she could get both. Among the trees along the north side of the garden there was an old yew, not a very large tree, but with thick branches. In the course of time the centre had decayed away, making a sort of natural chair or throne. Into this Anne climbed and there settled down contentedly. Behind and at each side the foliage screened her from the breeze, while in front a thin curtain of tiny leaves modified the strength of the sun.

It was very peaceful there in the garden, and soon Anne's head once more began to nod. She settled herself more comfortably and presently was sound asleep.

She suddenly awoke with the impression in her mind that something was happening. Instantly she was perfectly alert, listening intently. Yes, there was a voice, Grinsmead's voice, speaking softly from close behind her.

The yew tree immediately adjoined the thorn hedge which bounded the little estate. Outside the hedge was a lane which ran from the main road, round two sides of Frayle, and then back into the country. It led only to some fields, was seldom used, and on a Sunday afternoon was quite deserted.

Instantly Anne saw that she must reveal her presence. But before she could do so there came an answer in another voice which she also knew: Mrs Holt-Lancing's. And when she heard the words she knew that no matter what might follow, she could not admit knowledge of them. "No, Severus," she was saying, "we can't go on. I'm at the end of my tether. For a love like ours *any* risk is worthwhile."

"Dear Irene, I know and feel the same thing myself. But we mustn't lose our heads. We might so easily pull it off, get married after a decent interval, and then the crash would come. We mustn't risk – "

The voice got faint and died away to an indistinguishable murmur. Evidently the lovers were pacing slowly along, though their footsteps were inaudible on the grass-grown surface of the lane.

Anne's heart was beating rapidly. *What* was this that she had overheard? Risk of what? *Could* it be that Sybil's suspicions?…No; oh, no, it was impossible, utterly impossible. And yet …

The voices were coming back. She listened again. She would have fled had flight been possible. But it was not. While she was invisible from the lane as long as she remained within the shelter of the yew, any movement from it would have been seen through the hedge. Mrs Holt-Lancing was speaking.

"Yes, but in that case they managed it badly," she was saying. "We should have to be more careful. We could wait if we knew that the time was coming to an end. It's the knowledge that it's not coming to an end that's so unsupportable. I tell you, Severus, I can't go on like this any longer. If you love me you'll have to make a move."

"You know, Irene, that I love you – more than anything else in the world. It's not that. It's the difficulty, the almost impossibility – "

Again the voice died away as they passed in the opposite direction. Again Anne meditated flight, and again she was prevented by their return. They were evidently pacing this deserted portion of the lane in the belief that they were safe from eavesdroppers.

A cold shiver passed over Anne. That look which she had surprised on the evening of the dinner party! That look had revealed these two persons' souls, and now here was its confirmation in words.

But was that the only thing which these words confirmed? What about Sybil's fears? Was this their confirmation also? Sybil had –

But here were the voices again. Grinsmead was speaking. " – be sure of that. At the best it would be a dirty affair. And then what about my business? It's not the sort of business you can build up in a day. If I tried to start anywhere else it would be years before I was making enough to keep us. And then there's that cursed will that takes your money away if you remarry. No, Irene, it's not so easy. We must – "

They passed on. Anne could hear the murmur of Mrs Holt-Lancing's reply, but not the words.

Anne felt rather sick. What could all this mean but one thing? Was it not that Sybil was right? Suddenly to Anne her surroundings changed. The garden became a place of evil, the trees sinister monsters crouching to destroy. There was a foreboding in the stealthy rustle of the breeze through the leaves, even from the very sunlight the warmth and joy had gone, leaving it hard and pitiless. Anne shivered again. Was this how murder began?

But once more there was the sound of voices: Grinsmead's again.

" – take the necessary steps," he was saying. "I'll go into that case you mentioned. With care we should be able to avoid their mistakes. All right, Irene, we shall not have to wait much longer. If you'll face the chance of poverty the rest can be arranged. Assuming, of course, that your husband will divorce you when the time comes."

"He'll be only too glad," came Mrs Holt-Lancing's voice. Then followed faintly the sound of passionate kisses and the broken words, "My beloved, my beloved!"

They were standing just behind the tree. Presently Irene's voice came again: "I'll go now, Severus, that that's settled. We must be more careful than ever." There was the sound of a further embrace and the words, "My beloved, till Thursday"; Grinsmead's voice saying, "I'll wait till you're round the corner," and then silence.

Anne stealthily moved the branches surrounding her. She could see, not behind her, but some distance along the lane towards the garage. With the need for action she was once more cool and efficient. She had got to reach her room unseen before Grinsmead returned to the house.

For some moments the silence remained unbroken, then she heard a shoe strike a stone in the lane, and presently Grinsmead came into view, walking away from her. Mrs Holt-Lancing was evidently crossing the fields to her house. Anne waited till Grinsmead had disappeared behind the garage, then jumped from the yew and slipped quickly indoors.

Even when she had reached the shelter of her room her coolness did not desert her. Something still remained to be done. There would be time enough later to consider what she had heard and to analyse her impressions, but first she must get all this fragmentary conversation on paper. If Sybil's life were threatened, and if she, Anne, were to be of any use in the matter, she must at least be sure of her facts.

She wrote it on thin paper and for safety's sake sewed it into the lining of her cloak. Then she went back to bed again, glad to have the excuse of her headache to save her from having to go down and meet the others.

She felt physically sick, not from her bilious attack, but from sheer horror. For think as she might, she could conceive of no meaning to the words she had overheard than the unspeakably awful one that Sybil's death had been decided on.

She ran over the conversation in her mind. First there were those terribly suggestive references to risk. Irene Holt-Lancing saying that any risk was worthwhile, Grinsmead that they mustn't risk – whatever it was. Could that apply to anything except crime? And then there was the talk of other people having managed it badly, and of the need for greater care. Anne was no criminologist, but she remembered cases, poisoning cases in particular, to which these words might well refer. The bad management had led those concerned to the gallows. No wonder Grinsmead hesitated and talked about risk!

If Anne were right the matter was as urgent as it was serious, terribly urgent and terribly serious. If Anne were right, the crime had definitely been decided on. "We shall not have to wait much longer." There was no time to lose.

What form, she wondered, might the attempt take? This would surely depend on Grinsmead's opportunities of being alone with Sybil. There certainly were not many. A momentary grain of comfort came to Anne as she saw that Sybil actually allowed him no opportunities whatever. He never saw her till lunch or dinner, as the case might be, and from then till bedtime she was careful to remain in the company of Edith or Anne herself.

But this thought did not comfort Anne very long. Grinsmead's plan would surely never include an obvious clue of that kind. It would be something more subtle, something which would not connect him with the tragedy. Would he not somehow set causes at work which, after a safe time had elapsed, would fulfil his dreadful purpose? Something more like poison?

The more Anne thought over it, the more likely poison seemed to her. It was a hideous idea, so ghastly that she could scarcely bring herself to consider it at all. But she kept hammering the thought into her mind that it was Sybil, this young woman whom she had just made her friend, it was Sybil who was threatened with this awful fate. Anne couldn't face the idea of Sybil being dead. Dead! It was too horrible.

Anne saw that she must act, and act at once. She might make a mistake; she might put herself in the wrong; she might be ruined by a slander action; but she must risk that.

Sybil's safety far outweighed all personal considerations. But what was she to do?

At first she thought of reporting to the police what she had heard. But the more she considered this, the less she liked it. She felt sure they would do nothing. They would doubtless hear her politely enough, and then say that the conversation only proved that Grinsmead and Mrs Holt-Lancing were in love, not that they contemplated murder, and that in the absence of proof they could not act.

But she could not carry this terrible load herself. Was there anyone else to whom she could appeal?

Oh, if she had had a father or an uncle, or even some close man friend whom she could trust! But there was no one. She was so utterly alone. There was the doctor, of course. But he was a friend of Grinsmead's, and in any case he would not believe her either.

Her thoughts lingered longer on Mrs Alcock than on any other of her acquaintances. She at least was kindly and sympathetic. But she also was a friend of Grinsmead's, much more so, Anne imagined, than of Sybil's. Indeed it must be admitted that Sybil's unfortunate manner had made her anything but popular. No, Anne could not hope for real help from Mrs Alcock. She would inevitably take Grinsmead's side in the affair.

Finally, after a sleepless night of wrestling with the problem, Anne decided that nothing would be gained by speaking of the matter. She would, however, constitute herself more than ever Sybil's watchdog, keeping the keenest lookout for developments, seeing that Sybil was never left alone when Grinsmead was about, making sure that her door was bolted at night, contriving that it should be impossible for Grinsmead to put anything into her food. But the responsibility weighed heavily on Anne, and as the days passed her cheeks grew paler and her temper took on an unwonted sharpness.

As the days passed also and nothing occurred to upset the monotony of their lives, she began to wonder whether the whole thing had not been a mere piece of panic on her part. Grinsmead moved about as usual, looked as usual, in no way suggested a murderer preparing a horrible fate for his victim. She grew less and less able to think that this man, who seemed so kindly and thoughtful, really could intend to kill his wife. And this doubt was increased when one evening he surprised her in the drawing-room and began to talk in a more confidential way than he had ever before attempted.

"You've made friends with Sybil, have you not, Miss Day?" he remarked, after talking for a moment on other matters. "That will be good for her. In fact, I think she's the better for it already."

Anne murmured a non-committal reply. She really could not bring herself to be cordial. Whether there was, or was not, anything in her darker suspicion, there was no doubt that Grinsmead was a faithless husband. All the same he seemed to want sympathy.

"What do you think of her, Miss Day?" he went on presently, with a wistful look in his eyes. "You see more of her than anyone else. Do you think her health is improving?"

"I don't see very much change, Mr Grinsmead," she forced herself to reply.

"I'm sorry for that. I rather imagined she was more cheerful." He hesitated, then went on doubtfully, as if not sure of his reception. "Poor Sybil has had a hard time. There's no use in blinking facts: you must know how things are. You couldn't otherwise have made friends with her as you have. It's not Sybil's fault, the way things have gone. She tried hard. I don't know that it's my fault either; I tried hard too. But it was no good. We were temperamentally unsuited to one another, and we didn't find it out till it was too late."

Anne was embarrassed, and would much have preferred to leave the room, but she could scarcely walk away in the middle of the conversation. She forced herself to nod and say that she had imagined there might be something of the kind, and how sorry she was about it.

"I'm sure you are," he answered and paused. Then, as if speaking more to himself, he went on: "Of course you might say, if you weren't too polite, Why not get a divorce? But there are difficulties."

"Would not that be the best way in the end?" Anne replied in her blunt way.

"I've thought of it," he said slowly, "a thousand times. Unfortunately it's a matter of money; up to the present I've felt I couldn't afford it. A divorce is a costly thing, of course, but it's not that. The trouble is that a divorce would kill my business, and without my business we shouldn't have enough to live on. And she has only a little money of her own. No, Miss Day, up to the present I've considered a divorce impracticable."

Anne did not reply, and after a moment he went on: "And a separation would not give us the freedom that we want. I don't pretend to deny that I would remarry if I could, and so, I dare say, would she. I'm intensely sorry for the whole thing, both for her and for myself. But sorrow won't mend it."

Again he paused and again Anne not replying, he continued: "I know it is unfair to inflict all this on you, but I have been feeling increasingly that things cannot go on as they are. I have now come to the conclusion that so far as I am concerned I would be willing to risk a divorce and its possible loss of position and income, if only I could get free. Sybil would, of course, have to act, but I'd furnish the necessary evidence. I wonder if you are sufficiently in Sybil's confidence to know whether if this proposal were put up to her, she would be likely to agree to it? You see, she won't give me any chance to approach her about it direct. You don't happen to know her views?" He looked at Anne shamefacedly, but with a sort of veiled eagerness.

Anne was a good deal surprised. She remembered on the one occasion on which divorce had been mentioned between Sybil and herself how insistent Sybil had been that Grinsmead would never contemplate it, for the simple reason that he couldn't afford it. Anne felt it behoved her to be careful.

"I could scarcely say," she returned doubtfully. "She might be willing to consider it."

"You think so?" Again he hesitated. "I wonder would it be too much to ask you, if by any chance you got a favourable opportunity, whether you would sound her on the matter? All I would ask would be a chance of putting the thing before her. It wouldn't, of course, be an easy decision on her part. Is she willing to risk poverty to gain her freedom? She hasn't money; I don't think she could work. I would allow her what I could, but I mightn't have enough for myself. Sound her for me, Miss Day, and you will put me under an everlasting debt of gratitude."

Anne was impressed and embarrassed, but more than either she was surprised. This surely was not the manner nor the speech of a man with murder in his heart. Could he be what he represented himself – a man in trouble, trying to find as honourable a way out as the situation admitted?

Oh, how intensely she hoped so! What a fearful nightmare of dread and horror such a conclusion would banish. Poor man; if this were true all her sympathy would go out to him. And Sybil? Feeling as she did, would Sybil not jump at this chance to put an end, once and for all, to her fears?

It was characteristic of Anne that another side of the affair never occurred to her. If this new desire were consummated she would lose her job. Her thought however was not about herself. If poor unhappy Sybil could be delivered from her dreadful bondage, she, Anne, would take without murmuring what the gods sent her.

Next night, fearing greatly, she broached the subject to Sybil. She had formed the habit of going in to say good night to Sybil and see that all was right, after the latter had gone to bed. Sometimes on these occasions they sat talking for almost an hour. On this next evening after Grinsmead's request, Sybil seemed in a calm and softened mood, and Anne judged the time propitious.

She soon learned her mistake. The very mention of the word divorce, as suggested by Grinsmead, plunged Sybil into a state of extreme excitement and fear.

"Anne," she whispered fiercely, clutching the girl's wrist, "was it his own suggestion, entirely his own? You said nothing that led up to it?" Her eagerness was pitiable.

"He came over and deliberately started the conversation," Anne declared. "It was his own idea from beginning to end. Why, Sybil, what *do* you think of me?"

"I know, I know, of course!" She was terribly – and Anne thought unreasonably – upset. "But, Anne, don't you see what he means? Don't you see?"

"See what?" Anne questioned. "I only know what he said. What do you mean, Sybil?"

"That it's the end!" Sybil's voice rose into a little scream. "He's going to act! He wants to have your evidence on his side! Don't you see? He wants to have you on his side at the inquest! He wants you to say that he couldn't have intended it to happen as he was just about to open negotiations for a divorce. Think of it and you'll see how strong your evidence would be. Oh, he's clever, clever!" Sybil wrung her hands. Her terror was pitiable. But for the first time Anne found it unconvincing.

"Dear Sybil, do be calm," she urged. "You're perfectly safe at present at all events. And we'll take measures to keep you so. Don't give way. It won't help you to get upset and lose your sleep."

But Sybil had lost control of herself. There was another nervous burst of hysteria, another storm of tears, until to quiet her, Anne, on her own responsibility, gave her one of the sleeping draughts.

Anne was sorely puzzled. She no longer knew what to think. This last outburst seemed to her so unreasonable that against her will she wore round to Grinsmead's view that Sybil really was abnormal. It certainly did look as if all these fears were just the persecution mania which so often foreshadows a complete mental breakdown. Once again the burden of responsibility seemed almost more than Anne could bear. If Sybil were wholly sane, was it not a matter for the police? If she were not, should she not go away for treatment? Should Anne tell Grinsmead of Sybil's reception of his message and suggest such treatment?

Anne could not see her way clearly. Next morning, however, the problem seemed, if not less real, at least less pressing. Grinsmead was entirely unemotional and matter-of-fact, utterly removed from tragedy. Sybil even was once more comparatively normal. The whole idea of murder seemed as unsubstantial as a nightmare. Anne could no longer believe in it. There could not be any desperate cause for anxiety.

But Anne, like the rest of us, could not foresee the future.

6

DEATH

For some days after Grinsmead's approach to Anne on the matter of the divorce events at Frayle moved quietly. There were no further excursions or alarms. Grinsmead remained as before, quietly polite, apparently free from emotional stress. Sybil seemed slightly ashamed of her outburst and did not again refer to the matter. Gradually Anne's perplexities subsided.

She had been somewhat at a loss as to what reply to give to Grinsmead about the divorce. On the off chance that there might be some foundation for Sybil's fears, she did not wish to say that his wife would not even speak of his proposal. On the other hand, she could not arrange the meeting he desired. Finally, she compromised by saying that she had sounded Sybil, but so far had not received a decided answer.

The next event to upset the even tenor into which events had fallen was the arrival of old Mrs Grinsmead on a short visit. Anne had been told of her coming by both Sybil and Grinsmead, and she had been interested to notice the reactions of each towards the prospect. Sybil evidently disliked the old lady, and looked forward to entertaining her as a disagreeable duty, forced upon her by her position.

Grinsmead, on the other hand, seemed fond of his mother and glad she was coming.

"She's a wonderful old lady," Sybil declared; "cast in the heroic mould, one might almost say. I find her rather a strain to live up to. She's coming for ten days; she always does at this time of year. I expect it's a break for her. She doesn't seem to have much variety."

"She lives alone, then?" Anne said.

"Quite alone. A little village near Frome. Her husband was the doctor there; he died a couple of years ago. She has only one other child, a daughter, and she has some job in Vienna and doesn't often come over."

"Perhaps I could help to entertain her," Anne suggested. "What does she like to do?"

"Sit bolt upright on a high chair and knit and criticise adversely everything she sees," Sybil answered bitterly. Then, as if ashamed of herself, she added: "There, I shouldn't have said that. She means everything for the best. And she has this in her favour: she's passionately fond of her son. I expect that's why she doesn't like me."

Anne laughed. "I'm sure she's not so bad as all that," she said pleasantly. "She'll have the blue room, I suppose?"

"Yes, and I wish you'd go in with Hersey and meet her. She arrives about five tomorrow."

Next day at 4.42 Anne met the redoubtable old lady on the platform at Ashbridge. Anne identified her the moment she stepped from the train. A figure of medium height and build, surprisingly well-dressed in black and white, with a white face, white hair, small round eyes like those of a Harrison drawing, and a long, straight, pointed chin. Anne introduced herself, and the old lady held out her hand.

"So you're Miss Day, are you?" she said in sharp incisive tones. "Good of you to come to meet me. My son generally comes, but he wrote that he couldn't do so this time."

"No, Mr Grinsmead had to go to Town today," Anne answered. "Mrs Grinsmead is not very well, and she couldn't come in either. She asked me to take her place."

The old lady looked at her keenly. "How has Mrs Grinsmead been keeping?" she inquired. "I'm afraid she hasn't been well for a long time. Last time I was here I thought if anything she was worse."

"She's not worse than when I came," said Anne, "though I don't know that she's much better."

"It's very sad and very mysterious too. The doctors don't seem to be able to find out what's wrong. Are you a native of this country, Miss Day?"

Anne smiled and said she came from near Gloucester. "Near Gloucester?" repeated Mrs Grinsmead. "I knew a Dr Lambert near Gloucester. Ever heard of him?"

"Dr Lambert," cried Anne, with pleased surprise. "Why, yes, I know him well. He lives near Wicklesbury-on-the-Hill, my father's parish."

"That's the man. He was a friend of my husband's and often stayed with us. So your father was rector of Wicklesbury, was he? Then you know the neighbouring rector, Mr Oakley?"

Mr Oakley, it happened, had been a frequent visitor at Anne's old home. Whether because of this discovery of mutual friends, or whether Anne's ingenuous manner appealed to the old lady, she certainly seemed to Anne neither stiff nor censorious. Indeed, in an abrupt outspoken way she was friendly. But Sybil she evidently didn't like. Anne witnessed their meeting, and though both were coldly polite, it was clear that no love was lost between them.

Mrs Grinsmead, senior, struck Anne as an extra-ordinarily active person for her years. Not necessarily physically active, though she seemed, as Anne put it to herself, as hard as nails. But she was tremendously alert mentally, and there was a forcefulness about manner and speech such as few women of sixty could lay claim to. She had also, Anne gradually learned, a fund of unusual knowledge. In her early life she had helped her husband with his dispensing, and she knew quite a lot about drugs and medicine. Still more surprised was Anne by her mechanical knowledge. She seemed to know all about cars, and one day when the electric bells went wrong she did something to the batteries and put them right.

Anne witnessed her meeting with Grinsmead also. He was detained late in Town, and they were all assembled in the drawing-room, waiting for dinner, when he arrived. There was a slightly uncomfortable feeling in the air. Anne really did feel annoyed with Sybil. She was scarcely polite. She disliked and was bored by the old lady and she took very little trouble to hide it. Her manner reacted on Mrs Grinsmead, who became shorter and drier than ever. Edith was unusually silent, and Anne's strenuous efforts to keep the conversation alive fell flatter than they deserved.

It was a relief to all concerned when Grinsmead came in. He crossed the room, and to Anne's surprise kissed the old lady on the forehead.

"Hullo, mother," he said. "Nice to see you again. Sorry I couldn't meet you."

"You provided a satisfactory substitute," Mrs Grinsmead returned. "Miss Day greeted me with the appropriate enthusiasm." The voice was dry and colourless, but Anne surprised a look in her eyes which belied the coolness of her words. Yes, thought Anne, this old lady was fond of her son all right. Why, she doted on him! Pride, love, maternal yearning, shone unmistakably in her eyes.

As they stood there exchanging commonplaces, Anne could not help thinking how unlike mother and son were in externals, and how identical in essentials. He big and overwhelming, she comparatively small and slight; he florid and heavy of face, she white and thin and ascetic looking. But from both radiated force. Strong personalities, each of them. Anne felt that neither would be easily turned aside from his or her purpose. Character – that was it. They had character, these two. For good or evil they were people to be reckoned with.

Once again things settled down. Old Mrs Grinsmead dropped quickly into the ways of the house. She surprised Anne on her first morning by going out in sheets of rain for a fifteen-minute constitutional before breakfast. At breakfast she demanded, and read half Edith's paper. During the morning she wrote; it appeared that she did articles on a variety of subjects for the smaller magazines. In the afternoon she was ready enough to join in anything that was going on or to take a walk by herself, while in the evenings she played bridge. She played bridge well, better, a good deal, than any of the others.

Anne was glad that she had come, and she had to admit that she saw no signs of the old lady tending to sit upright in a straight-backed chair and knit and be censorious. Certainly her manner was sharp, and Anne could understand its putting the children off, but Anne did not think it meant more than a natural impatience for anything below her own standard.

As the days passed Anne found her friendship with her unhappy employer was becoming a larger and larger factor in her life. Sybil now absorbed by far the greater part of her time and more and more she leaned on her. Anne now saw her first thing in the morning as well as last thing at night. She had latterly formed the habit of making Sybil's morning tea, and taking it to her, instead of letting Gladys do so. In the evenings they had confidential chats after Sybil was in bed. But every night Anne waited outside the door till she heard the bolt shot, and then tried the door to make sure that it was properly fastened. To Anne, thinking afterwards over that period, it seemed that at no time had the affairs of the household gone more smoothly nor the atmosphere been more pleasant.

Then suddenly the blow fell.

About a week after old Mrs Grinsmead's arrival the Grinsmeads once more had some people to dinner and bridge. It happened that with two exceptions the guests were the same as had been present on that previous occasion immediately after Anne's coming. The Bolsovers had gone to Italy, and their places were taken by old Mrs Grinsmead and a Captain Panton, a friend of Merrow's. In addition there were Mr and Mrs Alcock, of whom Anne liked Mrs Alcock and tolerated her husband, Mrs Holt-Lancing, whom she could not endure; and Mr Merrow himself, who seemed to her so colourless that she didn't care whether he was present or absent. These, with Edith Cheame and herself, formed the party.

To a large extent history repeated itself on this occasion. Anne sat between Alcock and Merrow, and both in their several ways tried to be entertaining. Anne, though she didn't realise it, had become mildly popular among the Grinsmead's visitors.

After dinner came the inevitable bridge. Here arrangements were the same as on the previous occasion, except that when Sybil went to bed about ten Anne went with her, Edith taking Sybil's place at the tables. Once again Sybil was very much excited, her eyes having a wild expression and her cheeks bearing hectic patches. When the party broke up for drinks Anne moved close to Grinsmead.

"Don't you think it's a night for a sleeping draught?" she asked.

"I leave it to you," he answered. "What do you think?"

"I think she should have it."

"Good. Then give her one."

Upstairs Sybil was nervy and excited. She did not say so, but it was evidently the presence of Irene Holt-Lancing that upset her. She had scarcely been able to bring herself to speak to her, and yet her aim was to ignore, rather than call attention to, the part which Mrs Holt-Lancing was playing in her life.

However, by the time she had got into bed she had quieted down, though she assented with evident satisfaction to Anne's proposal about the draught. Anne thereupon prepared it, but Sybil seemed in no hurry to take it.

"Sit down and chat for a while," she invited, and Anne pulled a chair over to the bed and sat down.

This had now become a habit. Sybil seemed to relax and to enjoy their discussions. Latterly these had begun to embrace a wider range of subjects. They talked not of Sybil's position and her relations with her husband, but of music, literature, the drama – subjects of which no member of the household except Anne knew very much. But on this evening Sybil seemed to have her own affairs too heavily on her mind to venture into asides, and she talked principally of herself.

After half an hour Anne imagined Sybil had had enough. She therefore gave her the sleeping draught, said good night, tried the door and found it securely fastened, and then went to her own room. There, being tired, she got into bed, prepared to enjoy a few minutes with a book before going to sleep.

She was not, however, sleepy, and she read on longer than she had intended. A vague depression weighed on her spirits. She had a sort of uneasy, nightmarish feeling, as if something unpleasant was about to happen. The lobster, she thought; she should not have taken it, it usually upset her. Yet one didn't like to be conspicuous in these matters. Luckily she had an interesting book. She was very comfortable and she went on reading.

About midnight she heard the break-up of the party; the opening of doors, steps on the landing as the women came up to put on their things; voices in the hall; the starting up of motors; the shutting of the hall door; then silence.

Another ten minutes passed and there was a soft tap at her own door.

It was Edith Cheame, very apologetic and hoping that she was not disturbing Anne.

"I saw the light under your door as I came upstairs," she explained. "Those people have only just gone. I've been so longing to get to bed. I've got one of those wretched nervous headaches, you know, all twitchy and jumpy. What I wanted to know was about those sleeping draughts; could you by any chance spare me one? I know I'll not sleep if I don't get something."

"But of course! There's the box on the dressing-table. Take one."

"A thousand thanks, dear. But I thought you kept them locked up?"

"I do, of course. But I had them out tonight to give one to Sybil. I should have locked them away in the morning."

"Sybil looked as if she wanted one tonight."

"Yes, she was glad to get it herself. It was a good thought of yours."

"Well, I've been repaid for it now at all events. Got an interesting book there?"

"*Nights Errant.* I'm loving it. Mrs Alcock lent it to me. You read it?"

"No, but I have it on my list."

"I'll let you have it after I've finished. Mrs Alcock won't mind the few extra days."

"Good soul! Well, cheerio."

Presently the fascination of *Nights Errant* quietly vanished. Anne had grown drowsy. She put away the book, switched off her light and composed herself to sleep.

Next morning she awoke at her usual time, dressed quickly and went down to make Sybil's tea. It was a fine sunny morning, the sun a little thin and watery, as became it at this advanced time of autumn. But to Anne it seemed an ever-recurring symbol of hope. Her depression had vanished, and she felt vigorous and competent, ready to enjoy what the day might bring forth.

She made the tea, put it on its little tray, carried it to Sybil's door, and knocked for the bolt to be withdrawn. She had now done this for nearly a month, and she knew that Sybil appreciated the attention. Sybil never called "Come in!" The click of the moving bolt constituted her invitation.

But now there was no answering click, and after waiting for a moment Anne knocked again.

Still there was no reply. Evidently the effect of the sleeping draught had not worn off. Anne was slightly puzzled. She considered the four previous occasions on which she had given draughts. On all five the draught had been given about the same hour at night, and on each of the other mornings Sybil had been awake when Anne had come. However, it didn't follow that she would always be so. It was probably that the effect of these draughts depended upon something in one's self, one's precise state of health. She had better wait for half an hour and then try again.

She was turning away when she realised that there was an odd smell of gas in the corridor. She had noticed it subconsciously the moment she reached the door, but had not at first given it serious thought. Now it seemed to her quite strong. There were gas fires in all the upstairs rooms, and though the fittings were good, there was an occasional smell of gas, due usually to unskilful lighting. But Anne had never before smelled gas in the corridor.

She moved away to investigate, but immediately lost it. She turned back, wondering a little. It was strongest about the door, Sybil's door. Anne put the tray down on a side table which stood beside the door, and moved about, sniffing.

Yes, it was strongest at the door. She bent down and got a still stronger whiff. Suddenly her heart seemed to stand still. She dropped to her knees and put her nose to the keyhole. Gas was simply pouring out. For the tenth of a second she remained motionless, overwhelmed. Then as she tugged wildly at the door handle she screamed, shrilly, desperately.

There was a sudden movement in the house. Doors opened quickly, hurrying figures appeared. Grinsmead in a dressing-gown, his chin lathered for shaving, hurried up. Edith Cheame's door opened to reveal her, also in a dressing-gown, hastening out with frightened face. Old Mrs Grinsmead, fully dressed, appeared at the same moment. Gladys, pale and startled, was running upstairs.

"What is it?" Grinsmead asked quickly.

For answer Anne stabbed with her finger in the direction of the room. "Gas!" she cried. "Smell it!" She pointed to the keyhole.

Grinsmead stooped and took one sniff. "God!" Anne heard him ejaculate, then he cried: "Open the windows and someone turn the gas off at the meter!" He flung himself with all the weight of his heavy bulk on the door, prising with his bulldog shoulders.

But the door was solid and the bolt strong. He could not burst it. "Tools," he cried, darting downstairs in the direction of his workshop.

Mrs Grinsmead rushed to the windows, throwing wide open all those in the corridor, while Anne tore down to the little room under the stairs where the meter stood, and turned off the main tap. She was just in time to follow Grinsmead as he raced upstairs, a hammer in one hand and a cold chisel in the other. Mrs Meakin had now appeared, and white-faced, the five women watched while with furious blows Grinsmead drove the chisel in between the door and the frame at the bolt, and then prised with all his strength.

There was a grinding, tearing noise and the door opened jerkily, leaving the keeper hanging on the end of the bolt, with its screws sticking out as they had been drawn from the wood. Grinsmead threw it wide. A rush of gas poured out. Waiting to take a breath, Grinsmead plunged in. For a few seconds he was lost to view, then he reappeared, and in his arms a light, sagging figure.

"In here," Anne cried, flinging open the door of her room, which adjoined Sybil's, and then running to open the window.

Grinsmead bore in the figure, its face flushed a bright cherry red, while Anne flew downstairs to ring up the doctor. Fortunately Dr Roome was dressed. He answered the call himself, promising to be round in five minutes. Anne sped up again. Some one had shut Sybil's door to prevent the gas escaping into the corridor, and all had crowded into Anne's room, where Grinsmead and Edith were attempting artificial respiration. Mrs Grinsmead was with them, but as Anne entered, she stepped back. She caught Anne's eye and shook her head.

"Too late," she whispered. "She's dead. There's no hope."

Anne stared at her, scarcely able to comprehend the news. She marvelled that the old lady could be so calm, standing there with folded hands and compressed lips and with her emotions perfectly controlled. Could it be that she didn't care enough about Sybil to show even decent distress? Or could it be – Anne shuddered as a still more horrible thought shot through her mind. Could it be that the old lady was *glad*?

Impossible! And yet – Mrs Grinsmead idolised her son, and no doubt she believed Sybil was ruining her son's life – Was there something gloating in that veiled look? A sort of terrible evil joy on the pale features?

Anne did not know, and she did not care. Her thoughts went back to Sybil. She felt numb with horror. She could not believe that Sybil, poor, unhappy, distracted Sybil, could be *dead*. That she would never speak again. That her fears and hopes and joys and sorrows were over. Oh, it was too awful to think of!

For a few minutes she stood watching Grinsmead's pale, set face, as he worked desperately to try and induce breathing. He knew what he was about evidently, as also did Edith Cheame. Her face was as white and grim as his own as she helped him.

Suddenly there came the sound of wheels, and Anne flew down to open the door for the doctor. "Oh, doctor," she cried, "I'm afraid she's dead. Gas poisoning. Mr Grinsmead's trying artificial respiration. Come up."

Dr Roome was a practitioner of middle age, clever, kindly and efficient. Anne experienced a slight sense of relief as she saw his strong, reliable face. Instinctively she felt that everything possible would be done and without delay. The doctor shook his head to express his dismay and concern, but did not speak. Rapidly he followed Anne upstairs.

He shook his head again when he saw Sybil, though for an hour and more he continued the artificial respiration. At the end of that time he had to admit what he had known all the time. Sybil was dead.

A paralysis of horror held everyone in its stupefying grip. Grinsmead in particular seemed stunned. He appeared scarcely to hear the doctor's sympathetically worded statement. Anne felt as if she was in a dream, a hideous nightmare from which she must presently awake to find things normal. Edith seemed equally overwhelmed. Only Mrs Grinsmead appeared to have kept full command of her feelings and to realise to the full what had happened.

At last Grinsmead pulled himself together. "I knew it, doctor," he said in a low tone. "The moment I saw her I knew it. We found her too late."

"Come downstairs, Grinsmead," Dr Roome went on. "You can't do anymore here. Everyone should come away in the meantime. Come away, Miss Day." He shepherded them out of the room and shut the door. "I'm very sorry, Grinsmead," Anne heard him say, as the two men went down the corridor, "but I'm afraid this must be reported to the police. It's not death from natural causes, you know."

"I realise that," Grinsmead answered in a dull, toneless voice. "I'll ring them up now. I was just waiting for your report."

"I'll ring them up if you like," Roome offered. "Where's the telephone?"

They went downstairs, and Anne heard Roome's voice making his call. How dreadful that poor Sybil's tragedy could not be kept decently hidden! Surely all that had taken place need not be dragged into the horrid blaze of publicity. Anne felt sick as she thought of it.

Presently she heard Roome's voice calling her.

"It seems heartless, Miss Day, but every one must have some breakfast. Yes, you must," he went on, as Anne shook her head. "Have some hot coffee if you can't eat. It won't help matters for you to start a chill. Do you hear what I say, Grinsmead? Miss Day's getting breakfast, and you must have some."

Breakfast! Anne thought of it with loathing. She thought she never could look at food again.

But Roome insisted, and though all said they could not eat, they soon found they were mistaken.

By the time a little toast and a good deal of hot coffee had been disposed of there was a further sound of wheels and another ring.

"I'll go," said Dr Roome, and Anne presently heard him at the door. " 'Morning, inspector. 'Morning, sergeant. A bad business, I'm afraid." There were gruff murmurs in reply.

Grinsmead had followed the doctor out, and his voice came next, low, but clear and collected. "Good morning, Kendal. The doctor will show you everything. I know you'll keep things as quiet as you can." There were further murmurs, evidently expressions of sympathy, then the study door closed and heavy footsteps began going upstairs.

Anne, scarcely allowing herself to think, began automatically to help Gladys to clear the breakfast table. To do anything, no matter how unnecessary, was better than staying still. Action tended to prevent thought, and thought at present was too painful to endure. Sybil dead! It was too *awful*.

Poor, poor Sybil! How dreadful to have lived in such a state! How utterly dreadful to have died in it!

But death comes, and the living go on as before. Already the house was settling down. Though pale and shaken, the five women had taken up their daily tasks. The servants were getting on with their work and Anne was considering the day's catering. Edith had gone to keep the children out of the way. Grinsmead had shut himself up in his study, Mrs Grinsmead in her bedroom. Then Dr Roome suddenly made his appearance and asked Anne to go upstairs.

"The inspector wants to ask you a question or two, Miss Day," he explained. "You need have no uneasiness. You'll find him a very decent fellow."

Inspector Kendal saluted respectfully when Anne appeared. He began by expressing his sympathy and his regret at having to trouble her. "I just want a word or two about what you found this morning," he went on. "I shall have to get a detailed statement from you later, but now I only want a word so as to get the hang of things. You made the discovery, I believe?"

"Yes, it was I," Anne answered, and she went on to tell what had occurred.

The inspector nodded gravely. "Now we want to get into that room," he went on. "What about the windows? Did Mrs Grinsmead keep them open or shut?"

"Open. Invariably open, even on the coldest night. She was what is sometimes called a fresh air fiend."

"Then we must see if they're open now. Maybe, miss, you'd come out with us and point out Mrs Grinsmead's windows?"

They walked round to the tennis ground. All the windows in Sybil's room were tightly closed.

"I wonder if we shouldn't break the glass," the inspector observed. "It'll take the room the deuce of a while to clear otherwise." He rubbed his chin slowly, then decided he would make an attempt to open the window first.

Accordingly they came upstairs again, and having closed all the other doors on to the corridor, he opened that of Sybil's room. Then, taking a long breath, he rushed in and drew back the curtains. He had to rush out again, but after some deep breathing he made another attempt and got one window open. By hanging out of this he was able to breathe till all the sashes had been opened. Then he came out and shut the door.

"That room will be clear enough in a short time," he observed. "Here, constable, stay outside this door and don't allow any one in. In the meantime, I'll take statements. Where can I have the use of a table, miss?"

Anne showed him to the dining-room. He sat down and spread his notebook before him. The sergeant sat down beside him with another notebook. Kendal turned to Anne.

"Thank you, Miss Day, that will do in the meantime. I shall want you again later, but I'll take the doctor first, so that he can get away. Call Dr Roome, sergeant."

Anne left the room. She had never come in contact with the police before, and she was impressed by the unobtrusive but competent way Kendal had taken charge. With him there, all anxiety as to what should or should not be done, had vanished. Anne felt instinctively that he would not only see that every necessary formality was complied with decently and in order, but that he would also quietly but relentlessly ferret into things until he satisfied himself that no blame was attaching to anyone concerned.

This impression was strengthened when half an hour later the sergeant asked her if she would please come to the dining-room to make her statement. Kendal was polite, even kindly, yet he was none the less an official doing impersonally a distasteful job.

"Sit down, Miss Day, will you, please?" he began, standing up as Anne entered. "Now," he went on, "I'm sorry to say that there'll have to be an inquest, at which you'll have to give evidence. There's nothing, of course, in that in any way to alarm you, but I want to know now what your evidence will be. In accordance with our invariable routine, I'll take down your statement now and then ask you to sign it."

He began then asking questions, writing down skilfully-worded *précis* of the answers. How long had Miss Day been at Frayle? Under what circumstances had she come? What had her relations been with the deceased? Had she formed the impression that the deceased was happy in her mind? Oh, not altogether happy, was she not? And could Miss Day form any idea as to the cause of that unhappiness? A persecution complex? But that was rather a serious thing, wasn't it, closely allied to an affection of the mind? But Miss Day didn't think her mind was affected? Oh, the inspector followed, not more so than was consistent with a persecution complex! Quite so. Inspector Kendal put down his pen and slowly rubbed his chin.

"Now this persecution complex," he went on presently. "Did it ever occur to you that it might be a predisposing cause of suicide?"

Anne hesitated. "The idea has entered my mind," she said, "but not seriously. I never really imagined she might commit suicide."

"Quite so," the inspector returned, his pen running over the paper. " 'The idea of suicide had entered my mind, but I never seriously entertained it.' That correct? Now, Miss Day, can you tell me this? Was this persecution complex held against any one person more than any other?"

Anne was growing more and more troubled as she saw where this catechism was likely to lead. She need have no uneasiness, Dr Roome had said. Goodness, how little he knew! If this was a friendly and sympathetic police examination, what would one of the other kind be like? How much should she tell this inspector? Anne did not know what to do, but finally her commonsense came to her aid and she decided she would answer what she was asked, and volunteer nothing.

"It was directed against everyone, so far as I know," she said, "even against me," and she went on to tell of Sybil's sudden doubt as to whether she, Anne, were really against her, the inquiries Sybil had made at Gloucester, and her subsequent change of attitude towards Anne. Kendal nodded gravely as he wrote down the reply.

"But I don't think that quite answers my previous question," he went on respectfully, but relentlessly. "Do you mean to convey that there was no one person more than any other against whom this complex was directed?"

This seemed too point-blank a question to be evaded.

"I think it was principally directed against Mr Grinsmead," she answered.

Kendal wrote, then read his note aloud. " 'The complex was against everyone in the house, but principally against Mr Grinsmead, or more accurately, as a result of the complex Mrs Grinsmead felt that everyone in the house was against her, but particularly Mr Grinsmead.' Quite so, Miss Day. Now another question. Do you happen to know why the deceased imagined her husband was against her?"

"I suppose the disease," said Anne.

For the first time Kendal looked at her a trifle sternly.

"You have not quite got my meaning, Miss Day," he returned. "What I want to know is: Did the deceased in her own mind attribute to him any actual conduct or motives prejudicial to herself?"

Anne hesitated. "I don't know that I can answer that," she said. "If her mind wasn't quite normal, doesn't that cover it?"

"No, Miss Day, it does not," Kendal replied more sharply. "I must trouble you to answer my question."

"Well, if you must have it, she imagined Mr Grinsmead was not faithful to her."

"And to whom did she imagine he had transferred his affections?"

This was horrible. And Kendal was looking quite stern. He could be nasty, Anne was sure, if he were crossed. Not that she would have hesitated to do what she thought right because of that. But she did not know how much she ought to say. Then Kendal's voice broke in on her thoughts again.

"Remember, Miss Day, I am only asking you what the deceased lady imagined. I am not asking you what was the fact."

This was true. Anne felt she should reply. "To Mrs Holt-Lancing," she said in a low tone.

To her surprise Kendal nodded appreciatively.

"I'm glad you told me that, Miss Day," he declared. "For a moment I thought you were going to hedge. Now I may tell you for your peace of mind that Mr Grinsmead's little affair with Mrs Holt-Lancing is well known to the police. So you've given nothing away. Mrs Grinsmead was probably correct in her view, though mind you, whether she was or not wouldn't have mattered so far as her feelings towards Mr Grinsmead were concerned. In these cases it's usually the nearer and dearer the person, the more bitter the feeling against them."

Anne felt a weight roll off her shoulders. How thankful she was that she had spoken the truth! And how doubly thankful that she had been asked nothing which would have brought out that horrible affair in the lane. For Kendal now edged off this particular subject. He questioned Anne about Sybil's use of the gas fire, about the keeping open of the windows, about the bolt on the door, and other more or less relevant details of their daily life. Finally, he read over what he had written, asked Anne to sign it, thanked her for her help, and bowed her from the room.

Though the day was young, Anne ached from head to foot from sheer weariness. It was her first introduction to tragedy.

– 7 –

INQUEST

To Anne the rest of that day passed as a nightmare. The police spent a good deal of time in the house. After she left them they interviewed Edith Cheame, then Mrs Grinsmead, then the servants, and finally Grinsmead. Then she heard their heavy tread going up once more to the fatal room. For a couple of hours they stayed there, though what they were doing she could not imagine. At last they took themselves off, and their going was like the lifting from the house of some dark shadow of ill omen.

But they were succeeded by other visitors. Two women, sent by the doctor, who spoke in whispers and vanished silently upstairs. A melancholy man in black with a stealthy tread, the representative of the undertaker, who also disappeared upstairs. Sergeant Thatcher to say that the inquest had been fixed for ten o'clock next day. A mysterious, legal-looking man to see Grinsmead. And last, but not least, Mrs Alcock, who asked for Anne, but would not go in, and who merely called to express sympathy and to ask Anne to stay with her till she had time to look round, if she wanted to leave Frayle at once. She kissed Anne affectionately, thereby nearly sending that young woman off into a flood of tears.

Though at first Anne's mind was filled with the tragedy to the exclusion of all else, as the day wore on and the first shock passed away, her thoughts inevitably turned to the effect that it would have upon herself. This job, though it had had its serious drawbacks, had in many ways been ideal. Had she lost it? A vision of the London streets, now foggy, wet, and icy cold, seemed suddenly to spread out in front of her, broken only by registry offices, each more dismal, soul-destroying, hope-extinguishing, than the last. Small wonder that Anne shivered as she contemplated the prospect.

That she should stay on as Grinsmead's housekeeper never occurred to her, until that evening Edith Cheame suggested the possibility. Instinctively she shrank from any further association with Grinsmead. There was no doubt that, however indirectly, he had been the cause of his wife's death. Whether a woman of stronger character than Sybil would have allowed things to get into the state they had was not the question. Things had got into this state, and as a result Sybil had lost her life. Anne felt that in a sense Grinsmead had committed murder.

And yet, had he? Anne remembered the evening on which he had taken her into his confidence as to his marriage. If his story were to be believed, he had done all he could to make it happy. That he had failed, and that Sybil had failed, was according to him, their misfortune rather than the fault of either. And if Sybil had withdrawn herself from him, was it not only human that he should look elsewhere for consolation?

However, Anne felt that her desires in the matter were of little importance. It was not likely that she would have the chance to stay, even if she wanted to. No, for her it would be the London streets and the registry offices.

Edith Cheame, she found, was oppressed with the same fears. Edith appeared to have gone through an even worse time than had Anne, and she was now in correspondingly greater despair. She was shocked and sorry about Sybil's death, but she was clearly a good deal more shocked and sorry about herself. This, however, was understandable. Edith had never made friends with Sybil as Anne had. To the end Sybil had treated her with dislike and suspicion, and it was impossible that the governess could have felt warmly to her.

"My goodness, Anne," she declared during their talk, "I don't want to leave this place! It's not perfect, but compared to what I've been through, it's heaven. What on earth will the man do? I wish I were sure he'd keep us on."

"Would you stay?" Anne asked.

"Would I stay? Good heavens, Anne. What *do* you think? *Of course* I'd stay, and so would you. Both of us thankful to get the chance."

"I feel," said Anne, "that he was the cause of – upstairs."

"Rubbish!" Edith returned decisively. "How could he have been? He was extraordinarily decent to her, I think. It was she who was the cause of any trouble there was, with her notions and her suspicions and her superiority."

As they continued their talk it became increasingly evident to Anne that the Holt-Lancing side of the affair had never entered Edith's mind. Not surprising, Anne told herself. It would not have entered her own had it not been for those two accidents, the intercepting of that look at the bridge table and the overhearing of the conversation in the lane. There was no doubt that the two principals had been extraordinarily discreet. It was only, Anne felt sure, because of her abnormally quickened instincts that Sybil herself had come to suspect it.

"I'll tell you, Edith, what Grinsmead will do," Anne declared, a sudden idea striking her. "As sure as fate he'll get his mother to come and live here. She'll keep house for him. You'll be kept on, but I'll get the boot."

"As sure as fate, he won't," Edith returned. "You don't know the old lady. Why, by the end of a month he wouldn't be able to call his soul his own. He'd have to account for everything he did and she'd have everything going her own way. He knows her all right and he wouldn't be such a fool."

"I don't know," Anne demurred. "She doesn't seem to me as bad as she's made out."

That night Anne moved into one of the spare rooms. She did not expect to sleep, but the strain of the day had taken it out of her, and the moment her head touched the pillow she dropped into a heavy slumber from sheer exhaustion. But she had disturbing dreams, and when she awoke next morning it was unrefreshed and with a vague sense of impending ill.

The inquest was to be held in a small public hall some half-mile away on the road to Ashbridge. Only Grinsmead, Anne, Edith and Gladys were summoned, but Mrs Grinsmead wished to be present and accompanied them.

The crowd round the little building made respectful way for Grinsmead and the four women. With a similar respectful bearing a constable ushered them into the seats which had been reserved for them. It all seemed quite normal to Anne, like going to a concert or other entertainment.

But when she settled down and looked around her she saw that she had never before been at anything like this. Down the centre of the room was a long table, surrounded by chairs. At the head was the coroner, whom she recognised as Dr Heath, whom she had frequently met, and whom she liked. He was arranging papers on the table, but when he saw the Frayle party arrive, he got up and came over to express his sympathy.

Next to the coroner sat Inspector Kendal, who also rose and bowed to Grinsmead. All the remainder of the seats at the table were vacant, except for two young men with notebooks, reporters obviously. At the back of the hall stood a number of men and one or two women. Sergeant Thatcher seemed to be in charge and stood behind his chief, turning over some sheets of paper.

"It's ten o'clock," said the coroner. "If you're ready, sergeant, we'll begin."

"Ready, sir," the sergeant answered, and began fumbling more energetically than ever at his list. Then he called: "John Smallpiece!"

"Here," said a voice from the back of the room, and a stout round-faced man like a small shopkeeper or clerk, pushed forward.

"Take your seat, Mr Smallpiece." The sergeant pointed to the end chair at the table, and called "Joseph Turner!"

Turner followed his foreman, and after him came nine other good men and true. Then they were sworn and the proceedings proper began.

The first witness was Grinsmead. He went forward, was sworn, and sat down on a chair close to the coroner.

Sergeant Thatcher stood up to examine him. After extracting Grinsmead's name and profession, he went on to obtain from him formal evidence of identification.

"How long have you been married, Mr Grinsmead?" he went on.

"Just over seven years."

"And how would you describe your wife's temperament when you married her?"

"She was artistic and highly strung; inclined to moods of depression and elation. A little fanciful at times, but always good and kindly." Grinsmead spoke in a low though steady voice, as if he had made up his mind to go through a hateful job as quickly and unemotionally as possible.

"Her family were artistic?"

"That is so. Her brother was a well-known RA, and one of her sisters was both a novelist and a musician."

"Quite so. Now, Mr Grinsmead, was her health always quite good?"

"Her health was good when I married her and it continued good for four years or more. Then it began to deteriorate, in fact I may say that for the last three years it has slowly but steadily become worse."

"And what form did this illness take?"

Grinsmead hesitated. "Dr Roome was attending her," he said. "Perhaps he could tell you better than I."

"I shall ask the doctor, sir, certainly. In the meantime I should like to have your views about it."

"Uncalled-for excitement and apparent mental stress were symptoms," Grinsmead returned. "She worked herself up into a state of nerves without any real provocation, then became quite exhausted. She also became more fanciful."

It was evident that Grinsmead was finding these questions very painful, but he mastered his emotion and spoke quietly.

"And these symptoms grew worse?"

"Yes. Then she began to find running the household a strain. To relieve her I got, first a governess and then a housekeeper."

"Quite. And when did you get these?"

"The governess about sixteen months ago. The housekeeper about four months ago."

"I'm sorry, Mr Grinsmead, to ask you these questions, but I'm afraid they're material. Did the deceased's fancies ever grow so marked as to be called delusions?"

Once again Grinsmead hesitated. "I'm afraid they did," he said at last, bowing his head. "Unhappily she began to think that every man's hand was against her."

"Is that what's commonly called a persecution complex?"

"I believe so."

"And she was quite in error in that?"

"Absolutely and completely," Grinsmead returned decisively.

"She thought that your hand was against her, Mr Grinsmead?"

Again he bowed his head. "Unhappily she did."

"Was it for this reason that she insisted in having her own room?"

"I presume so."

"But she did have her own room at all events?"

"Yes."

"She had formed the habit of bolting the door at night?"

"Yes, she had an electric bolt put on which she could operate without getting out of bed."

"There was a gas fire in her room?"

"Yes."

"Do you know if she used it often?"

"Not to my knowledge."

"She didn't light it to go to bed by?"

"Not to my knowledge."

"But she liked the windows open?"

"So far as I know she always had the windows open, even on the coldest nights."

The sergeant went on to ask perfunctorily about the sleeping draughts, whose idea they had been, and whether Grinsmead knew that Sybil had had one on the fatal night. Then he passed to the dinner party, when Grinsmead had last seen his wife alive. He pressed him as to whether there had been any unpleasantness or disagreement between them, or if he could account in any way for Sybil being specially upset that night. To these latter questions Grinsmead replied that he knew of nothing which could have upset Sybil, and that she had seemed to him just as usual all the evening.

Anne, who was listening with troubled mind to this catechism, felt that those dreadful questions about Mrs Holt-Lancing could not now be longer delayed. But to her surprise there was no mention of Mrs Holt-Lancing. When the sergeant had extracted an account of Grinsmead's part in the discovery of the tragedy, he intimated that he had finished.

Some whispering took place between Inspector Kendal and the coroner, and then the latter asked if any of the jurors wished to put a question to the witness. None did so, and Grinsmead, after signing the record of his evidence, was told he might stand down.

Anne was surprised at being called next. In her turn she was sworn and took the chair which Grinsmead had vacated. She felt nervous, not because of her position, but because of the questions she feared she would be asked. Then she caught the coroner's eye and he smiled at her surreptitiously, as much as to say: "Don't worry; you have a friend at court."

This little action of the coroner's cheered Anne out of all proportion to its significance. She felt that he would see her through and would not allow her to be asked anything too horrible. The jury, too, seemed sympathetic to her. They looked what they evidently were, a collection of ordinary decent men, not too intelligent, but well-disposed and sorry for a young lady in a trying position.

The sergeant began respectfully enough. He asked Anne her name, how long she had been at Frayle and the circumstances of her going there. Then he went on to Sybil. How had Sybil's manner struck Anne on her arrival? Had she seemed to dislike and distrust Anne? Had she seemed to dislike and distrust the other members of the household? Did Anne think this dislike and distrust was well-founded? If not, was it what was commonly called a persecution complex? Quite so.

The sergeant then led Anne to describe her reconciliation with Sybil.

"I may understand then, Miss Day, that for the last few weeks you were on intimate and friendly terms with the deceased?"

"That is so."

"You then formed the habit of visiting her after she had gone to bed at night?"

"Yes."

"And you visited her on the night prior to her death?"

"Yes."

"Now will you tell the jury what condition she was in on that night?"

"A little excited," Anne replied. "There had been a dinner party that evening and dinner parties always excited her. But she was not more excited than after previous dinner parties."

The sergeant led Anne through all the events of the evening, the time Sybil went to bed, how long Anne sat with her, what they had conversed about, and finally the giving of the sleeping draught. Then he put her through a searching examination about the sleeping draughts, how many Sybil had had previously, the effect they had had on her, particularly whether on previous occasions on which Sybil had taken a draught she had been awake at her usual time in the morning.

"Now, Miss Day, how long was Mrs Grinsmead in bed before you left the room?"

"About half an hour, I should think. I didn't look."

"And when did you give her the sleeping draught?"

"Oh, just the last thing before coming out."

"Quite so," said Sergeant Thatcher, while the coroner and Inspector Kendal exchanged rapid glances.

"Can you tell me whether the windows were open or shut when you gave her the draught?" went on the sergeant.

"No," Anne answered. "I couldn't see them because they were covered with curtains. I should think open, because the room was cold, as Mrs Grinsmead liked it, but I don't know."

Thatcher then asked about the bolting of the door, getting Anne to describe the electric bolt to the jury.

"When you left the deceased that night did you hear the bolt being shot?"

"Yes, and I tried the door to make sure it was bolted."

"Oh," said the sergeant, "and why did you do that?"

"I did it every night. Mrs Grinsmead liked to be sure the bolt had worked."

Sergeant Thatcher then led Anne through the events of the following morning; her taking up Sybil's tea, her knocking, the absence of the click of the opening bolt, the smell of gas, her realisation that something serious was wrong and her cry for help. Then the sergeant intimated that he had finished and sat down.

Evidently, Anne thought with considerable relief, the question of Mrs Holt-Lancing was not going to be brought up. She was surprised as well as thankful, as the sergeant had made such a lot of it when examining her privately. But she found she was not quite done. The foreman of the jury wished to ask her a question.

"If we've understood the matter correctly," he said, evidently speaking for his colleagues as well as himself, "this young lady was more intimate with the deceased than anyone else. If so, I should like to ask her whether at any time she had been afraid of the deceased committing suicide?"

To this Anne replied precisely as she had to the sergeant when he asked her the same question. The idea had entered her mind, but she had not treated it seriously.

Edith Cheame and Gladys were next examined briefly. They had nothing fresh to say and stood down after confirming certain evidence of Grinsmead's and of Anne's.

Dr Roome deposed that he had been called by telephone to Frayle on the previous morning, to find the deceased already dead. He had, however, spent an hour in trying to induce artificial respiration. He could not say at what hour death had occurred, but he would place it comparatively late in the night, as there had been practically no cooling. The jury would have, however, to remember that in the conditions obtaining, cooling would be retarded. There were similar cases on record where eight to ten hours after death cooling remained inappreciable. In fact it was impossible to arrive at any accurate conclusion on the point. There was, however, no doubt that death had occurred from poisoning by carbon monoxide gas, such as is found in coal gas.

Dr Roome was quite definite in his manner up to this point, but when Sergeant Thatcher began to ask him about a persecution complex, he grew wary and reserved. He was not, he pointed out, an alienist. These questions of the mind were difficult. He was not prepared to say that the deceased's mind was affected because she harboured ideas that were unsubstantiated. She was not perhaps entirely normal, but very few of us were, and he could not say that such abnormality as she had shown was actually unbalanced. All the same, he agreed, speaking not as an expert, but as an ordinary practitioner, that such a frame of mind probably predisposed towards suicide.

This ended Sergeant Thatcher's catechism, but once again the foreman of the jury asked a question.

"Can the doctor tell us how soon a sleeping draught of the type used takes effect? What we want to know is, whether the deceased could have got up after Miss Day left her and shut the windows and turned on the gas, or whether she would have been too drowsy?"

As to this Roome was clear. The sleeping draught did not act quickly enough to have prevented the deceased performing these actions.

The next witness was Inspector Kendal. Sergeant Thatcher did not presume to examine his superior, and the coroner asked the inspector to make a statement in his own words.

"Yesterday at eight-five," he began, "I received a telephone from Frayle, telling me that the deceased had lost her life from gas poisoning. I at once proceeded to the place. The deceased had been taken from the room in which she had slept, which was full of gas. I opened the windows and when it had cleared away I examined the room."

"And what did you find?" prompted the coroner.

"I found, sir, that the door, which was of strong construction, was fitted with an electric bolt, as has been described. The door had been forcibly burst open, the screws holding the keeper of the bolt having drawn out of the wood. The appearance was in accordance with the evidence given by Mr Grinsmead. The windows were tightly shut and the curtains drawn. The tap of the gas fire was turned full on."

The inspector paused as if reaching the end of a paragraph. No one speaking, he resumed: "I then made some further investigations. I examined the tap of the gas fire and I found it marked with fingerprints. Then I took the fingerprints of the deceased lady and compared the two. I found they were the same. It is clear, therefore, that the gas was turned on by the deceased herself."

Public interest, which had increased on the mention of fingerprints, relapsed once more to normal. Inspector Kendal, after another momentary pause, went on.

"I tested the handles of the casement windows similarly for fingerprints, but I was unable to obtain any. Though I had no doubt on the subject, I was therefore unable to prove absolutely that they had been closed by the deceased."

Once again the foreman asked a question.

"I should like to ask the inspector whether he had any doubts that the deceased had turned on the gas, which caused him to take all that trouble about fingerprints?"

"No, sir," Kendal returned formally. "I had no doubt in my own mind as to what had happened, but in these cases it is best to obtain all the proof that's available."

This ended the evidence, and the coroner made a short speech summing up the case.

"I do not think, gentlemen," he concluded, "that you will have much difficulty in making up your minds on this unhappy tragedy. The door was bolted from within, and it would have been impossible for anyone to have entered to turn on the gas or to have left after doing so. Even, however, had the door not been bolted, this would not in any way have affected your finding. The fingerprints of the unhappy lady on the tap of the gas fire prove that it was she, and no one else, who turned it on. The closing of the windows, normally open, proves further the deliberate nature of the deed. I think you will agree that the deceased died by her own hand.

"There is, however, an alleviation in the case, that is, so far as anything can be an alleviation in these painful cases. There can be no doubt that the deceased was not of sound mind. She was not, in my humble opinion, responsible for her action.

"If you, gentlemen, are in agreement with these views, you will return a verdict of suicide while of unsound mind. If not, you will vary this verdict as you think proper."

The jury made a show of retiring to consider their verdict, but they got no further than the door. There they formed a knot, and after some whispering and nodding of heads the foreman faced round.

"The jury don't want to retire," he explained. "We're agreed on our verdict. We find that the deceased committed suicide while of unsound mind and that no blame attaches to anybody."

8

REPERCUSSION

That afternoon seemed to Anne the longest through which she had ever lived. Though the inquest was over comparatively early, she found herself quite unable to settle down to any of her usual pursuits. There was a sort of expectancy over everything. She felt herself like a person waiting for the footstep of a caller whose visit may bring incalculable consequences for good or ill.

The truth was that Anne had had a severe shock. The whole ghastly tragedy had stirred her in a way that she would not have believed possible, and for some time to come she would have to pay the price in her jangled nerves. Never could she get Sybil's face out of her mind as she had seen it when Grinsmead was carrying the body out of that awful room. Nor could she blot from her imagination the fears the unhappy woman had expressed. Poor Sybil! What a miserable end she had come to!

Against Grinsmead Anne's anger at first burned hot. The man had murdered his wife! Not directly, of course. Thank God, it was not so bad as that. Anne shuddered as she thought how unspeakably awful it would have been if Anne's fears and her own doubts had proved well-founded. But he had murdered her all the same. Anne felt certain that if it had not been for that wretched business with Mrs Holt-Lancing, Sybil would now have been alive.

She wondered if Grinsmead himself realised this. From his appearance she almost fancied that he did. The man had certainly been hard hit. In a day his face had seemed to grow old and his figure to fall in and become stooped. At least, she had to admit he was not callous. Possibly he had not realised, until it was too late, that Sybil was aware of what was going on and how terribly she felt it. Possibly that grim set face was a mask covering a mind torn by the torments of remorse.

Gradually Anne came to see that it was not for her to judge. She began to remember all Grinsmead's quiet kindness to herself, yes, and his kindness to Sybil. Perhaps he wasn't so bad. Perhaps this was one of those cases which seem preordained to end in disaster. In any case poor Sybil, unless she was entirely irresponsible, should not have taken so terrible a way out.

Anne, sick of her own company, tried to persuade Edith Cheame to go out for a walk with her. But Edith was engaged with the children and Anne had to go alone. She tramped for miles in the gathering gloom and felt the better for it. By dinnertime she had approached more nearly to her own sturdy self.

Dinner was an ordeal to all concerned, but Mrs Grinsmead, with grim insistence, kept a formal conversation going, and at length the meal was over. After it mother and son withdrew to the study, while Anne went with Edith to the latter's room. Anne was surprised to find how much the affair had shaken Edith. Anne had always looked on the governess as a rather hard woman, but now she revised her opinion. Edith was more upset than was Anne herself.

But the explanation soon came. It was about her own prospects that Edith was upset. Her terrible dread of poverty pursued her. She feared desperately that her job would come to an end. And Anne, in spite of her sorrow for Sybil, was so fully alive to the possibilities so far as she herself was concerned, that she readily returned to a discussion of their outlook.

It was as if the fates knew and sympathised with their uncertainties, that just as they had settled down to a desultory conversation Gladys should arrive with a message from Grinsmead. He would be grateful if the two ladies would come down and speak to him in the study.

"There," Edith cried. "We'll know now. He's going to tell us that we may look out for other jobs!"

Grinsmead was alone in the study. He stood up when they appeared. He did not ask them to sit down and the three remained standing throughout the interview.

"So sorry for asking you to come down," he began, "but I thought I would like to say to you at once that I hope you can both see your way to remain on here for the present. My mother, unfortunately, cannot stay more than a few days. I have made no plans yet, and I don't know what I shall do. I may eventually close the house and take a rest from my business and go and travel: I don't know. But in the meantime it would oblige me very much if you could both carry on. What do you both feel like?"

"Oh, but of course we'll stay, Mr Grinsmead," Edith answered, without giving Anne a chance to say anything. "We shouldn't dream of leaving you in the lurch. We'll carry on exactly as we have been until you've made your plans. Please don't worry about the house or the children. They'll be looked after exactly as if nothing had happened."

Anne looked at the governess in some surprise. There was a softness, a kindly, comforting, sympathetic quality in her manner usually conspicuous by its absence. It was as if she looked upon Grinsmead as a large boy who wanted mothering, as if she were offering him her support in his trouble. That Grinsmead felt her influence was obvious. Consciously or unconsciously, he reacted to it. An expression of satisfaction and relief passed over his face, and Anne felt instinctively that it was Edith's manner rather than her words that had called it forth.

Her best friend could not have called Edith Cheame a handsome woman, yet at that moment she looked very nearly beautiful. That Grinsmead admired her was obvious. Quietly he thanked her for her attitude, then turned to Anne and asked if Miss Cheame had been speaking for her also.

Anne reassured him, he thanked them both, said he would advise them directly he had made his plans, and the interview was over.

Edith was in high delight as they reached her room. "That's all right," she exclaimed, throwing herself back in an armchair and lighting a cigarette. "So far nothing could be better. Now, I'll tell you, Anne, what we've got to do. We've got to run this house as it never was run before. If we do everything with our own hands, we've got to make it go perfectly. We keep out of his way unless he wants to talk to us. He has no trouble about house or servants or children. His meals are ready when he wants them and they're good meals that he likes. You ought to know what he likes by this time. His study will always be inviting, a bright fire, whisky to his hand, everything clean, but his papers not disturbed. I'll tell you, Anne, we'll make him so comfortable that he'll not want to change. It's our only chance."

Anne, in spite of herself, could not help feeling slightly shocked. "You don't think much of poor Sybil, Edith," she remonstrated.

"Anne, dear, you make me tired," Edith said impatiently. "Poor Sybil could have done much better for herself if she had tried. The man was as good to her as the average husband, better indeed, if she had only had the sense to see it. Poor Sybil, indeed! If you or I had had her chance we'd have made a different thing out of the marriage. Sorry," she went on with a change of manner, "you liked her. Well, I didn't: I've never pretended otherwise. And she didn't like me and she never pretended otherwise. She treated me as if I was a thief and an interloper, and all the time I was doing my best for her. There, don't mind what I say about her. But don't you agree about what we should do?"

"Well, of course," said Anne. "We should do our best in any case, I suppose."

Edith contemplated her with an expression of weariness. "Well, well," she said, "if you like to take up that attitude you can. As a matter of fact," she added as an afterthought, "I suppose you're wise."

The next two days dragged slowly and heavily away, and on the third the funeral took place. It was private and a simple ceremony. Grinsmead and his mother went in his own car, Anne and Edith following in one of the hired vehicles. The day was dark and wet. A drizzling rain swept across the countryside, driven by a cold wind from the southeast. It was a sad little party that streamed across the wet grass, and stood while all that remained of unhappy Sybil Grinsmead was laid to its last rest. Yet when it was over and the blinds were raised and the house began to settle down to its new conditions, Anne was conscious of a want, as if her only real friend in the establishment was gone.

To Anne the funeral marked the definite end of an episode in her life. While poor Sybil's body lay upstairs, she in a sense was still there. But now she was gone. The last link was broken. Henceforward things at Frayle could never be quite the same. Anne had the same feeling when her father died. Until the funeral he was there, upstairs. After it she was alone. Her whole life had changed with the ceremony.

Next day Anne had occasion to go into Ashbridge to make some household purchases. She did not want to take Hersey from his work, so she walked to the crossroads and travelled in by bus. In due course she completed her business, and was returning to the bus starting place when she heard her name called.

"How do you do, Miss Day?" said the voice, and looking round, Anne saw that it was Dr Heath, the coroner.

He shook hands pleasantly. "I was so sorry you had to go through all that distressing business," he went on. "It must have been an ordeal for you. All the same, if you'll allow me to say so, you acquitted yourself admirably. An ideal witness, you proved."

Anne was not proof against flattery. She smiled.

"It didn't turn out so bad as I had feared," she rejoined. "I always imagined that giving evidence was a terrible thing, but everyone was so kind it made it easy."

"Giving evidence is easy enough," the old doctor replied. "It's cross-examination by a hostile counsel that's the trying business."

They chatted for a few moments and then Anne said she would have to run to catch her bus.

"Now," said Dr Heath, "I want you to give an old man some pleasure. Will you not come and have tea with me and I'll run you home after it in my car?"

Anne accepted at once. She had met Dr Heath on different occasions, and liked him.

He chose a quiet table at one of the restaurants, and for a time they talked generalities. Then he inquired whether Sybil's death was going to make any change in her prospects. Finally he turned the conversation back to the inquest.

"I was very much struck with your evidence, Miss Day," he said. "As I said, I thought you gave it uncommonly well. But there was something else that I thought too." He drew a little closer and sank his voice. "Please do not think me impertinent, but I formed a very strong impression that you knew something that you did not tell us. Was I right? I hope you'll tell me."

Anne was startled. Was this business in the lane which she hoped had closed forever, about to be reopened? She shivered involuntarily.

"Ah," the doctor went on, but in the kindest way, "I see I was right. You do know something. I thought so before, now I'm sure of it. You are a very honest young lady, Miss Day, and your face reflects your thoughts." He paused and held out a cigarette case. "Now," he went on, "we're here together really in private; no one is near enough to overhear what we say. I want you to tell me what's in your mind. If it's something which ought to go no farther, I give you my word that it will go no farther. But I think you ought to tell it. These are serious matters in which you have become involved, and you have a duty to the community."

Suddenly Anne saw that this encounter which she had supposed to be chance, was not chance at all. This old wizard had seen her relief when the trying questions were not asked, and he was going to get to the bottom of it. She thought hurriedly. Why should she not tell him? After all, if there was anything wrong, why should she protect Grinsmead? Because she was taking his money? No. She would be the best housekeeper she could because she was taking his money. But there her liabilities began and ended. If there was anything in it, Sybil was her friend, not Grinsmead.

All the same, Anne loathed the thought of, as she put it to herself, becoming a traitor to her employer. It is possible, indeed, that she would have temporised had not Dr Heath suddenly made this impossible.

"The death of Mrs Grinsmead," he said gravely, "came as a blow and a shock to us all, and from what I have heard, it probably came as a greater blow and shock to you than to anyone else. Now I should tell you that during that inquest it was my firm opinion that we didn't get the whole truth. There was a reason for the suicide which we didn't hear. I knew poor Sybil Grinsmead fairly well, and I don't believe that without some strong urge she would have taken her life. I may tell you, Miss Day, I was not satisfied with the evidence we received. According to everyone's statement, your own included, she was in a normal frame of mind that evening, even allowing for the extra excitement of the dinner party. Yet she takes this terrible step within a few minutes of your leaving her. Now, Miss Day, if you suspect what may have been in her mind which caused her to take this step, it is your duty to tell it. I admit the hatefulness of doing such a thing. But you must not allow your own feelings to come between you and your duty."

Anne was sorely troubled. The more she thought of describing that scene in the lane, while she remained a trusted member of Grinsmead's household, the more she hated the idea. Besides, what could it matter now? Nothing would bring Sybil back to life. Nor could Grinsmead be punished, if his conduct had caused her death. He had broken no law. Surely the thing might be let die.

But the old doctor evidently thought otherwise. He smoked quietly for some moments, then had another try.

"Inspector Kendal told me of your statement to him about Mrs Grinsmead's suspicion of her husband. It's a nasty subject to discuss, but I'm afraid we must discuss it. I should like to ask you, Have you any special knowledge on this subject?"

"Must I answer that question?" Anne said desperately.

Dr Heath continued to smoke gravely. "I'll put all my cards on the table, Miss Day," he went on presently. "If you mean, Can I legally compel you to answer? Of course I cannot. It's a question of your duty as a citizen. Indeed we're pretty well in the same boat. I have been deeply distressed in trying to settle the question of my own duty in the matter. It might be argued that my business as coroner was ended as soon as the jury returned their verdict. However, I greatly fear that in that verdict justice may not have been done, and rightly or wrongly I have decided that it is my duty to try to make sure."

He paused, but Anne not replying, continued: "Not to mince matters, Miss Day. I have a strong feeling that her husband was indirectly responsible for Mrs Grinsmead's death. I want to know whether that is capable of proof, or whether it remains merely my suspicion. You must see for yourself that if I'm right, it should be known. If that cannot be punished by law, it can and ought to and must be punished by public opinion. I put it to you that you must answer my question, not because I can legally compel you, but because it is your duty. Remember if you refuse, you are associating yourself with Mr Grinsmead against his wife."

This view of the situation had not struck Anne. It now occurred to her that it was the view the law would take under such circumstances. What was the phrase? Accessory after the fact? She could not, of course –

"What was poor Sybil Grinsmead afraid of?" Dr Heath's voice broke in on her reflections.

Suddenly temptation seized Anne. As things were, she held her job. Grinsmead certainly wouldn't marry Mrs Holt-Lancing for several months, probably a year. He would want to keep the house open for her, and in all probability would be glad of her, Anne's, services. Another year's happy and well-paid employment! But if Dr Heath seriously pushed his views it might mean that Grinsmead would have to leave the locality. Her job would be gone. Anne saw that she would be a fool not to keep her own counsel.

But soon there came a revulsion of feeling. Anne seemed to see once again Sybil's terrible distress on that day on which she had broken down and sobbed so heartrendingly. She had clung desperately to Anne as if for support. And now here was Anne, for the sake of her own money and comfort, about to screen the man who had been responsible for the poor woman's misery. She couldn't do it. No, no matter what it cost her, she just couldn't do it.

Dr Heath, seeing the struggle which was taking place in her mind, had remained discreetly silent. But he now gently repeated his question: "What was Sybil afraid of, Miss Day?"

"She was really unbalanced," Anne answered slowly. "She was afraid she was in physical danger from Mr Grinsmead."

Dr Heath nodded. "I thought so," he said. "That was exactly the idea that occurred to me on one occasion when I saw them together. She was afraid of him. Afraid for her life probably?"

"Yes, I think she was," Anne admitted.

"She also knew that he was carrying on an intrigue with Mrs Holt-Lancing?"

Anne nodded. "She knew that, yes."

"And you knew it too," Dr Heath returned quickly. "Otherwise you would have said, 'She thought so,' not 'She knew it.' Tell me how you found it out, Miss Day?"

Anne told him. The old man did not say much in reply. He seemed, indeed, disappointed rather than otherwise, as if he had been expecting some much more incriminating disclosure. Anne felt relieved by this attitude, for she was human enough to hope that her statement would lead to no serious result.

"I'm glad you told me that," he declared. "It's always best to know the worst, isn't it? And when you do know it, nine times out of ten it's not so bad as you had feared. A sound philosophy, Miss Day?"

Dr Heath drove Anne back to Frayle. She felt a good deal happier in her mind, now that she had shared the weight of her secret. And now that she had shared it, she thought that it really had not been so much of a secret after all; nothing to justify the thought she had given it. Dr Heath evidently had not thought much of it. She was greatly comforted and relieved. She had now, she felt sure, done with the whole horrid episode.

On one other occasion, however, it was recalled to her, again in Ashbridge. In a shop she met Mrs Holt-Lancing with her husband, the captain, who was home on leave. They were coldly polite, made some colourless remarks, and passed on. Anne was not prepossessed with Captain Holt-Lancing's appearance. He looked thoroughly bad-tempered. Indeed Mrs Holt-Lancing herself was looking badly also, old and haggard and worried.

Once again the days began to slip uneventfully past. Mrs Grinsmead returned to her home near Frome, and then after a few days came back. She made no attempt to interfere with the running of the house, Anne and Edith remaining in control. She explained indeed that she had only returned for a short time to keep her son company and if possible to prevent him from brooding too much over the tragedy.

Grinsmead had, however, become much less approachable. He made no reference to Anne or Edith finding another job, or to his giving up the house. Things settled down. The vision of the London streets and their registry offices faded from the minds of both women.

And then something happened which jerked them suddenly out of their complacency and left them full of dread for the present and of doubt for the future. A stoutish, comfortable-looking man with keen blue eyes called one day. He said he was from Scotland Yard and that he wanted some information relative to the death of Sybil Grinsmead.

PART 2

As Inspector French Saw It

9

INITIATION

Inspector Joseph French stood at the window of his room at New Scotland Yard, looking out at the blue-black sky which made it now at midday so dark that the electric light was necessary if work were to be carried on. Ah, he was right! From early morning he had been prophesying a fall of snow, and there it was. A tiny white flake was slowly edging its way downwards, making little halting movements from side to side like a particularly somnolent moth, as if it couldn't make up its mind where it really wanted to go. It hovered down, then another appeared and then another, all in the most leisurely way possible floating past on their way to the ground.

French watched till the air was dotted with white flakes, falling with steady and business-like regularity. It always impressed him, the gentle beginning of a snowstorm. It seemed to him a model of how a symphony should begin; a faint, high-pitched melody from some soft instrument, wavering uncertainly down from the ceiling, being joined by instrument after instrument, till at length the entire orchestra, with strength and decision, was thundering out some striking theme. That would be when the snow, driven by a screaming wind, was flying horizontally across the window with the speed of an express train.

French was not usually whimsical, and now he reminded himself that he had something better to do than to stand at his window and indulge in fancies. But after all there was some excuse for him. Till now he had not lifted his head from his desk during the entire morning, and a neat pile of closely-written sheets bore testimony to his industry. It was symbolic, that pile of paper. It meant achievement; something attempted, something done. It represented the completion of his investigation into that terrible case of the murder of a whole family, father, mother, and three children, which had taken place shortly before at Westbury and which even in these days of callous murders, had shocked the entire country. From the first there had been little doubt as to the murderer – a dangerous inmate of a local mental home had escaped on the previous evening – but to find the unhappy maniac had proved an extraordinarily difficult task. However, French had succeeded in running him to earth, and these sheets contained the evidence to be submitted to the public prosecutor. Ten minutes earlier French had written the last word.

For the moment, therefore, he was out of a job. But only for the moment. It had been arranged that after lunch he was to go down to Chelmsford to obtain some information relative to a burglary which was believed to have been committed by a gang on which the Yard had long had its eye. Well, he would go and have lunch now, so as to get down to Chelmsford, and therefore back to his home, as soon as possible.

But alas for the plans of mice and men! He had no sooner picked up his hat and coat when his telephone bell sounded. His immediate superior, Chief Inspector Mitchell, wished to see him. Mitchell telephoned that he was with the Assistant Commissioner, Sir Mortimer Ellison, and French was to join them in the AC's room.

While Sir Mortimer was always a model of the strictest fairness, he had recently shown more appreciation of French's work than formerly. This dated from that important case of the Moxon's Securities frauds and the consequent murders in the Channel, when, owing to exceptional causes, French had worked directly under his orders. He had been pleased with French's handling of that case, and the result was that when anything of exceptional difficulty arose, his reaction was to put French on to it.

"Come in, French," he said pleasantly. "Got a job for you."

"Chelmsford's off," Chief Inspector Mitchell put in. "I'll send someone else."

Sir Mortimer was seated at his desk, a cigarette between his lips and his rather tired-looking eyes bent on a file of correspondence which comprised the only papers on the desk. Mitchell, also with a cigarette, sat opposite him in one of the two large leather-lined armchairs the room boasted. Sir Mortimer's left forefinger made two little stabs towards the cigarette box and the other armchair.

"Help yourself and sit down, French," he said, "and listen to me." He turned to Mitchell. "I'll begin again so that French may hear the thing from the start. I'm going to victimise you, French; I hope you won't mind. Sacrifice you on the altar of friendship and all that. Are you good at wild goose chases? Never mind, you needn't answer that question. I want you to go on one now, and we'll see how well you'll do it."

Sir Mortimer laid down the file of papers, sat back in his chair, and went on: "I don't know if you've ever met my old friend, Major Oliver? He's chief constable of Ashbridge, and a first-rate fellow. He called in to see me yesterday and started a hare. I want you to chase it, but I shouldn't be surprised if you find it turn into that wild goose I was speaking of. But we can't refuse to look into his problem, particularly as he's gone through all the formalities to get our help."

French had never met Major Oliver, but he had heard of him as an efficient officer, thought a deal of by his men.

"It seems they've had a suicide near Ashbridge," went on Sir Mortimer. "A Mrs Grinsmead, the wife of a local solicitor, killed herself by gas poisoning. So far as I can see, looking through the evidence given at the inquest, it was a perfectly clear case. But for some reason the Ashbridge police are not satisfied. They hint at murder. They put forward what seems to me a quite trumpery tale about the husband being in love with another woman and so on. But if every case of a triangle drama ended in someone's death, the population of the world would show an alarming shrinkage, eh, Mitchell?"

Mitchell ejected a cloud of blue smoke. "There must be more than that in it, sir," he declared.

"Doesn't seem to be," Sir Mortimer returned. "I've waded through this stuff with quite remarkable concentration, and I can't find a single fact to support it."

"I expect there's something that they haven't put in writing," Mitchell persisted.

"May be. All I know is they haven't put it in writing. However, we needn't worry about that. I've had to promise to look into the thing. My satisfaction is that neither you nor I shall have to do it personally. French is a traveller. It's a nice day for a trip to the country. I thought French would like to go."

French grinned. "You want me to report to the Ashbridge police, sir?"

"Precisely. Take this file and you can read it up in the train. Ring up Superintendent Godfrey and tell him when you'll arrive. Anything else? No, I think that's everything."

The weather in London was bad, but when French got to Ashbridge he found it was worse there. A south-easterly gale was blowing, tearing in across the country, and the wind had an edge on it like a knife. The snow was dry and powdery, and was already drifting deeply. The streets were deserted, save for an occasional taxi or a wrapped-up individual, striving with bent head to force his way against the storm. French was thankful to find a car had been sent to meet him, and more thankful still to get to the fire in the superintendent's room at police headquarters.

"How are you, inspector?" the superintendent greeted him. "Some time now since we met."

Some years earlier French had been sent to assist the Ashbridge police in connection with a burglary case. He had then found Superintendent Godfrey a good fellow, and he was glad to see him again.

"That's so, sir," French returned. "From my recollection Ashbridge is a better place in summer than now."

"We keep all kinds of weather here," the superintendent assured him, "so that everyone is catered for. Weather as well as pleasure to suit all kinds of tastes. Well, what do you think of the case?"

"As far as the evidence at the inquest goes, it seems to me a pretty obvious one," French answered cautiously. "I take it, sir, you have some other facts up your sleeve."

The superintendent bent forward. He lowered his voice and became confidential.

"As a matter of fact," he said, "it's the coroner that's raised all this dust. He's rather friends with Major Oliver, our chief constable. He went to the major and said he was not satisfied about the suicide, and what he told him impressed the major so much that he wants to have the case reopened, or at least he wants to consider reopening it. Then as luck would have it, the major met your Sir Mortimer Ellison somewhere, and talked to him about it. Result: Inspector French visits Ashbridge on a snowy day."

"I know that part of it," French declared. "May I ask, sir, if you're impressed with the coroner's arguments?"

Superintendent Godfrey shrugged. "I'm not expressing an opinion," he returned. "Better that you should hear the facts for yourself and form your own. The major would like to talk to you about it himself. He'll be here directly. In fact," he glanced out of the window, "there's his car."

A few moments later the door opened and two men walked into the room. One, middle-aged and with an alert military bearing, French guessed was Major Oliver. The other, quite an old man, had a strong rugged face, and medico written all over him.

"Afternoon, Godfrey. Afternoon, inspector; so you've turned up? Beastly day."

The superintendent sprang up to take the newcomers' coats and to pull forward a couple of chairs.

"Good afternoon, sir. Good afternoon, Dr Heath," he greeted them. "Won't you pull in to the fire, gentlemen? It's as cold as ever I've felt it."

"We've not been out long," the major answered. "Dr Heath has been giving me lunch. Doctor, this is Inspector French from the Yard. Our coroner, French, Dr Heath."

"I'm afraid I'm the cause of your having to come down on this delightful afternoon," said the doctor, holding out his hand. "The major'll tell you you've come on a wild goose chase, but after all he's responsible for bringing you, so I don't mind."

"Sir Mortimer Ellison was telling me about French. He said he liked chasing wild geese," Major Oliver declared genially. "It's fine exercise. Keeps you fit, so that you don't need doctors. Busy at the Yard, French?"

"Pretty fair, sir," French returned. "I've just finished that Westbury case. Before that I was on routine."

"Ghastly business, that at Westbury. Well, this case will be either routine and a wash-out at that, or else it'll attract a deal of attention. The parties move in good society here."

"So I gathered, sir, from the depositions. You have some further information, I understand?"

"The doctor has," Major Oliver said slowly. "The doctor called to see me a few days ago and said he was uneasy about the case. Uneasy, was all he would say. Well, his information made me uneasy, too. We both admit it may be all right, but we both think it should be looked into again. There, I'm afraid Superintendent Godfrey doesn't agree with us; he thinks it's OK. Probably he's right, but there seems to be just the chance that there may be something wrong, and I think we'd be wiser to make sure."

There seemed to be nothing to be said to this. French therefore marked time by remarking, "Quite so, sir."

"Inspector Kendal did go into it pretty thoroughly, I admit," Major Oliver went on, "and came to the conclusion that it was suicide all right. By the way," he looked at Godfrey, "does French know why we got Kendal to go into it so carefully?"

"I've not told him anything, sir."

"Well, French, it was for this reason. Near the Grinsmeads there lives an attractive grass-widow, a Mrs Holt-Lancing. Her husband is master of the Orient liner Oratorio, and conveniently spends most of his time at sea. Now about half-past four one morning about a month before Mrs Grinsmead's death, one of our patrols was passing this lady's house and he saw a man leave it and walk stealthily down the drive. The patrol at once thought of burglary, and he slipped behind a shrub to watch. The man passed within six feet of him, and who do you think it was? It was this man Grinsmead. The patrol shadowed him to his house, where he let himself in with every appearance of secrecy."

"Not often one gets such direct evidence as that, sir," French remarked.

"No, is it? Well, when Grinsmead's wife died suddenly a short time later, the superintendent remembered the incident. It made us suspicious about the death. There was no evidence of any crime, you understand, but there was a possible motive. For that reason we told Kendal to make a thorough inquiry."

"Quite natural, sir. But he got nothing?"

"He got nothing," the major admitted. "As I said, he came to the conclusion that it was suicide. But Kendal didn't know what we know now, what Dr Heath has since discovered. Unfortunately Kendal is engaged on the Entrican murder and we've no one else that I'd care to put on it. So I saw Sir Mortimer, and – here you are."

"I'll be glad to do anything I can, sir."

"Good. Now I thought, and Dr Heath thought, that you should hear what he has to say from his own mouth. That's why he came in with me. But before he begins, I think I should remind you, French, that we're dealing with an influential family. You'll have to be very tactful in any inquiries you may make."

"I quite understand, sir. You wish inquiries made as quietly as possible?"

"That's it. Now I take it you've read the evidence given at the inquest? You don't want to be posted on that?"

French reassured him.

"Very well," Major Oliver went on, "then I'll ask Dr Heath to tell you what's been troubling him."

He lit a cigarette, passing his case to the others. It was pleasant enough in the office. Superintendent Godfrey had stoked up the fire till it glowed a bright red and the contrast between it and the whirling snow without added beauty to the dingy walls and comfort to the somewhat adamantine chairs.

Dr Heath seemed to find a little difficulty in getting under way. He smoked in silence for some moments, then suddenly he turned to French.

"I must begin on a personal note," he said. "I want to explain that my chief difficulty in this affair was to decide my own line of conduct. I was not satisfied with the verdict at the inquest. But I saw that the verdict wasn't my responsibility. On the evidence the police supplied, the jury decided the affair was suicide. Was I not therefore clear of it?"

He paused as if for an answer.

"Subject to these gentlemen's correction, sir," French observed, "I should say that if you felt a reasonable doubt of the correctness of the verdict, it was your bounden duty as a citizen to pursue the matter further."

"You think so? Well, I don't know. However, rightly or wrongly, that's what I did. I couldn't believe that poor woman had been murdered, and do nothing about it. If I was wrong, I am sorry."

"You were not wrong, doctor," Major Oliver said crisply. "Put that doubt out of your mind and explain the affair to French."

The doctor inclined his head. "I'm glad to have your opinion," he answered, then turned to French. "Well, inspector," he went on, "what first aroused my interest in the case was the fact that it touched me personally. I was very well acquainted with the late Mrs Grinsmead."

He paused. French felt somewhat surprised and a trifle troubled, he did not know exactly why. But before he had time to analyse his feelings, the old man resumed.

"Mrs Grinsmead was a Miss Sybil Courland. Her father was a landed proprietor near Northampton. His ground joined on to my father's much smaller place. The two families were great friends. As a boy I constantly played with the Courlands, Sybil's father among the others. He and I grew up together and only drew apart when we went to different colleges. I've known Sybil herself since she was a baby, and as she was growing up I kept more or less in touch with her. She lived at home, then during a holiday at Bognor she met Grinsmead. She married him within the year. From one point of view it was well she did so, for her father lost a lot of money as a result of certain frauds, and had to sell the place and live in a smaller way.

"Now," went on the doctor, looking round on the others, "you must not here jump to any false conclusion. There was not at that time nor at any other time anything in the nature of an attachment between myself and Sybil Courland. The reason why my previous knowledge of her seems to affect the case is quite otherwise. It is this: I feel absolutely convinced that Sybil Grinsmead would not in any conceivable circumstances have committed suicide."

French was immediately disappointed. Then it was a wild goose chase after all. If this was all the doctor could bring forward, he, French, might as well have stayed at home. He knew these ideas; obsessions, he called them. Sheer nonsense, ninety-nine times out of a hundred.

"This, of course, will seem nonsense to you" – French felt slightly guilty – "but I have tried to weigh up my knowledge of the woman as dispassionately as possible, and the more I do so, the more utterly I feel assured that I am right."

"According to the evidence, sir," French essayed, "Mrs Grinsmead had been in bad health for some three years and was gradually getting worse. Do you think this illness might have changed her character?"

"Very reasonable, inspector, but not in this case true: I am convinced of it. I occasionally met Mrs Grinsmead after her marriage, though I didn't attend her professionally. I met her within the last year, probably – let me see – four or five months before her death, and though she was obviously changed, I feel sure her character had not altered. I hope all of you understand that I am making no claim to omniscience. I may be wrong, though I feel perfectly satisfied in my own mind that I am right."

The doctor paused, a twisted smile upon his lips. The others made dutiful murmurs of sympathy. French believed the man had a bee in his bonnet. But he felt that this belief would be more wisely kept locked up in his own breast.

"When therefore," Dr Heath went on, "I heard of the death, I at once doubted the suicide theory. First, I thought of accident, then when this seemed unlikely, a much more unpleasant suspicion came into my mind.

"I knew – one does know these things – that the marriage had not been a success. I had guessed it from the manner of each of the Grinsmeads. Then I knew Grinsmead. He is, as you know, a solicitor. I had come across him both in business and socially. I never could trust him. Besides that,

I have seen a look of cruelty in his eye that has very strongly repelled me. I don't say that he would be guilty of serious crime: I say that this knowledge of him has made it seem possible to me."

Again the doctor paused, and again French felt he was listening to nonsense. He was surprised indeed that any sensible man would seriously put these fancies forward as arguments.

"So far," Heath resumed, "a suspicion that all might not be right was all that passed through my mind. I had no proof and of course I could take no action. What I could do, however, and did, was to ask the superintendent here to have the thing very carefully gone into, so as to make sure it was suicide and not murder. Superintendent Godfrey then told me about Grinsmead having been seen leaving Mrs Holt-Lancing's house in the middle of the night. I needn't tell how this strengthened my own conviction of the need for investigation. The superintendent, however, said that he had felt this so much himself that he had already instructed Kendal to go into it thoroughly. Kendal did excellent work, I admit, and he came to the conclusion that it was suicide. But Kendal had not my knowledge of the two parties. While he mightn't be so impolite as to say he disbelieved me," the doctor gave another twisted smile, "he would not attach much weight to my opinion. I don't blame him either."

"But, sir, didn't the facts brought out at the inquest rule out anything but suicide? I don't, sir, mean to question your opinion," French smiled in his turn, "I'm merely asking to get a difficulty cleared up in my own mind."

"Quite right, inspector. That's what I like. All the facts brought out at the inquest pointed to suicide, except two. I don't know how much weight you would attach to these facts, but to me they are significant. The first is this: all the witnesses without exception swore that Sybil Grinsmead was in a quite normal frame of mind on that evening. Dinner and bridge parties excited her a little, but she was not abnormally excited. She had made friends with and trusted the housekeeper, Miss Day, whom everybody says is a most capable, level-headed young lady. Now Miss Day was with Mrs Grinsmead after she went to bed; she gave her the sleeping draught after Mrs Grinsmead was actually in bed. And then at that time, Miss Day swears positively that she was normal. These sleeping draughts do not act instantaneously, but they act reasonably quickly. What I mean is that there was no chance of Mrs Grinsmead lying awake for any time and worrying herself into an unhappy frame of mind. If she committed suicide she must have done so in the frame of mind in which Miss Day left her. Now I put it to you, gentlemen: If Mrs Grinsmead intended to commit suicide would she not have shown some difference of manner? I cannot but believe that she would. At the same time I must admit that it was not till thinking over the case after the inquest that the full weight of the argument struck me."

It was certainly a point. French did not think there was a great deal in it, but undoubtedly there was something. These people who said the deceased was normal were simply unobservant. And yet, French had to admit, they must have been very unobservant.

"That," Dr Heath went on, "is my first point. My second is this: During Miss Day's evidence I formed the opinion that she was keeping something back; no, perhaps that is scarcely fair – that she knew something that she did not tell. I didn't think she was necessarily to blame; I saw that it might be something about which she had not been asked.

In any case I formed the opinion that she could tell us something. Another notion, you gentlemen will think? Well, wait till you hear."

The others made disclaiming murmurs.

"This was a case in which I could put my opinion to the test," and the doctor described his interview with Anne in the Ashbridge teashop. "Now, gentlemen," he continued, "this conversation between Grinsmead and Mrs Holt-Lancing in the lane seems to me to have contained some very significant phrases. Admittedly what Miss Day heard was disjointed; at the same time what do you make out of phrases like these: 'A love like ours is worth any risk.' Now I ask you, what is the significance of the word 'risk'? Again, 'We might get married after a proper interval and then the crash might come.' What does 'crash' mean? Again, 'In that case they managed it badly. We should have to be more careful.' Again, 'At the best it would be a dirty business.' And again, 'We shall not have to wait much longer.' What do all these phrases mean, gentlemen," he paused, then added slowly, "*but one thing*?"

French was impressed. The old man had spoken well. He had made quite a case. If it hadn't been that the details of the death pointed so unmistakably to suicide, he would have proved his case for further investigation.

There was silence for some moments while the four men smoked meditatively. Then Major Oliver summed up.

"Dr Heath told me all this some days ago," he said. "I admit it impressed me a lot. Not alone, because of its own weight: there was another reason. I had never met the deceased lady, but I had come across Grinsmead on different occasions, and my estimate of his character was just the same as the doctor's. In addition I knew that he was an extremely able man, quite capable of putting up a plant to deceive the police. Eventually I went up to Town and saw my friend, Sir Mortimer Ellison. He made no bones about it at all. 'I'll send you a man,' he said, and the inspector here is the result. Now what about it, inspector? Let's have your opinion. Have we, or have we not, made a case for further investigation?"

French smiled. "If you'll excuse my saying so, sir, I don't think that question arises. I've been sent down to make a further investigation."

"No, French, that's where you're wrong." The chief constable smiled also. "You've been sent down to discuss the affair with us and give us the benefit of your experience and advice."

"Sir Mortimer thought I should look into the thing, sir."

Major Oliver laughed. "Well," he said, "that's the kind of tact I've been asking for, so I can't now object to it. I take it, then, that means you'll make your investigation?"

"I think Sir Mortimer wouldn't be pleased if I went back without doing so, sir."

The major rose. "Right; we'll let it go at that. That satisfactory to you, doctor?"

"Perfectly satisfactory to me," Heath answered. "All I wanted was to be sure."

They chatted for a few minutes and then Major Oliver and the doctor left. Superintendent Godfrey turned to French.

"You better see Kendal before you do anything else. Where are you staying? I'll get him to call round and see you this evening."

"Wouldn't he come and dine with me?" French suggested. "We could go into it then."

"Right. I'll tell him. Here's the file of the case. The Atherton Arms at seven o'clock. Right."

10

CONSULTATION

"Well, now, what about it?"

Dinner was over at the Atherton Arms and French and Kendal had found a roaring fire in the deserted smoking-room. The wind had veered and the snow was turning into sleet, with a prospect of rain before morning. But it was still bitterly cold, and the two men had drawn their chairs close to the fire with sighs of satisfaction. Kendal had just lighted a pipeful of French's own special mixture, and was tactfully amazed at its magnificent aroma.

"Yes, it's not bad," French admitted. "Fellow in a little shop near Charing Cross mixes it for me. I've read through your file. You seem to have taken the deuce of a lot of trouble over the case."

"Had to," Kendal explained. "The chief got this notion and what could I do? All a piece of nonsense, if you ask me."

"You think so? It didn't seem very convincing to me, though of course that conversation does sound a bit fishy."

"We didn't know about that when I made my investigation."

"That was the point the chief made about having the thing looked into again. He was going to ask you to do it, then you were full up with the Entrican murder, and he went to Sir Mortimer."

"That's all right," Kendal returned, answering French's thought rather than his words. "I'm jolly glad to be out of it. I wish you luck and all that, but I'm afraid you won't get much."

"There's not the slightest chance of my getting anything," French returned. "However, I'm in the same boat as you; instructions. I'd like any views you have on the thing."

Inspector Kendal settled himself more comfortably in his armchair. "To me," he began, "the outstanding feature of the case is that the deceased woman must have turned on the gas herself. Her fingerprints were clear on the tap. You've seen the photo?"

"Oh, you photoed it, did you? Good. No, I've not seen it."

Kendal took some papers from an attache case he had brought. "Here is my sketch of the tap," he said, "and here a photographic enlargement of the print on the tap. Here," he pulled out another photograph, "is an enlargement of the print of Sybil Grinsmead's right thumb. There's no doubt they're the same."

"None," French agreed, after a close scrutiny. "That's certainly pretty convincing."

"Yes, there's no question she turned on the tap all right."

French put down the photograph and took up the sketch. "I see it was that batswing tap which sticks out from the right side of the stove; the secondary tap, not the main one on the supply pipe. Also it turns through one right angle only. Any prints on the main tap?"

"None."

French sat staring fixedly at the sketch. "I suppose," he said presently, "I suppose nothing of this kind is possible. Suppose Mrs Grinsmead turned on the gas and lit the fire. Then suppose some one else turned it off at the meter, either thoughtlessly or of malice aforethought, immediately turning it on again. The deceased's fire would go out, and when the meter tap was turned on again, gas would escape into the room."

"I thought of that," Kendal answered. "I dismissed it for three reasons. First, everyone agreed that the deceased

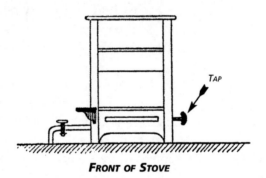

FRONT OF STOVE

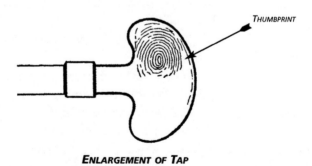

ENLARGEMENT OF TAP

didn't like the gas fire and practically never used it. The night of her death was cold, but only moderately. There had been dozens of colder nights previously, and on none of these had she had the fire. Second, Miss Day, who was in the deceased's room until a few minutes before the deceased went to sleep, states positively that it was not lighted. And of course there was no reason why the deceased should have lighted it after Miss Day left. Both of these points I think have a good deal of weight, but what puts the lid on the thing is the third. The cook, who is an exceptionally reliable woman, was not feeling well that night, and she kept her own gas fire on all night, turned low admittedly, but burning continuously. Now she stated – and I see no reason to doubt her statement – that she lighted that fire about half-past nine, when she went to bed. She swears positively she heard ten o'clock strike after she was in bed. The deceased, you remember, did not go up to her room till ten, and Miss Day was with her till after half-past ten. So it follows that the cook's fire was lit before the deceased went up, and it stayed lit till the morning. Therefore no one turned off the meter after the deceased had gone to bed."

"I suppose the one meter does control both fires?"

"Yes, I tried that. But I'll tell you what I didn't try, not having Dr Heath's evidence to spur me on. I didn't try whether there wasn't some other tap controlling the deceased's fire: a subsidiary tap shutting off, let us say, that section of the building. That's a thing you could look into."

"I'll do so," said French, making a note.

"That's the matter of the gas tap," Kendal went on. "Now the next thing is the bolt. You've seen an electric bolt?"

"I've seen them in the Lyon Palace Hotel in Paris. You work them from a couple of buttons at the bed; one bolts and the other unbolts."

"Well, you'll have noticed the bolt also. It's an enclosed affair that you couldn't very well tamper with, certainly not from outside. But beside that I made a very careful examination of the bolt, and I'm quite satisfied it was not tampered with. There were no marks of any kind."

"I suppose it couldn't have been tampered with electrically?"

"Meaning?"

"Meaning that some one connected another pair of wires to those between it and the bed, and operated it from outside the room?"

"No. I thought of that too. There was no place where such wires could have been attached. The wires had obviously been there for a considerable time, and the insulation was good throughout."

"Seems overwhelming, that." French smoked thoughtfully. "First you prove that the deceased turned on the gas herself, then you show that no one else could have done it. Pretty convincing, I must admit." Again he paused, then added suddenly: "But look here; what is there to prevent some one fitting a flat tool over the tap with a cord leading out beneath the door, and pulling the tap round after everyone was asleep?"

"Our minds run in the same groove," Kendal smiled. "That's exactly what I asked myself. But I soon found the answer. It just wasn't possible. I tried it for long enough, and I satisfied myself it hadn't been done. In the first place the tap was stiff from disuse. If you pulled one wing, as you would with a cord, it wouldn't go round, you had to pull both wings in opposite directions before it would move.

138

Besides that, French, you know as well as I do that if anyone had been trying on any game of that kind, he would have first greased the tap and got it moving easily. And there was another thing more conclusive still. The pull of a cord would have been parallel to the shaft of the tap, not at right angles to it. The cord would therefore have tended to pull the tap in to the stove, not to turn it. You follow me?"

"Clearly. There was nothing, I suppose, to act as a pulley, round which a cord could have been passed to change the direction of the pull?"

"Nothing. I thought of that too."

Once again French sat silent. Then he turned to another point. "I suppose," he asked, "there is no doubt that the bolt was fastened?"

"Absolutely none. Grinsmead forced it in the morning."

"Ah," said French, "but how do you know that? Suppose Grinsmead forced it, yes, but not in the morning. Suppose after everyone was asleep he forced it, ever so slowly and silently. Then suppose he went in and somehow turned on the tap without destroying the fingerprints. I think this could be done with a spanner, provided you were there beside it. He would then go out, closing the door after him. In the morning he would make a great show of forcing it, but it would be only show."

"That's ingenious, French; I confess I hadn't thought of it." Kendal relapsed into silence, both men smoking meditatively. Then Kendal went on: "I'm afraid that's no go for this reason: Grinsmead says he put his shoulder with all his strength to the door in the morning and that he couldn't burst it open. This doesn't stand on his own word. Both Miss Day and the maid saw him do it. And what's more, both heard a grinding noise as the screws drew out of the wood. By Jove, now I remember that Miss Day tried it herself before raising the alarm, and she couldn't open it."

"It couldn't have been forced, and after the gas had been turned on, made fast in some other way?"

"No, because there would have been traces of that other way, and there weren't any."

"All right," said French, "that's a wash-out. There doesn't seem to be much for me to do in this job. That's the gas tap and the bolt covered pretty completely. What was the other thing the coroner laid such stress on? Oh, yes, the windows being closed. Did you get anything from that?"

Kendal looked at him, French thought, a trifle strangely.

"Well, you've read the evidence," he said. "It was stated that the deceased was a fresh air fiend and that even on the coldest nights she slept with her windows open. Everyone was agreed about this, so I think we may take it as true. I saw Gladys, the maid, and she swears that when she pulled the curtains, before the deceased went up to dress for dinner, the windows were wide open. They are casement windows, you know. They were too widely open for the night, and Gladys closed them partially. She left them about four inches open. Then she drew the curtains. After that no one saw them, for they were hidden by the curtains."

"But you failed to get fingerprints on the handles?" Kendal made a sudden gesture. "You're on to it now, French. That was the one thing in the whole case that bothered me. It was because of it that I went into everything so carefully. It was because of it that the chief paid so much attention to Dr Heath."

"You found no prints at all?"

"None. I couldn't understand it."

"But you had opened the window yourself?"

"Oh, well, I'm not altogether a fool. I held the handles by the extreme end, the little knob, you know."

"Perhaps whoever closed them did the same."

"No, French, don't you see? Gladys' fingerprints should have been on them if no one else's were."

"Ah," said French. "Go on."

"I got Gladys up and made her close them to the same extent as she had that night, and then tried again. She had left prints. Not very clear, you know, because you really grasp a handle like that by the middle of the fingers. But there was a good print of her thumb. I asked her had she been wearing gloves that night, or had a cloth in her hand. She hadn't; was quite positive she had closed them with her bare hands exactly as she had just done. So what do you make of that, French?"

French considered. "Did the deceased wear gloves that evening? Do ladies wear gloves with evening dress now?"

"She didn't. I asked that."

French whistled slowly. "Then the position is that before dinner these windows were four inches open with Gladys' fingerprints on the handles. In the morning they were shut with no prints on the handles. That is, whoever closed them wiped off the prints at the same time. Well, why shouldn't the deceased have done that? Suppose she thought the handles dirty or cold or wet; why shouldn't she have grasped them in a handkerchief?"

"That's what in the end I assumed she had done. I don't see any other way out of it. I tell you, French, I went into this case with a perfectly open mind. If anything, I was biased against the suicide theory because of the chief's attitude, and I was forced round by the facts to accept it. Just look at it. Here you have a lady with abnormal mental tendencies which the doctor tells us would predispose her to suicide. Her husband is running after another woman and her life is so unhappy that she has ample motive to commit it. Then the details of the actual death are consistent with suicide and with suicide only. Summing up, there's not a fact in the entire case which can't be explained by the suicide theory, and there are several that can't be explained in any other way. Rightly or wrongly, French, that's my opinion."

"I'm inclined to think it's mine also," said French. "I'll have to go into it, of course, to justify my existence, but after what you've done it'll be only a matter of form." He got up and rang the bell. "You'll have a drink?"

For some time they sat chatting over their whiskies, and then Kendal took himself off. French was impressed with the thorough way in which the man had done his job. He didn't seem to have left many loose ends to be straightened out.

However, as he had said, this would not absolve him, French, from making a fresh investigation. He began to consider how he should attack the problem.

French had already formed a theory, though as yet he had been careful to keep it to himself. It had flashed into his mind on the way down, when he was looking over the dossier of the case. He had been inclined to dismiss it as untenable for the simple reason that it did not seem to have occurred to the local men. But now Dr Heath's story had so much strengthened it that he could no longer dismiss it untested.

Anne Day!

What if Anne Day had murdered her employer? The whole of the evidence of suicide hinged on Anne. She could unquestionably have murdered Sybil Grinsmead, and invented her story to make it seem like suicide.

142

First, there was Sybil's alleged distrust of Anne, followed by the reconciliation and subsequent friendship. That would have been put in to show that the two women were on good terms and that there could have been no bad feeling on Anne's part. Then Anne had said that she had sat with Sybil for about half an hour after Sybil had gone to bed on the night of her death, giving her the sleeping draught at the end of that time, and just before she, Anne, had left the room. What if that were a lie? Suppose Anne had given Sybil the draught immediately and had sat watching her till she became drowsy. Then suppose Anne had shut the windows and turned on the gas. Sybil through force of habit would have bolted the door, but by the time she smelled the gas she would have been too sleepy to take action. This would account for the entire affair.

Then there was the attempt to throw suspicion on Grinsmead. These hints about Grinsmead and Mrs Holt-Lancing had come from Anne. Might there not be a reason for this?

So much had occurred to French in the train, but now to this evidence was added that of the conversation in the lane. Anne Day again! Might not this tale of the conversation be just an invention to drive home the probability of Grinsmead's guilt?

Of course French had recognised the difficulty of motive, but as he considered the matter further he saw that motive was by no means such a difficulty as he had imagined. There might indeed be an extremely adequate motive. Suppose Anne imagined, or even knew, that Grinsmead was attracted, not by Mrs Holt-Lancing, but by herself? Anne was poor, she might well make any endeavour and take any risk to achieve security. Admit that she thought Grinsmead might marry her if the way were clear, and it was easy to see that she might have taken steps to clear the way.

Yes, French thought, the theory was certainly likely enough to require a thorough testing. And what was the best way to do it?

He imagined, through the conversation in the lane. If that conversation had really taken place as Anne stated, it would go a long way towards clearing her, as well as justifying the coroner's suspicion of Grinsmead. How could he find out about this conversation?

After a good deal of thought, French decided to try the "confidential" method on Grinsmead. It had the obvious defect of putting the man on his guard, were he guilty, but that risk had to be taken.

Next morning therefore, French went down to see Grinsmead at his office. He was in luck as to his weather. The rain was over, the snow had vanished, and the sun was struggling to break through a mass of untidy clouds. It was still cold, but fresh and pleasant.

In accordance with the "confidential" policy, French sent in his private card to Grinsmead. He had to wait for an interview, but not very long. Grinsmead, when he did reach his room, was formally polite and businesslike, but French could not help thinking, not at all attractive.

"I should begin, sir," said French, subsiding into the chair which the other indicated, "by showing you my professional card. As this call is confidential, I did not wish to let your clerk see it."

Grinsmead raised his eyebrows slightly. Did a flicker of alarm show in his eyes? French could not be certain, but he rather thought so. Grinsmead had the legal, tight-lipped, expressionless face, though of the somewhat fleshy type. He

144

answered immediately with a sort of careless attention, "Well, inspector, what can I do for you?"

"I'm sorry to say," French went on, "that my business is rather unpleasant. I will therefore try to get it over as quickly as possible. It concerns certain rumours which have been in circulation. I expect you know what I'm referring to."

"I'm hanged if I do," Grinsmead said unhelpfully.

"I dare say, sir, now I come to think of it, you would be the last to hear them. Then I must tell you. These rumours refer to the death of the late Mrs Grinsmead."

Grinsmead blenched as if French had touched him on the raw. Whether the man's reaction arose from sorrow or remorse or fear, French did not know, but it was at least certain that strong emotion had been aroused. But Grinsmead quickly pulled himself together.

"I don't know what you're talking about, inspector," he answered. "I heard no rumours."

"These rumours hint at a definite cause for the suicide."

Grinsmead made a gesture of annoyance. "Good Lord, what if they do? There are always people prepared to hint lies about everything. Doesn't your own experience tell you that?"

"Of course, sir," French said smoothly, "but these stories are both direct and persistent. In fact, not to put too fine a point on it, it is freely stated that it was your conduct that drove your wife to suicide."

Grinsmead sat back in his chair and stared. "For heaven's sake," he said slowly, "say what you have to say and be done with it. What were the stories?"

"I'll tell you, sir," French returned. "If you want the direct truth, it is said that Mrs Grinsmead was driven to suicide because of your intimacy with Mrs Holt-Lancing."

It was a blow. Grinsmead wilted, but only for a moment. Then slowly he grew, or pretended to grow, angry.

"What the blazes is that to you?" he growled savagely, but keeping his voice well lowered. "The thing's a damned lie, but even if it were true, what is it to you?"

"Not much, if the rumours stopped there," French answered quietly. "Unfortunately, they don't. It's suggested that this intimacy was deliberately used to force Mrs Grinsmead into suicide. That it was, as you might say, thrust into her face; that she was baited with it. That's the rumour, sir, and quite apart from me, you've got to meet it, or you'll lose your job and be driven out of the Town."

Grinsmead made a furious gesture.

"Damn your impudence, I can look after my own affairs! But what I want to know is, where do you come in? And if you can't tell me that, will you leave the room, now, at once!"

"I come in here, Mr Grinsmead. If anything of the kind is proved, it will be pretty close to attempted murder. Now, *I* don't suspect that, and the superintendent doesn't suspect it, but we've got to satisfy other people above us who have taken these rumours seriously. Do as you like, of course, sir, but if you take my advice you'll treat them seriously too, and give me the satisfaction I need."

Grinsmead glared, while he turned this over in his mind. His principal feeling, French could have sworn, was uneasiness, and this uneasiness was growing with every moment that passed. He was taking French's remarks just as French had meant him to take them, as camouflage covering some more definite and deadly accusation. At last he seemed to come to some decision. He looked venomously at French, then growled: "What do you want me to do?"

"Answer some questions, sir."

"Go ahead," said Grinsmead, after some thought.

"Thank you, sir. I needn't tell a gentleman of your legal knowledge that you're not bound to answer my questions unless you like. With that proviso I ask whether you deny that a mutual attachment existed between yourself and Mrs Holt-Lancing?"

"Of course I don't deny it," Grinsmead answered angrily. "It was true. We were attached, and are. And what of it?"

"Did Mrs Grinsmead know of it?"

"Not to my knowledge. Never by word or deed did she suggest it. If she suspected it she kept it to herself. I asked you, what of it?"

"Only, sir, that if Mrs Grinsmead had known of it, it might justify the rumours."

"Well, that's just where you're wrong, Mr Inspector, with your suggestions and your rumours and your hints and your grandmotherly nonsense. It did nothing of the kind."

"How do you know that, sir?"

"I know it for this reason. Mrs Grinsmead was ill; her mind was affected. That was the cause of her suicide. I don't know whether you prefer rumour to the testimony of the doctor who attended her, but you'll find that the doctor'll back me up." He paused, then his anger apparently breaking out afresh, he went on, "I'll hear from Sir Mortimer Ellison what he thinks of your coming here and presuming to question my relations with a lady. It's the most confounded piece of insolence I ever heard of in my life. I'll see if that's the duty of Scotland Yard officers. Anything more you want to ask?"

"Yes, sir," said French, unperturbed by this outburst. "It is suggested that shortly before Mrs Grinsmead's death you and Mrs Holt-Lancing planned a scheme to get yourselves out of your difficulties. I should like to know what that scheme was?"

This proved a second blow, heavier than the first. Grinsmead's jaw dropped, and he sat back with fear, unmistakable, on his features. In a considerably shaken voice he answered, "You're wrong there, inspector. We had no such scheme in view."

"We are not wrong, sir. We have convincing evidence of it. You may not wish, however, to speak of it. If so, that is your own business. But I give you the option of explaining it. I'll put my question in another way: What, for example, did you mean by saying to Mrs Holt-Lancing, 'We'll not have to wait much longer'? Wait for what?"

Gone was Grinsmead's haughtiness, his anger, simulated or real, his desire to interview Sir Mortimer. Instead was fear, a desire to propitiate, a willingness to discuss, an eagerness indeed to discuss.

"I see, inspector, you know too much," he said in rather shaky tones. "I shall have to tell you everything. I know legally I needn't say anything, but if I don't, you'll begin to suspect me of something serious. What happened was this."

French was a good judge of character. Long experience had taught him to recognise at a glance whether a witness was lying or telling the truth. But in the present instance he found himself baffled. So far as he could tell from the man's manner, Grinsmead might have been doing either. With considerable interest French settled himself to listen.

"It's quite true," Grinsmead began. "However you knew of it, it's quite true. We were fond of each other, and the situation was getting unbearable. I'm not trying to justify my conduct to you, but it's only fair to mention that my friendship with Mrs Holt-Lancing was the direct and inevitable consequence of my wife's coldness. I say quite definitely it was not the other way round. It was because I couldn't get any sympathy from my wife that I turned elsewhere.

"Well, as I said, the situation was getting unbearable. I determined to end it. But not as you seem to imagine. I determined to end it by a divorce. I was prepared, if there was no other way out, to fake the evidence which would have enabled my wife to divorce me. It was in reference to this decision that I said to Mrs Holt-Lancing, 'We'll not have to wait much longer.' "

"There was some reference to a risk," French suggested.

"Of course there was. If there had been no risk in the thing I should have done it long before. There was every risk. There was the risk that we mightn't get the divorce. There was the risk that, if we did, my business would be ruined, and then how should we have lived? People are pretty old-fashioned in a place of this size, and they might easily have taken a divorce seriously."

French considered. The man had certainly been open. These admissions covered facts which would have been difficult to prove, and which in themselves were damning. On the other hand, so far as French could see, his explanation did really cover the facts, and might be true or false. French thought his obvious policy was to accept it as true.

At the same time he saw that he could make a little test.

"Thank you, Mr Grinsmead," he said, "that was what I wanted. Unfortunately, it's only half my business. I also want permission to examine the gas fittings in your house to set at rest some further suggestions about the tragedy. Now I could get a plumber and go as an inspector from the Yard, or if you would prefer the business kept secret, I could go as a plumber myself. What do you say, sir?"

"What in hades do you want to see?" Grinsmead returned irritably.

"Just the run of the pipes and fittings."

"Oh, all right," Grinsmead returned. "It seems to me idiotic, but I suppose you know your own business."

"Perhaps, sir, you'd telephone out and tell your people that you've given instructions for the gas fittings to be overhauled?"

With a bad grace Grinsmead did so. French thanked him formally, wished him good day, and left the office. Reaching the street, he turned into the first telephone booth he saw and rang up the Yard. Could Sergeant Ormsby be sent down by the first train with two sets of plumbers' clothes and a kit of tools?

11

INVESTIGATION

French's interview with Grinsmead had had considerable value, but of a negative kind. The man's admission of his attachment to Irene Holt-Lancing and of the conversation in the lane had proven the truth of Anne Day's statements and given a knock-out blow to French's theory of her guilt. To this extent the interview represented progress.

But Grinsmead had said little to help French constructively. Still less had he given himself away. French, indeed, was disappointed with the result. He wondered if he could get more out of Mrs Holt-Lancing. There would just be time to pay her a visit before Ormsby could arrive.

He took a taxi out to the lady's house. It proved to be a small cottage of the kind usually described by agents as a bijou residence, standing in its own tiny but well-kept grounds. By a stroke of luck Mrs Holt-Lancing was at home, and French was shown into the drawing-room. It was a restful room. The furniture was good, the fire bright, while flowers and books gave it an inviting atmosphere.

The mistress of the house struck French as a woman of determination and character. He felt also that she was one with a strong appeal to men. He could not but admire her, with her dark hair and eyes, delicate features and perfect complexion. He thought indeed that he had never seen a brunette with so charming a colouring.

Following his procedure with Grinsmead, French sent in his private card, reserving his official title for the lady's private eye. However, she betrayed no interest in his profession, merely asking shortly what she could do for him.

French opened by expressing regret at the unpleasant nature of his business. To this, however, she made no reply, except by a grave and expectant nod. French therefore went on: "My business is concerned with the recent death of Mrs Grinsmead. It is known, madam, that you and Mr Grinsmead were embarrassed by the existence of Mrs Grinsmead, and that you agreed to take certain steps to get rid of your embarrassment. I want to know what those steps were."

Mrs Holt-Lancing's face was not very expressive, but now it registered first amazement and then indignation. "I am aware neither of the steps nor of the embarrassment to which you refer," she said coldly. "Will you kindly explain yourself?"

"I think you understand, madam, but I shall try to make myself still clearer. The police are aware of the attachment between you and Mr Grinsmead and that Mrs Grinsmead stood in the way of your mutual happiness. Also that you and he had fixed up a scheme to overcome this obstacle. I want to know what that scheme was and how it affected Mrs Grinsmead? Stop!" he said sternly, as she seemed about to flame out on him. "Before you answer I must caution you that anything you say may be used in evidence against you."

This last phrase did it. She knew enough about police matters to recognise it as one usually associated with arrest.

She paled, and the anger in her eyes faded and anxiety took its place.

"I don't understand you," she faltered. "Mr Grinsmead is nothing to me."

This gave French his opportunity.

"I've already warned you that you needn't reply to my questions," he said in a lower voice. "For your own sake I may now add that if you make any false statements it may be a very serious matter for you. You may take it from me that I would not come here and ask the questions I have unless I was sure of my ground. Think again, Mrs Holt-Lancing. Do you care to amend your answer?"

"Mr Grinsmead is nothing to me," she repeated, though less firmly.

"Very well," said French grimly. "Do you know the lane at the back of the Grinsmead house?"

"I know there is a lane."

"On Sunday, the twenty-fifth of October at half-past four in the afternoon you and Mr Grinsmead met in this lane and had a conversation?"

French thought at first that she was going to deny it, but from his resolute manner she evidently realised this would be useless.

"Well," she murmured, "and what if we had?"

"Only this, madam. The police happen to have a fairly complete record of that conversation. Is it necessary for me to remind you of it?"

"There was nothing in the conversation of which I am ashamed."

"Possibly not, madam. But there was something you'll require to explain: your decision with Mr Grinsmead to take a decisive action to ease the situation in which you found yourselves; your references to the risk of this action;

your references to waiting for a decent interval, after which the crash might come; it being at the best a dirty business; avoiding the mistakes of predecessors; and finally, your decision not to wait much longer."

She stared at him, amazed at his knowledge. But she did not speak, and French continued: "Now, madam, your difficulty, referred to in this conversation, was the existence of Mrs Grinsmead. You decide that you will shortly take means to get yourselves out of your difficulty. Now follow me," French raised his finger and spoke very emphatically, "a short time after that conversation Mrs Grinsmead dies under extremely suspicious circumstances, circumstances indeed which point to murder. I make no accusation whatever. I simply point out that the police must have an explanation of the scheme referred to in that conversation. You will see this for yourself."

As French mentioned the word "murder," Mrs Holt-Lancing gave a low moan. "Oh, no, no, no!" she cried brokenly. "Such a thing never entered our minds. It's too horrible!"

French spoke more gently. "Well, madam, all you have to do is to explain."

"I see I must," she returned. "You know too much, though how you know it I can't imagine. We did meet on that Sunday afternoon and we did have that conversation. We were," she hesitated, "fond of each other, and we did want to end our unhappy situation. I admit all that because it's true. But your dreadful interpretation is absolutely and entirely false. We had a scheme, but it was for divorce – a double divorce. We were, I see I must tell you, going to fake up some evidence which would allow Mrs Grinsmead to divorce her husband and my husband to divorce me. That was the whole thing. I swear it. Ask Mr Grinsmead and he'll tell you the same thing."

French went on putting questions until he had satisfied himself that she and Grinsmead told the same tale. Then he obtained from her a statement as to her own movements on the night of the tragedy. She had been present at the dinner party and had played bridge afterwards. About midnight the party had broken up and the Alcocks had driven her home.

Before leaving, French set himself to quiet the lady's mind. He reminded her that all he had asked from her was an explanation, that she had given him this, that so far as he could see it was satisfactory, and that he was obliged for her information and regretted having had to trouble her. In fact they parted on outwardly amicable terms.

French, however, was dissatisfied with the interview. He had really learned nothing. Whether Mrs Holt-Lancing and Grinsmead were innocent or guilty, they would have told him just the tale they had. If they were guilty, they would obviously prepare an explanation of their conversation, for use in the unlikely event of its becoming known. And what more obvious explanation could they think of?

French returned to Ashbridge to find Ormsby, a plumber to the life, waiting for him. French took his bundle of clothes into the station lavatory and emerged as a passable imitation of a plumber's mate. Then with their kits, which contained – strange tool for a plumber – a large camera, they took the first bus running in the direction of Frayle, completing the journey on foot.

Grinsmead's telephone had evidently been sent in good faith, for no surprise was exhibited at their arrival. On the way out, French had explained what was required and they lost no time in concentrating on just those points. After a general walk through the house and a good deal of heavy tramping up and down stairs between the meter and the various rooms, they settled down in the room which had been Sybil's. First they examined the gas stove. It was of a rather old flueless pattern. French took a couple of photographs of it, as well as general views of the room. The batswing tap came in for special scrutiny. The supply pipe ran out from the opposite side of the fire, and in a couple of feet disappeared beneath the floor, as had been indicated in Kendal's sketch.

French next turned to the door bolt. A short examination of the bolt, the pushes and the connecting wires, convinced him of the accuracy of Kendal's statement that it had not been interfered with.

He gave a good deal of thought to the door. It was strongly made and well-fitting, except for the usual space below it to enable it to clear the carpet when open. The marks where it had been forced were clear, and an examination of them convinced him that the door had only been forced once, that is, that his theory that Grinsmead had forced it in the middle of the night was untenable. If Grinsmead had done so, and if he had then fastened it strongly enough to resist Miss Day's thrusts, marks would have shown of the forcing of this second fastening.

The windows didn't occupy French long. There was nothing remarkable about them and an almost casual inspection sufficed. Then he turned to Ormsby and nodded.

"Na, then, Bill," Ormsby said loudly for the benefit of passers-by, "get that there board up, will you, so's I can 'ave a look at the joint."

As he spoke, Ormsby, who was almost a tradesman, so handy was he with tools, began lifting the board covering the pipe leading to the fire. Soon it was up, and they followed the pipe along till it passed out into the corridor. So far no extra tap was disclosed.

Having replaced the board, they repeated their operations in the corridor. Here were junctions on the pipe leading to other rooms, but no taps. Laboriously they worked right back to the meter, finding that the same conditions obtained throughout.

This upset another of French's theories. There was no way in which, had the fire in Sybil's room been lighted, the gas could have been cut off and then turned on again, without at the same time extinguishing the fire in the cook's room.

It was in a meditative mood that the two men walked back to the bus. French from the beginning had really believed the affair to be suicide. Now he felt that the evidence was proving it. Kendal had been right all through. He was certainly right in saying that the suicide theory covered all the facts, for the most suggestive, that of the Grinsmead–Holt-Lancing conversation, could now be explained on that hypothesis. The absence of finger marks on the window handles, the other puzzling feature of the case, could also be accounted for. It was reasonable enough to assume that the dead woman had imagined that the handles might be cold or dirty, and had held a handkerchief in her hand while operating them.

French determined that next morning he would go back to Frayle in his own personality and check the statements of all concerned. If he learned nothing fresh, he would report that in his opinion all was OK, and return to London.

That night French sat in his hotel trying to get his ideas straightened out. The more he considered the affair, the stronger he thought was the case for suicide. Apart from the actual details of Mrs Grinsmead's death – and these could only be accounted for on the suicide theory – the general circumstances fitted in and the motive was entirely adequate.

All the same, he saw that one of the serious difficulties to the suicide theory still remained: the fact that the deceased lady had shown no special mental stress on the evening of her death. It really was difficult to believe that in this normal state and under the quieting influence of the sleeping draught, she would take this tremendous decision to end her life, and not only take it, but arouse herself sufficiently to get out of bed, close the windows and turn on the gas. French swore. It wasn't so straightforward as he had imagined.

He saw that he hadn't sufficient information as to the action of the draught. Before doing anything further he must get this point squared up.

Next morning, therefore, he was early in Dr Roome's consulting room. He pledged the doctor to secrecy, told him the developments, and asked his help.

Dr Roome did not say much, though he evidently considered the coroner's ideas as the merest moonshine. However, he answered French's questions without hesitation. The draughts were merely a quite ordinary mild hypnotic. It was not possible to say how long a time would intervene between the taking of the dose and drowsiness setting in, as this depended on the patient's constitution, health and tolerance to the drug. But under normal conditions he would estimate from ten minutes to half an hour.

Dr Roome thought it would have been possible for Sybil Grinsmead to get up and turn on the gas after Anne Day had left the room. She was certainly awake and in possession of her full powers since she had bolted the door. All the same, he admitted that performing such unfamiliar operations was a very different thing from merely pressing a button, which she might do in a drowsy condition from force of habit. The doctor was non-committal, but on the whole his view was that this particular point of view showed suicide possible, but unlikely.

French thought it might be wise to ask Dr Heath the same questions, so as to see whether a contrary bias would affect the replies. But he found he had wronged the doctor. Heath told him just the same as Roome.

French, therefore, carried out his previous programme. He went out to Frayle and interviewed the inmates. Blandly ignoring the surprised stares of those who had seen him in his previous incarnation of plumber's mate, he asked his questions. But all he achieved was the complete corroboration of Kendal's views.

On returning to the hotel that night French busied himself in getting out a draft of his report to Sir Mortimer Ellison. In this he proposed to review the evidence and give it as his considered opinion that the late Sybil Grinsmead had committed suicide as Inspector Kendal had already suggested. He worked steadily, with the result that by nine o'clock the draft was finished.

It occurred to him that Kendal would be interested in his results. Kendal, he knew, lived comparatively close, and French thought he would call in then and there for a chat. Ten minutes later he was knocking at the other's door.

Kendal was glad to see him. He welcomed him with effusion and got out whisky and tobacco. Soon French was installed in the most comfortable chair while Kendal poked the fire to a still more fervent heat.

"I'm going back tomorrow," French said, when they had talked for some time. "I thought you might like to see my report first."

Kendal said he would like nothing better.

"What's your general conclusion?" he asked. "Suicide or murder?"

"Suicide," French answered decisively. "I agree entirely with you. I've been through the whole case and got exactly what you got. These new facts brought out by Dr Heath don't affect the affair. They can be explained on the suicide theory quite easily. On the other hand, on the murder theory many facts can't be explained at all."

"I'm glad you agree. Now that the thing is closed, I don't mind confessing that I was a good deal worried about it. If you had found out that it was murder after my reporting it was suicide, it wouldn't have been any too good for me."

"I'm glad too," French admitted. "Not that there was at any time the least chance that you had made a mistake. You went into it too thoroughly for that."

"I did it as well as I saw how," Kendal agreed. "Will you let me see the report?"

"I don't think there's any need for you to wade through it, but I'll give you a rough outline. I begin by pointing out," and French summarised what he had said.

"And here," he concluded, "I've copied your sketch showing the fingermarks on the tap. Hope you don't mind?"

He put the sketch down on the table before Kendal and stood staring at it. Kendal was complimentary about the completeness with which French had summarised the case, but pointed out that of course French could have had copies of his photographs. French said he was going to ask for these as well.

For a moment they remained motionless, Kendal looking at the draft and French standing beside him with his eyes fixed on the sketch. It was very still in the little house. Mrs Kendal was out, as was also Kendal's one daughter. No sound indeed was to be heard but the soft murmuring of the little tongues of flame in the fire.

Suddenly an idea darted into French's mind. He stiffened. He grew rigid, as now with round eyes and an expression of incredulous amazement he stared at the sketch as if he could never see enough of it. Kendal, sensing a change in the emotional atmosphere, glanced at him.

"Gosh, French! What's up?" he exclaimed. "What are you looking at?"

For a moment French seemed unable to move. Then he pointed wildly to the sketch. "See it!"* he cried excitedly. "See it! See what it means! Good Lord, man, don't you see it?"

Kendal evidently thought his visitor had gone dotty.

He looked from French's eager, excited face to the sketch and back again from the sketch to French's face. "See what?" he asked. "I don't see anything. I don't know what you're talking about."

"Why," said French, tapping the paper, "this sketch! I've only noticed it this minute. We've missed it, you and I, and there was the key of the whole thing in our hands! Don't you see now?"

Kendal shook his head helplessly, some annoyance beginning to creep into his manner. But French was thinking only of his discovery. "Why, man," he went on impatiently, "look at it! Don't you see that there in that sketch is the proof of murder?"

* For sketch, see page 136

Kendal's jaw dropped. "Murder!" he repeated slowly, adding in the same conversational way a short but pithy oath. "Good Lord, French, how do you make that out?"

"Here," said French, "take the sketch in your hand and look at it! That tap was turned clockwise."

Kendal obeyed as a man in a dream. Then suddenly another oath burst from him. "I see it," he cried, "I see it! The print's at the wrong end of the handle! She turned the tap off, not on! How in hades did I miss that?"

12

EXPLANATION

Further thought convinced both inspectors that this discovery of French's did really prove that the case was one of murder. If Sybil Grinsmead had turned the tap off, some one else had turned it on, using great care first, that his own fingerprints should not be left, and second, that the prints already there should be preserved. With one object and with one object only could this have been done.

"But hang it all, French," Kendal said, when they had discussed the thing for some time. "Even yet I don't understand it. Why should the deceased have turned it off? Who turned it on?"

"The murderer," French returned. "As I now visualise it, the murderer wanted Sybil Grinsmead's fingerprints on the tap. Very well, how could he get them there? Only, surely, in one way. He would light the fire, wipe the tap, and let the lady turn it out again."

"But we've heard nothing about the fire having been lit."

"I know we've not. But that doesn't mean it wasn't done. As a matter of fact it would be part of the murderer's plan to keep it quiet."

"Naturally, so far as he was concerned himself. But how would he insure that the lady wouldn't mention it?"

French shook his head. "I don't know. Probably if he explained the thing so clearly to her as to leave no question in her mind, she would not think it worthwhile repeating."

"If it was Grinsmead he might have annoyed her at the same time so that she might not wish to repeat it."

"That's so, Kendal. That's a good notion. And there's another thing. The tap must have been turned on with a tool; something like a spanner which would only grip the edges. That wouldn't affect the fingerprints."

Kendal ruefully agreed. He was evidently a good deal upset by the discovery.

"Curse it all, French," he said. "This will be a feather in your cap all right, but it won't do me much good. Here I've gone into the thing and given it as my considered opinion that it was suicide, and now it turns out that I was wrong! It'll be some time before I live it down."

"Nonsense," French returned. "We're in the same boat. Here was I about to report the same thing. I'll tell that to the super, and that it was only chance at the last minute that prevented my putting it in writing. Don't you worry, old man. It'll be all right."

"Very decent of you and all that, French. But we can't change facts. However, that's not the point. What'll you do next?"

"Go out and have another shot at Frayle, I suppose. I don't really know. Between this and tomorrow I'll have to think up something. I suppose I'll have to try and find out about that fire being turned on, though of course if only the murderer knows about it that won't be easy."

"Won't you tell the super what you're doing?"

"I don't usually report till I'm sure of my ground. However, there would seem to be no doubt so far as it's being murder goes. Have you the 'phone?"

"In the hall."

"I was going to suggest that you ring him up now and tell him that I'm here and that we've been talking the thing over and come to the conclusion the coroner was right."

Kendal rose. "I'll get him for you, but you must speak to him. I needn't warn you that these local offices can overhear you."

"So they can in Town, but I'll be careful."

Superintendent Godfrey was extremely surprised when with veiled hints French succeeded in conveying to him the news. But he quickly congratulated French and expressed his agreement with the proposed programme.

"It's always a miracle to me, Kendal," French remarked, when the telephoning was done, "how often murderers with an elaborate plan fall short in some tiny detail. Look at this Grinsmead, if it was he, taking all that trouble to get his victim's fingerprints on the tap, and then getting them on the wrong half of the handle! It's always the same. The committing of the murder must excite them so as to destroy their power of thought."

"That's so. I say, French, has it occurred to you that that poor woman knew what was coming to her? She was no more of weak mind than you or I. She knew what that ruffian meant."

"It was a put-up job between the two of them, Grinsmead and that Holt-Lancing woman," said French. "There's no doubt they settled it in the lane that Sunday. And they fixed up the divorce yarn in case questions should be asked. And they – " French stopped suddenly. "By Jove, Kendal," he went on, "there's another thing we've missed till now! Upon my soul, there's evidence that it was murder without the prints on the tap at all! Look here, the plan those two discussed couldn't have been divorce."

Kendal stared.

"Don't you see?" French went on. "They couldn't have afforded it. In the conversation itself Grinsmead referred to some will under which Mrs Holt-Lancing would lose her money if she married a second time. And in my interview with him this morning he said that without the income from his profession he couldn't live. Divorce, as he admitted himself, might easily have ruined his business. Therefore if they were divorced and remarried they couldn't have lived. Besides, a divorce from her own husband would cost her something. Therefore it was not divorce those two were discussing. Therefore it was murder, because murder was the only alternative."

"I wonder," said Kendal doubtfully. "You may be right."

"I must be right," French returned. "I tell you, Kendal, it was murder. And what's more, we'll get them both. Whichever of them actually did it, they're equally guilty."

"I'm only sorry I'm on this Entrican business and not working with you," Kendal returned. "I'd like to see it through now."

"If you can fix it up I should be only too delighted," French invited, as he collected his papers prior to taking his leave.

Next morning he was early at Frayle. There one by one he interviewed the whole household. Did anyone know of the gas fire in the late Mrs Grinsmead's room having been lighted within a reasonable time of her death? If not, had anyone other than a member of the household had an opportunity of lighting it?

In reply to the first of these questions French learned nothing whatever. But in answer to the second everyone reminded him that on the night of the tragedy there was a dinner party with five guests. Except for these five, no one had visited the house within a week of its mistress' death.

French was perfectly aware of the five guests, and particularly that Mrs Holt-Lancing was one of them. But though he had asked for the information, he did not see how a guest could have worked the trick with the gas fire.

For the time being he switched his mind off the fire and turned once again to the question of the windows. The murder theory involved Mrs Grinsmead having neither shut the windows herself, nor known they were shut. Some one had therefore gone into the room for this purpose. Could he find out who?

Gladys, the maid, said she had partially closed the windows and drawn the curtains about seven o'clock. At ten Sybil had gone to her room. The windows must therefore have been closed between those hours. Who had closed them?

Ensued another interview with each member of the household. The result was again disappointing. Everyone in the house could have gone unseen into that room and closed the windows, but everyone denied having done so.

French, however, did learn one significant fact. The possibilities as to the closing of the windows were not confined to the members of the household. The two ladies who had attended the dinner party had gone up to the pink spare room on arrival. Either of them could have done it.

French saw that if Mrs Holt-Lancing were a party to the crime, this might prove an important discovery. Further questions showed that she had been the last to arrive. As she knew the house so well, Gladys had not shown her upstairs, but had simply said to her, "The pink room, madam, if you please." As Mrs Holt-Lancing had gone upstairs, Mrs Alcock had come down. Irene Holt-Lancing

167

had therefore had ample opportunity to go into Sybil's room and close the windows.

So far, so good. Grinsmead might have lit the fire and got his wife to turn it off; either Grinsmead or Irene Holt-Lancing might have closed the windows. But had they done so? French saw that he would have to interview them both again, when perhaps he would be able to surprise an admission out of one or other.

Wearily he turned back to that puzzling point, the turning on of the gas. He felt that before he saw his suspects he must have some theory as to how it could have been done.

He sat down at a table in Sybil's room to think the thing out. And first, was it possible that the tap could have been turned on before Sybil bolted the door?

This meant, he was positive, before Sybil bolted the door on Anne's departure. Anne's room was next door, and the walls of houses of this type are not thick. It would have been impossible for anyone to have knocked at Sybil's door and had the door unbolted, after Ann had left and before Sybil had gone to sleep, without Anne hearing it. To settle the point French questioned Anne. No one, she declared positively, had entered Sybil's room after she had left. Before accepting the evidence French satisfied himself that the click of the bolt could be plainly heard in Anne's room.

If, then, Anne herself were not guilty, and French now felt satisfied about this, the gas *must* have been turned on after the door was bolted. How could it have been done?

He thought again of the obvious idea of fixing some tool to the tap with a cord leading out under the door, which would pull the tap open and then slip off and be drawn out under the door. But the more he considered it, the more firmly convinced he became that Kendal was right and that this had not been done. There were two taps in question: on the left of the fireplace the main one on the approach pipe, which cut off both fire and ring; and on the right the batswing tap, which controlled the fire alone and on which Sybil's fingerprints had been found. The door was in the corner of the room to the left, so that a pull on a cord would have been from right to left across the front of the fireplace. Both the taps were very stiff, so that only an extremely strong apparatus would have operated them. The main tap could not have been turned *fully* on, that is, parallel to the pull on the cord, as it was found. Even supposing a tool could have been made to turn it at all, this would certainly have disengaged itself while the tap was still at a considerable angle to the pull. In the case of the batswing tap the thing was even more impossible. The pull was in the wrong direction – parallel to the shaft of the tap. It would have tended to draw the tap as a whole towards the fire, and not to turn it round. And there was no fulcrum or leverage or pulley which could have been employed to alter the direction of the pull.

French spent a couple of hours considering and experimenting, and at the end of his investigation he found himself more than ever convinced of the impracticability of the scheme.

His next move, however, seemed more promising. He took out the two little side screws and lifted away the casting covering the bottom of the fire. At once he experienced a thrill of eager satisfaction. There were marks in the dust covering the pipes. Some one, not so long since, had been working with these pipes!

But wait a moment. Was he going too fast? No use in building up a theory on false premises. Ormsby, he knew, had not had the front off; had Kendal?

He replaced the casting and went down to the telephone. After considerable trouble he located Kendal and put his question. No, Kendal had not touched the casting; he had had no occasion to do so. Good! that was all French wanted.

French returned to Sybil's room, and locking himself in, once again removed the casting. His reaction to dust marks was almost automatic. He got his fingerprint apparatus and dusted the entire fittings with white powder. But here he drew blank. The surfaces were too rough to retain impressions.

French sat back on his heels and examined the fittings. The main pipe, coming in at the left side of the fireplace, ran across near the floor to the right side, then turned up. In this vertical portion was the tap controlled by the batswing handle. The pipe then ran back across the fireplace towards the left, but at a higher level. Near the centre of the fireplace it ended in a sort of rosehead or nozzle like that of a garden hose, a brass cap pierced with a number of small holes. Through these holes the gas issued into the atmosphere when the taps were on. In front of the cap was a larger pipe with an open end towards the nozzle, which led on across the fireplace to the left, and thence to the burners. The gas entered this pipe, carrying with it sufficient air to make the correct burning mixture. The nozzle was about ¾ in. in diameter, the inlet pipe about 1¼ in. diameter, and the two pipes were about ⅜ in. apart. A thin removable hood was sprung on to the inlet pipe, which projected back over the upper part of the nozzle. French slipped the hood off and the pipes with the space between them became fully exposed.

Absently French's hand stole to his pocket and he drew out his pouch and pipe and began automatically to fill the latter. Here certainly was a place at which the gas could be stopped. If something soft like a pad of rubber were pressed firmly on the face of the nozzle, it would close the little holes and do the trick. But how could such a pad be fixed? Well, that wasn't so difficult. Wedges driven in between it and the inlet pipe would do it. Yes, that seemed possible.

French lit his pipe and began slowly to smoke. That seemed all right so far. If the gas exit at the nozzle were closed, the gas could then be turned on and no gas could escape. If then the pad were pulled out by means of a cord from the door, the gas would escape into the room.

But how could the wedges be pulled out? French saw that here was the difficulty. The cord would pull, not in the direction in which the wedges should be drawn, but at right angles to it. The cord would not move them.

And then he saw a further difficulty. Wedges could scarcely be driven in while the hood was in place. And he had found it in place.

At the same time the marks in the dust showed that something of the kind had been done. French retired to an armchair in the corner of the room and smoked stolidly while he continued thinking the matter over.

Presently he attacked the problem from a new angle. Whatever was done, whether the nozzle was padded up or not, apparatus of some kind would have been required. Could he find that apparatus?

Suppose Grinsmead were guilty. He would have withdrawn the apparatus beneath the door. What would he have done with it?

He would not have kept it, as that would be dangerous. How could he have disposed of it?

French tried to put himself in Grinsmead's place. There he was in the middle of the night with some compromising materials. How could he get rid of them?

The kitchen range? No, the fire would be out before the apparatus would be available. So would the other downstairs fires, and upstairs there was only gas.

But would the downstairs fires be out? Could Grinsmead not have built up the necessary fire before going to bed?

If any part of the apparatus were metal or rubber, French thought an attempt to burn it would be unlikely. But if it had been made of wood and leather this might have proved the solution. French knocked out his pipe and went down to interview the servants.

But from them he learned nothing. None of the fireplaces on the tragic morning held an exceptional amount of ashes, nor was the unburnt coal in the boxes lower than usual. Nor were any pieces of metal or other material found in the ashes.

French had provided himself with a search warrant, and he now took advantage of it. He settled down to hunt for the apparatus. Grinsmead's bedroom, his study, his workshop – all were examined with scrupulous care, but without result. Nor did French's careful searches elsewhere nor his veiled inquiries lead to anything whatever.

A hopeless case, he thought at length. Whatever had been used had been destroyed. However, the point was so important that as a last resource he got down into the ashpit and began turning over the household debris. He had a nasty couple of hours among old tins, broken crockery, cinders and dirty rubbish of all kinds. But even this self-sacrifice remained unrewarded.

On his way back to the house he turned rather hopelessly into the garden. Was there any rubbish heap or other place in which something might have been buried in the middle of the night? He did not think so. Such work could not have been done in the dark without fear of leaving traces, and a light would have been dangerous. No, there was no help there.

He decided unhappily that this promising clue had petered out and that he must try something else. And then as he turned to the door his eye fell on a large water barrel at the corner of the house. It was fed from the roof and used for water for the garden. Without hesitation French walked over and turned on the tap. The water spouted out and began to creep across the grass.

It ran for an hour, leaving the entire surroundings in a sea, and then at last only a couple of inches of water was left. French threw in a piece of wood and with difficulty and bad language scrambled in. Standing on the wood, he bent down and began feeling through the water.

Ten seconds later his fingers touched a small object. He drew it out and stared at it wonderingly.

It was a bit of thin metal about half an inch wide and four inches long, curved into a quadrant. At one end a hole had been drilled, through which a cord had been passed and knotted, leaving two ends each about six inches long. A peculiar cord, that. As French cleaned it, he thought it was made of black silk. The metal was covered with a thin skin of rust, as if it had been in the barrel a comparatively short time only.

A bit of clock spring, French thought, and then suddenly his heart leaped. Clock spring! Yes, a bit of clock spring would solve his problem. A pad of rubber held over the gas nozzle, not by wedges which could not be pulled out, but by clock spring, which could! And there was the explanation of the two cords: one would pass out under the door and pull the spring out, the other would be attached to the pad, so that as soon as it was released and dropped from the nozzle it would also be drawn out of the room. French climbed out of the barrel, wiped his hands, and made a sketch. Yes, he had it at last!

Here A was the gas nozzle and B the air intake pipe. The pad C, of rubber and pear-shaped, was placed across the nozzle and fixed firmly in position by the clock spring D. If now the cord F were pulled, the spring would be drawn out, the pad would drop to the floor, and would in its turn be pulled out by the cord E. Both spring and pad would pull noiselessly across the floor and would easily pass under the door.

French could scarcely contain his delight. Here was not only proof of his theory, but a highly promising clue. Who had bought some yards of this heavy black silk cord? Who had had a hole drilled in a piece of clock spring? Surely these purchases would be traceable and would lead straight to the murderer!

He decided that his first step must, however, be to test the apparatus out. Accordingly he left Frayle and took the first bus to Ashbridge. There he bought six yards of a strong, smooth, dark-coloured cord – not indeed silk, but good enough for his purpose. Next at a plumber's he got a scrap of fine sheet rubber, about 3-16th inches thick. From this he cut a pear-shaped piece large enough to cover the nozzle, while leaving a projection to which the cord could be attached. He drilled a hole in the projection, passed the end of the cord through and tied it, cleaned the clock spring and tied it also on to the cord about a foot from the pad, and the apparatus was ready. Then he went to the police station, told Superintendent Godfrey of the experiment he wished to try, and asked for the help of Kendal that

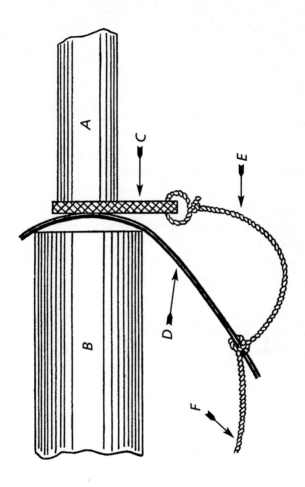

evening. Finally he rang up Anne Day to say that he was returning to Frayle about nine that night, and asking that she and Gladys should remain in to meet him.

Kendal was eager to know their business, but French would not enlighten him. "Bit of an experiment," was all he would say. "It wouldn't be so valuable if you knew what to expect."

Shortly before nine the two men left Ashbridge on Kendal's motor bicycle combination. At Frayle French left Kendal downstairs, going up alone to Sybil's room. There he fixed his pad and spring and led the cord across the floor to the door, passed it underneath, and hid the end of it under the mat in the corridor. Then he turned on the tap of the fire, and having waited to make sure that the pad was gas-tight, he called Kendal and Gladys.

"I want you, Gladys," he said, "to go into that room and fix the windows exactly as you did that night. Do everything else in the room that you did on that night, exactly as you did then. Look about you to the same extent. If you see anything unusual, tell me at once. Kendal, you're to be observer in the matter. Don't interfere, but note what is done. It's just an experiment, you understand, Gladys."

Gladys and Kendal went into the room, and Gladys fussed about at various jobs. Then she came out to French and said she had finished.

"And you saw nothing unusual?" French insisted. She had seen nothing. Everything seemed exactly as on the night of the tragedy.

"I'm much obliged to you, Gladys," French said. "That's all. Now will you please ask Miss Day if she will come here."

Gladys disappeared, and presently Anne arrived, curious and slightly resentful. French, as usual, was polite.

"We want your help in a small experiment, Miss Day," he explained, going on to make the same request of her as he had of Gladys. Again Kendal was to be observer.

Anne did as she was asked, without, however, noticing anything unusual. French thanked her, and let her go downstairs. So far everything had gone well. As French had foreseen, neither of these women had noticed the cord.

French was even more pleased that Kendal had not observed it. Of course it wasn't easy to see; the murderer had been depending on that. The direct light of the electric lamp above the bed did not fall on it, and owing to its dark colour it was almost indistinguishable among the shadows.

"Now, Kendal," French went on, "I want you to go into that room and have a stretch on the bed. You may read, but you are not to look carefully about. You are, indeed, to be Sybil Grinsmead, and you will therefore get quickly drowsy. I'm sorry, but you may have to stay there an hour or more. But directly you notice anything strange, come out and tell me."

Kendal grinned. "You're not doing it badly, French," he declared. "It seems like the Speckled Band over again. What am I to expect? A gentle hiss like steam passing from a kettle?"

"If you hear that," French answered, "come out and tell me."

French saw his colleague satisfactorily settled, then came out and shut the door. He had determined to do nothing for an hour, so as to demonstrate that the fire was quite gas-tight at first. Accordingly, when the hour had passed, he stole softly to the door, lifted the mat, and was about to pull the cord, when he stopped.

He saw suddenly that he was making his test under much more severe conditions than those which had obtained at the time of the murder. The clock spring, falling on the tiled hearth and being drawn over the kerb, might make a very faint sound. This sound, of course, could not have been heard by Sybil, who was drugged and asleep. Still less could it have been audible to anyone outside the room. But Kendal, awake and alert, might hear it.

For a moment French stood in thought. Then he went to the bathroom next door and turned on the water. This sound, he felt sure, would be sufficient to drown any slight noise the spring might make, thus making his test fairer.

His idea proved correct. When he went back to the door and pulled the cord it came out quite easily, inch by inch, making no appreciable sound and bringing out the spring and pad. French replaced the mat, put the apparatus in his pocket, and stood waiting.

But not for long. In two or three minutes he heard a sudden movement and Kendal strode to the door and flung it open. "Gas!" he said in amazed tones.

"Right," French answered, pushing him back and following him into the room. "Let's cut it off."

With his torch French showed Kendal the open tap. Then closing it, he went to the window, and threw all the sashes fully open. "Come out," he said, "till the room clears."

Here was all the proof anyone could desire as to the feasibility of French's theory.

"Would it be too late to see the super tonight?" French asked, when after closing the windows on a room only slightly smelling of gas, they were returning to Ashbridge. Kendal said Godfrey would be only too glad to hear their news, and ten minutes later they were at his house.

He listened attentively while French explained his discovery, and though he didn't say much, he was evidently impressed.

"That should be a useful line, the purchase of those materials," he said, when the story was finished.

"I wanted to see you about that, sir," French answered. "I thought your men could perhaps take that in hand, so far as the local shops are concerned. Of course the stuff might have been got in London or anywhere. If your men can make nothing of it here, I should suggest a couple of advertisements in the trade journals."

"We'll have a try for it here," Superintendent Godfrey decided. "At the same time you go ahead with your ads. Nothing more tonight? Good! Keep me advised how you get on."

French, tired but jubilant, wrote his query about the clock spring to the various watchmakers' papers, and turned in.

– 13 –

JUBILATION

Next morning French found himself in less exuberant spirits. He did not see his way clear. Up to the present he had certainly done well. He had completed the first stage in his investigation; he had proved that murder had been done, and he had shown how. But so far he had got no proof as to the identity of the murderer. How was this to be obtained?

Assume it was Grinsmead or Irene Holt-Lancing, or both. Who might have seen these two together. If he could trace out their meetings he might learn something.

It occurred to him that perhaps Hersey, the Grinsmeads' man, might, in his capacity of chauffeur, be able to help him. Hersey, of course, had been interrogated, but it had not been supposed that he could know anything material, and the interrogation had not been pressed. Perhaps further judicious questioning might bring something useful to light.

Accordingly, after breakfast, French went out once again to Frayle. He found Hersey greasing the car in the garage. French summoned up all his knowledge of cars, and talked greasing technique till the ice was broken.

"I want to get a bit of information from you, Hersey," he went on, when the time seemed propitious. "It's very private and very important also. I may tell you in confidence that a serious charge may arise as a result of these inquiries I'm making. You follow me?"

French looked knowing, and Hersey, not to be outdone, looked knowing also.

"I see you understand me," French went on mendaciously. "Now I want you to tell me anything, no matter how slight, which seemed to you strange or abnormal and which occurred about the time of Mrs Grinsmead's death. It doesn't matter whether you see a connection or not. If anything out of the common happened, let me know about it."

French, thus blindly casting bread upon the waters, found it, not after many days, but immediately. To his surprise Hersey gave indications that he was disturbed by his visitor's question, and from that, if French knew anything of the type, it followed that the man really had something to tell.

"I see you're going to help me," French went on pleasantly. "Get along, like a good chap, and let's hear it."

"I don't know nothing about the mistress' death," said Hersey. "Is there anything fresh about that?"

French hesitated momentarily. "Well, yes," he answered, "there is. We think that she was driven to her death by certain persons. There will probably be a criminal charge against them. You must tell me what's in your mind, Hersey. I don't for a moment threaten, but you probably know that in these cases to keep anything back may mean a charge of accessory after the fact."

Hersey shook his head. "I'll not be charged," he declared. "I thought a deal of the mistress, though she did get a bit strange in her manner. Very good to me, she was always. If anyone had done her any 'arm, and I knew about it, I wouldn't 'old it back. But I don't."

"No," said French understandingly, "I know that, because if you knew anything of that sort you'd have come forward with it before now. But I want you to tell me that little incident that you are thinking of, even if you don't see any connection with the death."

"I didn't say there was an incident," said Hersey, with a hint of truculence in his voice.

"Not with your lips, Hersey," French returned confidentially, "but you did by your manner. Come now; neither you nor anyone else can afford to keep things back in a murder case."

Hersey was startled. He moved uneasily. "Well, it isn't much, mister, to make a song about. However, it was a bit queer and no mistake. It's been on my mind that I should have mentioned it to somebody, and then I thought it wasn't my business and I didn't know what to do. So 'ere goes."

"Good," said French.

"I'm a bit of a mechanic," went on Hersey, "and I do most of the running repairs to the car, more than most chauffeurs, though I say it myself. That day before the mistress' death it 'appened that I'd noticed the brakes a bit out of adjustment – I'd applied them sharply to save a dog, and I'd found that they'd slued 'er round. So I was afraid she'd skid if it was slippery. Well, the master wanted to go up to London the next day, and I thought I'd better adjust them that night. I 'ad an engagement in the evening, so I came back 'ere a bit before eleven and got to work. I 'ad the devil's own job with it. One of the brake pins on the back off 'ub 'ad seized, and I couldn't get it out, not for a couple of hours. It was close on two o'clock before I 'ad the job done."

French was interested. This was a promising beginning. He nodded encouragement and Hersey resumed: "It was a few minutes before two when I put off the light 'ere in the garage and started for 'ome. I lodge with a family about a quarter of a mile down the road. I came across the yard and opened the wicket quietly, so as not to be 'eard if anyone was awake in the 'ouse, and 'ave them thinking there were burglars. As I stepped out of the wicket I saw a light. Some one was standing under that clump of bushes out there, and shining a torch up against the wall of the 'ouse. I thought, 'Burglars, as I'm a sinner!' I slipped round behind the bushes, but before I could get near the light it went out and the figure 'urried away towards the front. It wasn't a very dark night; there was no moon, but the stars were bright. I couldn't see enough to be sure who it was, but I could see enough to know it was a woman. As I say, she went round the front corner of the 'ouse."

French pictured the place. The yard wall ran on from the back of the house in line with the side of the building, that is, the side next the tennis ground. In this yard wall was the large gate used by the car, containing the wicket of which Hersey had spoken. On stepping out of the wicket one could see along the side of the house. The bushes referred to stood about fifteen feet from the wall, between the house and the tennis ground.

"That's interesting," French said. "Did you follow the woman?"

Hersey looked as sly as a rather benevolent fox. He shook his head.

"Oh," said French, "you didn't find out who she was?"

"Not me," Hersey declared knowingly. "It weren't no business of mine, it weren't."

"But if you thought she was a burglar, wasn't it your business to alarm the household?"

"She weren't no burglar. It weren't no business of mine and I didn't interfere."

"What did you do?"

"I went back to the yard and waited there a while and then I went 'ome."

It was obvious that the chauffeur knew more than he had stated. French was sure he had a very good idea both of the identity and the business of the woman. But for a long time Hersey wouldn't admit it. Finally French got quite sharp.

"Now, Hersey, you listen to me," he said. "If this story of yours is connected with a crime, you'll be in it if you don't tell. If it's not connected with a crime, everything you say will be kept secret. Now you'll either say who you thought the woman was, or you'll come in with me to the police station in Ashbridge and be put through it there."

Hersey, now sullen and aggrieved, refused to reply at all, and it was not till French put up the bluff of formally cautioning him and asking him to accompany him to the police station that he gave way.

"I thought it was Mrs Holt-Lancing, but I didn't know for sure," he said sulkily.

French's heart leaped, but he crushed down any sign of interest.

"Why in hades couldn't you have said that before?" he asked testily. "I knew it was she. There's nothing in it."

Hersey unreasonably seemed disconcerted, particularly when French added: "But why did you think it was she?"

French had more trouble getting a satisfactory answer to this question than to the first. It took quite a lot of persuasion before Hersey replied. But at last he did so.

It seemed that he and Rose Unwin, Mrs Holt-Lancing's servant, were "walking out." On the occasion of these walks, when not discussing themselves, the conversation was wont to turn to their respective employers. Rose it was who had first suggested that there was something between the two, founding her opinion on a few words she had overheard during one of Grinsmead's calls. These calls, which at one time had been fairly frequent, had afterwards practically ceased, but the servants had noticed instead a series of singular coincidences. It became a commonplace for Hersey to tell Rose that the master was staying in London or Brighton or Bournemouth overnight and ask her could she come out and meet him early that evening, and for Rose to reply that she could, as her mistress was going to spend that night at Canterbury, or Winchester, or Oxford. But Hersey and Rose had been absolutely discreet. Not to a single individual had they breathed their thoughts. So far as Hersey knew, no one shared their suspicions.

When therefore Hersey had seen this woman, who in the dim light looked like Mrs Holt-Lancing, shining an electric torch on what he now admitted he believed was Grinsmead's window, he assumed that it was really Mrs Holt-Lancing, signalling to Grinsmead for some purpose of her own. He had not mentioned the affair to anyone, not even to Rose. He valued his situation, and he believed that knowledge of such matters would lose it for him.

"That's all right," French finally approved. "Now I'll tell you something. I won't use that information unless it becomes absolutely necessary, and if I do use it I'll see that it doesn't injure you. See?"

Hersey seemed glad to have his secret off his mind. But he wasn't as pleased as French. French indeed was secretly chuckling with delight. For here was the first item of his proof. Hersey didn't understand its significance, but French did. He not only saw what that light was for, but he even saw that he should have foretold its use.

The murderer, he already believed, had gone into Sybil's room to shut the windows. The shutting of the windows was necessary for his scheme, as had they been open, it was questionable whether the gas mixture would have become deadly soon enough. Besides, with the windows open there would have been a danger of the gas being smelt from an adjoining room. Now how was the murderer to know whether Sybil had or had not noticed them shut and opened them? Only in one way: by going outside the house with a torch and flashing the light up on them. And that, French dared swear, was what was done. Grinsmead's window was in that wall, true, and almost certainly a signal from that torch was received through it. But Sybil's window was there also.

But why, French wondered, could Grinsmead not have gone out and made his own investigation? For some time French puzzled over this, then he saw what might prove to have been the reason.

Could it not, he wondered, be that some alibi or other proof of innocence was thereby made possible? Something perhaps in connection with the opening of the house doors or ground-floor windows? Could Grinsmead have wished to prove that going out of the house was necessary to the crime, and that he did not go out? French had to admit that this was not a very satisfactory theory, but he hoped further thought would improve it.

How he wished he had been on the job on the morning after the crime, before footprints had been obliterated! However, there was no use in worrying about that; he must be thankful for the information he had.

Again warning Hersey to be silent on the matter, French walked down to Mrs Holt-Lancing's cottage. The lady was at home and saw him at once.

"I'm sorry to trouble you again, Mrs Holt-Lancing," he began, "but I'm afraid I have to ask you another question. It has been suggested to the police that you were at Frayle shortly before two o'clock on the morning of Mrs Grinsmead's death. It is not said that you were in the house; the suggestion is that you were in the grounds near the house. Now, what I want to ask you is, Do you wish to make any statement about this suggestion, either to deny or to explain it?"

Mrs Holt-Lancing seemed utterly taken aback. If she was not genuinely surprised by the question, French felt she was a serious loss to the British stage. She registered amazement extraordinarily well. Then she began to talk. She expressed the utmost indignation that such a thing should have been said; she denied the suggestion *in toto*; and she asked for the name of whoever had made it with a view to instituting proceedings for slander. In fact, Mrs Holt-Lancing gave a highly convincing and artistic representation of injured innocence.

When French was able to get a word in, he pointed out mildly that he made no accusation, but merely asked a question; that he was obliged to Mrs Holt-Lancing for answering it, which she had not been bound to do; that he fully accepted her statement; but that in such serious matters, as she knew herself, it was customary to ask for confirmation, and this he now did.

The lady, however, could give him no confirmation. She had left Frayle after the party on the night in question in company with Mr and Mrs Alcock, who had kindly driven her home. She had gone to bed at once, and had not got up till eight next morning.

French realised that it would have been quite possible for Mrs Holt-Lancing to have reached home, as she said, and gone noisily to her room. But about half-past one she could have slipped silently out again, walked to Frayle, inspected Sybil's window and given the signal to Grinsmead, returned, and entered her own house without anyone being a bit the wiser.

As French brought the interview to an end by thanking the lady for her information and bidding her a courteous good day, he was well pleased with his progress. What he had got was not proof of his theory, but taken with the other facts, it was uncommonly near it. He debated with himself as to whether he should not go at once into Ashbridge and see Godfrey with a view to arresting Grinsmead and Mrs Holt-Lancing. There would certainly be full justification for such a step.

Then he wondered whether he could not possibly do a little better first. Was there no line of investigation as yet unworked, no source of information untapped?

He thought again of the unexpected fruit his interrogation of Hersey had brought forth. It was, of course, unlikely that anyone else at Frayle had been up that night or had seen anything unusual, as in this case he or she would certainly have come forward with the information. However, it was just possible that he might learn something further by a few more questions. It would be well worth a little extra trouble if he could put a complete case before Godfrey.

Of all the inmates of the house, Mrs Meakin, the cook, had appeared least in the limelight in connection with the tragedy. Except for having had her gas fire lit all night she had had nothing of interest to tell the police. It had somehow come to be assumed that she could know nothing about it, and she had not therefore been so exhaustively questioned as the others. For this reason French determined that he would begin his forlorn hope with her.

He walked back to Frayle and saw the cook. After chatting for some moments he reminded her that he was still working on the case, and that he hoped to get some further information about the events of that night of tragedy.

"We believe, Mrs Meakin, that something took place that night which we don't yet fully understand. When I tell you, please, in the strictest confidence, that there were people about the grounds that night who were carrying out some very mysterious operations, you will see that my questions are justified. Now what I want to find out is, was anyone in the house awake that night? If so, did they look out of the windows? If so, did they see anyone outside? You follow me? I begin with you because you said you were not very well that night. You may have lain awake?"

"I wasn't well," Mrs Meakin answered, "and I didn't sleep for some time after I went to bed. But I didn't look out of my window, and I neither saw nor heard anyone outside, or inside, for that matter."

"And you don't know of anyone else who might have been awake or up?"

Mrs Meakin considered. "You've seen Miss Cheame, of course?" she asked presently. "She was up getting herself some food in the middle of the night."

This was news to French. However, he concealed his satisfaction.

"No," he said, "not yet, but of course I'm going to. As a matter of fact, how did you know she was up?"

"The food was gone, and I asked about it."

French nodded. "Now was there anyone else? I knew about Miss Cheame."

There was no one. Mrs Meakin could give no further help. But French could see that her sympathies had been with Sybil Grinsmead, and he felt convinced that if she had known anything, she would have told it.

With somewhat more interest, though still not expecting to learn anything, French next asked for an interview with Edith Cheame. She handed the children over to Anne and received him in the schoolroom.

"As you see, Miss Cheame," he began, "I'm still carrying on inquiries about this unhappy tragedy. The police have got hold of some information which they don't understand, and I have to report on it," and he mentioned that mysterious strangers had been in the grounds during the night. "Now I understand that you were about that night, and I should be glad to know if you heard or saw anything unusual?"

"I was about, inspector?" she returned, with evident surprise. "I don't know what you mean by that. Are you suggesting that I was out during the night?"

French shook his head. "No, Miss Cheame, of course not. But I'm suggesting that you were downstairs. Were you not?"

A light seemed to dawn on Edith. "You're quite right," she admitted, "I was. I couldn't think at first what you meant. Yes, I was down in the pantry. But only for a minute or two. I went to get something to eat."

"Yes? You were hungry then in the night?"

"Yes, I was hungry and I went down for food."

"I wish you'd give me all the details, Miss Cheame." Edith seemed still more surprised, but she answered without hesitation.

"If you think it's important, of course I will. As a matter of fact, I was unwell all that afternoon, a nasty bilious headache. I couldn't eat anything either at tea or dinner. Then there was the bridge party afterwards, at which I relieved Mrs Grinsmead. That didn't help it. Of course I could have said I was ill and gone to bed, but you know in these cases you'd rather put up with things than make a fuss. After the people went home I thought I shouldn't be able to sleep, so I went and got a sleeping draught from Miss Day. She had gone up with Mrs Grinsmead, but I saw by the light under her door that she wasn't asleep. She was in bed, but she gave me a draught. However, in the end I didn't take it, as when I got into bed I began at once to feel drowsy. I fell asleep, but woke shortly. My headache was better, but I was hungry. I went down and got something to eat in the pantry. Then I went up to bed again and fell asleep and didn't wake till morning."

This was clear enough, and there was no reason to doubt it. French, however, made it an invariable rule to assume that all statements made to him were suspect, and to try to obtain corroborative details.

"I follow," he said pleasantly. "Now, Miss Cheame, you went to bed, I suppose, shortly after midnight?"

"About that, yes."

"And what time did you wake up and go for the food?"

"About two. As a matter of fact it was just five minutes to two, for I looked at my watch."

"Now, did you look out of any of the windows when you were up?"

"No. It was dark, you see."

"You saw no lights outside or any suggestion of people being about?"

"Nothing of the kind."

"Did you hear anything?"

"Not a sound."

"You neither saw nor heard anything, inside or out?"

Edith looked up sharply. "Oh, I'm sorry," she said. "I thought you were asking me about people outside the house only. Inside, yes, I saw Mr Grinsmead."

French was startled. Was he going to get something after all.

"Oh," he said. "You saw Mr Grinsmead, did you? Where was he?"

"In the corridor outside my door."

French remembered that outside Miss Cheame's door was also very nearly outside Sybil's. The doors almost faced one another.

"And when did you see him?"

"When I opened my door."

"What was he doing?"

For the first time Edith hesitated. "Hadn't you better ask him?" she said.

"I shall do so, but I want to hear your statement as well."

"I think he can tell you better about himself. I'll tell you about myself."

"I appreciate your delicate feelings, Miss Cheame," French said dryly, "but unfortunately in a police inquiry they are out of place. I shall ask both of you the same questions and check your statements against one another. This does not mean that I doubt either of you; it is the police routine which must be carried out. You will therefore please tell me what Mr Grinsmead was doing when you saw him, and he shall tell me what you were doing at the same time."

"He can't tell you what I was doing, because he didn't see me."

"But didn't he hear you opening your door?"

"No, I opened it very quietly, so as not to disturb anyone."

"Very well, he didn't see you, but you saw him. Just answer my question, please."

"He was standing in the corridor with his back to me. He was rolling up a piece of cord or wire."

French's heart gave a sudden leap. A cord or wire! "Yes? And what did you think the cord or wire was?"

"I thought perhaps it might be an electric flex."

"And what did you think Mr Grinsmead might be doing with an electric flex at that hour of the night?"

"I thought possibly he wanted to read and his light had failed, and he was getting current from the plug on the corridor, but I didn't really know. I didn't see that it was my business and I was only anxious that he should go away so that I could slip downstairs to the pantry."

"Quite. Well, that's reasonable enough. And what did you do then?"

"I drew back into my room and closed the door until he should go away."

"And he did go away?"

"Yes, in a minute or two he went to his own room."

"I see. That may be a help to me, for he may have seen some one outside. What happened then?"

"That was all. When he went away I went down and got the food."

"How did you know it was Mr Grinsmead?" French went on.

"I saw his dressing-gown," Edith answered. "It is a Chinese one with blue dragons on it."

"Did you not see his face?"

"No, but I'm certain it was he from his figure. I couldn't be mistaken."

"Oh," said French. He paused in thought, then resumed: "By what light did you see him?"

"My torch."

"Was the light on in your room?"

"No."

"Was the light on in the passage?"

"No."

"Then how did he see to roll up the wire?"

"He also had a torch."

"But could he hold a torch and roll up at the same time? I'm not trying to pick holes, Miss Cheame, but only to get the thing clear in my mind."

Edith nodded. "He wasn't holding the torch," she answered. "He had placed it on its side on the edge of the table, so that it would shine on to his hands."

French remembered the table. It was a small one standing against the wall just beside Sybil's door.

"I follow," he said. "Did you happen to notice what colour the flex was?"

"I couldn't tell exactly. You see, it was between me and the wall, and it simply looked dark."

French nodded and got up. "Well, thank you very much, Miss Cheame. I'm obliged for your statement, though I'm afraid it doesn't help me as much as I had hoped. Now, I'd be glad if you could take the children again, so that I might ask the same questions of Miss Day."

As French waited for Anne he found it hard to control his jubilation. But he fought it down and little trace of it remained in his manner as he repeated his questions, first to Anne, and then to Gladys. From neither, however, did he learn anything fresh.

To French this statement of Edith Cheame's seemed about as important as any he could have well received, though it was evident that the governess did not realise its significance. Why, it was nothing more nor less than the proof he required! It practically amounted to taking Grinsmead in the act. French had him! The man would never be able to explain away so damning an action.

French was interested to notice how evenly divided was the responsibility for the evidence against his two suspects. From Anne Day had come the story of the conversation in the lane, from Hersey that of the woman shining the torch on the window, and now Edith Cheame had told of Grinsmead's rolling up of the cord in the corridor. This spreading of the evidence over three witnesses undoubtedly added immensely to its strength.

In spite of his own common sense, French for a moment could not resist allowing himself to indulge in daydreams. If this really were the end, he had certainly handled the case well. It had been gone into by a quite efficient brother inspector, who had come to a reasonable, but entirely false conclusion. But when he, French, had come on the job, he had quickly discerned the true inwardness of the affair. He had seen it for what it really was – wilful murder. And now he had got his proof, and in an extraordinary short time at that! Moreover, it was a neat proof; one of the type everyone must admire. He had considered the circumstances, he had evolved a theory, he had tested it, and now he had proved it true. Some work!

The next thing was to get the credit for his work. He took the first bus to Ashbridge and saw the superintendent.

Godfrey was gratifyingly impressed by French's story. He considered it for some minutes and then announced that there was now sufficient evidence to make the arrests. "I'll just ring up Major Oliver," he went on. "He likes to be consulted in these matters."

The chief constable was, it appeared, in full agreement with the proposal, and Godfrey began at once to arrange details. They would make the arrests late that night, so that the affair might be carried out secretly. Eleven o'clock, Godfrey thought, would be a suitable time. At that hour Kendal and a constable would take Mrs Holt-Lancing, while he, Godfrey, and French would bring in Grinsmead. After that, statements could be taken, if necessary.

French, full of self-satisfaction, went to his hotel for dinner and to kill time till he should be required again.

PART 3

As Anne Day Saw It

HORROR

The coming of Inspector French to Frayle had given Anne Day a nasty shock. Just when she and the other members of the household had come to believe that the dreadful episode of the death of Sybil Grinsmead was over and they were settling down into something like peace of mind, the whole horrible affair was reopened.

This reopening was terrible in its very vagueness. There were interrogations, there were suspicions, there were imaginings, but there was no knowledge of what was really going on. It was felt by all concerned that a blow was about to fall, but it was not known how, or from where, or of what kind. The atmosphere became tense, weighted with unde-fined ills, and the nerves of everyone suffered.

To Anne Day and Edith Cheame in particular the spectre of unemployment loomed up once more, not by any means in the distance, but close at hand. If their terrible suspicions were to prove well-founded, it would mean the break-up of the Grinsmead home, and for them the soul-destroying disappointments of the registry offices. Life at Frayle had indeed become a nightmare.

Inspector French himself was not without terror to Anne. While personally he was invariably polite and considerate, there was an insistent, remorseless fixity of purpose about him which amazed, even as it dismayed, her. She felt that he must inevitably get what he wanted, if only because of his unconquerable pertinacity. He had evidently got it into his head that the death of Sybil was no suicide, that it was murder, and that some one must be brought to book for it. Anne felt that some one would be; even, she almost imagined, if it were suicide after all. The man would not stop till he had found a victim. She shivered as she thought of it.

That Inspector French had already got some quite definite suspicions she felt sure, though she had no idea as to what form they took. He had interrogated her on different occasions. On all of these except one she had simply repeated what she had told the other inspector, Kendal. French had not on these occasions conveyed any special idea to her by his manner. But on one occasion he had done so. He had asked her to go into Sybil's room one evening with Inspector Kendal and go through every operation which she had gone through on the night of Sybil's death. That evening she could have sworn French had some quite definite motive behind his request. It had seemed to her that he had known something and was expecting confirmation of his theory from her actions. It had puzzled her, because he, French, had not seen what she did. He had remained outside the room. And when he dismissed her nothing seemed to have happened. However, something had probably happened after she had left, for the two inspectors had remained upstairs for a long time.

On this very afternoon French had had a further interview with her, at which he had definitely intimated that he was following some clue. He had asked her whether she had been awake on the night of the tragedy, and if so, whether she had heard or seen any movements inside or outside the house. Of course she had not. Then he had told her that there was evidence that people were about the grounds that night, and he was trying to find out if anyone had seen them from the house. This had surprised Anne extremely. Whatever she might herself have feared, it was not persons from without. But French had given no explanations, merely asking his questions in his unemotional, unhurried, painstaking way.

The whole thing had got badly on Anne's nerves, and she knew that Edith Cheame was suffering in the same way. In fact, as the two women sat chatting in Anne's room after tea on the same afternoon, Edith was the more outspoken of the two.

"I can tell you, Anne," she was saying, "I'm about fed up with this place. I've got to hate the very sight of it, and of everyone in it. Suspicions and questionings and fears and doubts; there's no end to it. God knows how I fear being out of a job, but I don't believe I'll be able to stick it here much longer. And we may be pretty sure there's worse to follow."

This was unlike Edith, who generally took calmly enough the evils which the gods sent other people.

Anne agreed.

"In a way," Edith went on, moving restlessly in her chair, "I don't suppose it matters whether we want to stay here or not. I don't believe we'll get the choice. Have you noticed how Grinsmead has been looking lately?"

"Ten years older since Sybil's death. Yes, I've noticed it. Every day he seems older and grimmer. Whatever the truth of this business, he's feeling it terribly."

"That's it. He'll not stick it much longer. And then we'll get the sack."

"You mean he'll sell the place?"

"Yes, sure. Don't you think so?"

"If he goes elsewhere he may ask us to go with him."

"Not on your life," Edith said. "He'll want to see the last of us. And 'pon my soul, Anne, I'm not sure that I don't want to see the last of him. I hate the sight of everything connected with the place. I want to get away. I want to see new people. Oh dear, how I would like a sea voyage!"

"Not much chance of that," said Anne. "I feel just as you do. But we'd be silly to make any move at present. These feelings will pass away. Let's just sit tight and say nothing."

Edith agreed that this was undoubtedly wisdom, and they relapsed into one of their usual discussions of the crime.

"What on earth has reopened the question?" Anne wondered for the hundredth time. "It was found to be suicide by the coroner's jury, and why can't they let it stand at that?"

"Heaven knows," Edith said uneasily. "I didn't tell you I got another horrible fright this afternoon; I thought I'd told French something that would back up their suspicions."

Anne looked up with troubled face. What fresh evil was coming now?

"You didn't, Edith? What on earth was that?"

Edith Cheame made a gesture of mystification. "It was something I saw that night," she answered, "and how I came to forget it I absolutely can't think. The tragedy put it completely out of my head. It was Grinsmead. I saw him about two that morning. He was in the corridor with something like a cord in his hands. He was winding it up."

Anne's face expressed amazement.

"Grinsmead!" she repeated. "Winding up a cord in the corridor? Edith, you weren't dreaming, I suppose? What on earth was he doing that for?"

"My dear, ask me something easier. How should I know? I told French that I supposed his lamp had failed and that the cord was a flex which he was connecting to the landing plug. But, of course, I didn't really know."

Anne stared, while something like horror slowly grew in her eyes.

"Edith, do you mean that you don't see? Oh, dear, how awful! What do you really think he was doing?"

"My dear Anne, as I say, how do I know? What do you think yourself?"

Anne shivered. She looked fixedly at Edith. Then she put her thought into words.

"If they think him guilty," she said in low tones, "they must suppose he somehow turned on the gas without opening the door. I've wondered about that again and again. If so, don't you see what follows? This'll be the proof they want. A cord! Some apparatus for turning on the tap!"

Edith's eyes dilated as she stared at Anne.

"Oh, no, no, no," she cried in distress. "Oh, no, Anne; you're wrong; you're wrong! How horrible to suggest such a thing! I don't believe it."

"But what else could it mean?" Anne persisted in a whisper.

"Oh, I don't know; but not that, not that! French made nothing of it. If it was what you suggest he would have been impressed. But he wasn't. Besides, he thinks it was some-one outside."

Anne remembered French's questions. "What can he mean by that?" she wondered.

"I don't know, but that's how the thing arose. He'd found out somehow that I'd been down getting food that night, and he said some one had been seen outside the house during the night, and had I seen anyone?"

Anne shook her head. She understood now why this question had been raised.

"Edith, it was a trick," she cried. "Don't believe it! They saw no one outside. It was a trick to find out what you knew. Oh, need you have told them that?"

"Anne, don't be silly. How could I help myself? He asked me the direct question: 'Did you see anyone when you went for food?' What could I say? I don't think that's fair of you, Anne. If Grinsmead is guilty and it was found out afterwards that I'd seen him and that I'd kept it back, I'd be accused of murder too."

"Did he see you?"

"No, I slipped back into my room till he'd gone."

Anne wrung her hands. "Oh, dear," she cried, "there's no end to the awfulness of this thing. It's not your fault, of course; I shouldn't have said that. But, Edith, how did you come to *forget* such a vital thing?"

"I didn't really forget it. I forgot it that first time the police were making inquiries, that morning we found Sybil. The tragedy must just have put it out of my mind. Then at once I remembered it, but the thing was over and done with, as I thought; as we all thought; and it didn't seem to matter. Then when this new inquiry started I didn't feel called upon to volunteer a statement, but when I was asked the direct question, of course, it was a different thing."

Anne saw that. She saw also that if Edith had kept her information to herself, it was what she, Anne, would have done under the same circumstances. In fact, it was what she had done. She had not volunteered about the conversation in the lane, and it was only when asked the direct question that she had told about it. Indeed she had been less communicative than Edith. Anne had never mentioned the

204

conversation to Edith, and even now she did not do so, and it was far more damning evidence than Edith's.

Whether it was the result of this conversation, of French's questions, or of the generally unhappy situation in which they found themselves, Anne had seldom felt so weighed down by foreboding as on this evening. The very air seemed to be charged with horror, like the oppression which so often comes before a storm. It was as if she was waiting, almost breathlessly expectant, for something dreadful to happen. And the others were evidently suffering from a similar unease. Dinner was a nightmare. Both Edith and Grinsmead were unusually silent, and only for Anne's determined efforts the conversation would have died altogether. Mrs Grinsmead, who on such occasions always proved a host in herself, was away. She had gone to London for the day and was not expected back till quite late.

By the time Anne reached her room she had developed a nervous headache, and she determined to go early to bed. But Edith followed her into her room. Edith appeared anxious for a chat, or as Anne shrewdly suspected, she didn't want to be alone. Anne, on her part, was not sorry. It was too early to go to bed, and she felt she couldn't settle down with a book.

They talked in a desultory way about nothing in particular, Anne sitting propped up with pillows on her bed, while Edith pottered listlessly with a piece of sewing. It was perhaps the best thing they could have done, and gradually Anne found her nerves quieting down and her outlook growing more normal. Indeed she was just considering getting her book when a knock came to the door.

It was Gladys to say that Mr Grinsmead would be obliged if Miss Cheame would step down and speak to him for a moment at her convenience.

Edith exchanged glances with Anne. "Here it is," she declared. "A hint to look out for some other job. What did I tell you?"

"No," said Anne. "If it was that he'd have sent for us both. Go on, Edith, and find out."

Ten minutes later Edith returned, looking a good deal excited.

"He's thinking of sending the children away for two or three weeks," she reported. "He wanted to know if I would take them to Bournemouth. If I'd take them, Anne! What do you think of that? If he'd overheard us talking before dinner, he wouldn't have asked."

"I shouldn't mind going with you," said Anne.

"Hard lines, old thing. But you're too valuable here. But it's rather wonderful luck, isn't it? I was just saying I wanted a sea voyage, and here the next best thing turns up within an hour or two."

Anne was pleased for Edith's sake, but a little hurt that Edith should think so obviously of herself alone. However, Edith was like that.

"I've never been to Bournemouth," she went on. "They say it's *the* place in winter. Maybe with luck – " She didn't finish her sentence, and Anne ragged her on the millionaire she was going to meet and marry.

"You never know," said Edith darkly.

They went on chatting for a few moments, then Edith got up.

"Nearly ten," she said. "I'm going to have a good long hot soak in my bath. It quiets you when you're feeling jumpy."

Anne sat on alone, now dreamily unwilling to move. Dully she considered following Edith's example. She need not wait till Edith was done, as Sybil's bathroom was now available. Then she thought a bath was too much of a fag. She would content herself with her morning tub. She felt she really must read a little before turning in, but she made no move to get her book. To get up was more trouble than it was worth.

It was very still in the house. Earlier there had been a wind which had whistled round the gables and chimneys, but it had gone down. There were no sounds from downstairs. Not that there was anyone there likely to make a noise. The children were in bed and presumably asleep. Mrs Meakin and Gladys had probably also gone to bed. Grinsmead was in his study, but as Mrs Grinsmead was not yet back from Town, he had no one to talk to.

Suddenly Anne started. What was that? The sound of a shot, surely? A shot, muffled indeed, but still near; in the house, Anne could have sworn.

She sprang to her feet, her heart beating rapidly, and ran out into the corridor. There was no further sound, and pausing only for a moment to listen, she raced downstairs. As she did so she thought she heard a faint indeterminate sound. For a moment she thought it was the locking of a door, then she recognised it as the opening of the door from the kitchen quarters. She reached the hall as Gladys appeared, startled-looking and rather pale.

"What is it, Gladys?" Anne cried in a low voice.

"The study, miss," Gladys whispered tremulously, pointing to the door. "A shot – in there."

Anne, her heart pounding almost to suffocation, ran to the door and knocked. There was no answer. She knocked again. "Mr Grinsmead!" she called. She tried the door. It was locked.

"Was he in there?" Anne asked, but she knew even as she did so that it was a silly question. How else could the door have become fastened? Gladys nodded without speaking.

"Oh, my God," cried Anne, almost sick with foreboding. "We'll have to break open the door. Ring for Hersey."

There was an extension telephone from the hall to Hersey's lodgings.

"Hersey's in the garage. I saw the light from the kitchen," Gladys cried, instantly vanishing.

Anne automatically went on knocking and trying the door. "Mr Grinsmead! Mr Grinsmead!" she cried despairingly. "Open the door! Open the door!"

But there was no answering sound or movement. Then it occurred to Anne to put her eye to the keyhole. The room was lighted up, and she could see a small patch of the opposite wall down to the skirting, with the *Encyclopedia Britannica* stand and the edge of the large wall bookcase on the right. But she could see neither Grinsmead nor any other person.

Anne felt herself sick and unhinged. "Oh, God, not another murder!" she cried aloud. Then with all the force of her will she pulled herself together. She listened breathlessly at the keyhole for sounds of movement within. There were none, and she realised the truth. Grinsmead had killed himself.

For what seemed an eternity she waited, though it could not at most have been more than two or three minutes. Then Gladys appeared running, followed by Hersey with a small crowbar in his hand.

"Break it open, Hersey," Anne ordered, and stood back.

Hersey approached, and inserting the chisel point of his bar between the door and the jamb, levered strongly. The door was solidly made, but slowly it gave way, opening with a tearing sound, as the lock keeper was forced through the splintering wood.

To Anne it brought back poignantly that terrible morning, not so long ago, when she had smelled gas in the corridor. It was not often that one saw a door forced, and here was the second within a time which could be measured in days rather than weeks. That first forcing had led to tragedy and she feared terribly that this was the prelude to tragedy also. So much so that as the door swung back she felt an overwhelming reluctance to enter the room.

But she nerved herself to do it, and followed by Hersey and Gladys, she passed in through the open door.

The study was a fair-sized room, expensively furnished and decorated. The door was close to the right wall, and this wall was entirely covered with bookshelves. It was the front of these shelves that Anne had seen through the keyhole. In the wall facing the door was a large bow window, with an opening section forming a French window which gave on to the tennis ground. Another window, glazed with obscure glass, looked out into the yard. In the wall behind the door was the fireplace, and on each side of this were large cabinets in which Mr Grinsmead had stored legal journals which he had at one time intended to have bound. In front of the bow window was a table desk and chair, another table stood between the windows, while in the corresponding corner on the right of the bow window was the stand containing a recent edition of the *Encyclopedia Britannica*. Two deep leathered-covered armchairs were drawn up to the fire, and other chairs were placed here and there about the room.

But it was not on these objects, all of which were pretty well known to Anne, that her gaze fell. On his back on the floor between the desk and the encyclopedia stand lay Grinsmead, a small, evil-looking hole in his forehead, just above the right eye, from which a tiny drop of blood had trickled down to the carpet. That he was dead was only too clear. Apart from the position of the wound, there was that in his wax-like features and glazing eyes which precluded doubt. He lay sprawled on his back, and on the floor near his right hand was an automatic pistol.

Anne and her two companions, rigid with horror at this second tragedy, stood motionless like soldiers in a line, looking down on the tragic figure. Grinsmead looked peaceful enough now, more so than for a long time; strangely peaceful, Anne thought, having regard to the manner of his end. She could not help wondering whether, for him, this was not for the best. If he were guilty of his wife's murder, as after Edith's evidence about the cord it was hard to doubt, he had doubtless seen in suicide the easiest way out. Probably he had felt the inspector's net growing tighter and tighter. Perhaps he had learned that arrest was imminent. Poor man! Whatever his crimes, Anne could not help pitying him. He had paid a large part of the price if his life had become too terrible to support.

There was a sudden step behind them and Edith hurried up. As her eyes fell on the prostrate figure she gasped. For a moment she stopped and gazed speechless with the others, her hand gripping Anne's arm as in a vice, then she dropped quickly to her knees and felt Grinsmead's heart.

"No hope," she said in a dull husky voice. "Nothing can be done. He's dead." Her eyes followed Grinsmead's right arm and came to rest on the pistol. "No one has touched anything, I suppose?"

Anne shook her head. For the moment she was past speech. Edith, slowly getting up, went on: "Well, we'd better leave everything as it is. But we must have the doctor at once. I'll ring him up. That'll do; we'd better come away. Gladys, go and get us all some whisky."

Edith, always efficient, quietly took charge. She rang up Dr Roome and then the police. She made everyone drink a stiff peg of whisky, and she had a fire lit in the dining-room, in case they would be kept up by the police to make statements and answer questions.

PART 4

As Inspector French Saw It

– 15 –

DEMONSTRATION

French's feelings were mixed as, shortly before eleven that same night, he walked back to the police station in Ashbridge, ready to assist Superintendent Godfrey in his unpleasant task of arresting Grinsmead. He was pleased because of the progress of his case. The most difficult part was over – the long tedious investigation – and not only over, but over brilliantly. He had proved that murder had been committed and he had got his criminals. There now remained little more than routine; the building up of the case in detail and putting it in a form in which it could be placed before the public prosecutor.

On the other hand, he greatly disliked dealing with his victims. He hated the actual making of the arrests. He hated to see misery and terror grow in the eyes of his fellows, no matter how much they deserved their fate. He hated also those subsequent long hours, usually in the night, during which statements were obtained from the prisoners. All this was a part of his job which he would willingly have left to someone else.

To his amazement, on reaching the station he found it humming with excitement.

"Oh, there you are, French," Godfrey exclaimed as French appeared. "We're late. Grinsmead's done us in the eye."

French stared. "Bunked?" he queried laconically.

"No – suicide. Just had a 'phone. I'm going out now. Will you come along? You come too, Pendlebury," he added to a constable; then turning to Kendal, continued: "Look sharp, Kendal, will you, and bring in Mrs Holt-Lancing. We don't want to lose her too. You're ready, French. Then come along."

That Godfrey was deeply upset by this development French could see clearly. He obviously felt himself to blame for letting Grinsmead slip through his fingers. French, indeed, saw that he was to blame, and what was more, would undoubtedly so be held by the authorities. An error of judgment, of course. But the consequences of an error of judgment usually prove just as disastrous to a man's career as carelessness or even deliberate fraud.

"He must have got wind of what was coming to him," Godfrey said grimly as they drove along.

French wondered if this was an incipient attempt to shift the responsibility. "Not through me, sir," he declared decidedly.

"I didn't say through you," Godfrey returned acidly, "though as a matter of fact, how do you know? You got the information about the cord from that governess woman. No chance of that getting round to Grinsmead?"

"You mean through Miss Cheame?"

"How else?"

"I suppose it's possible, sir. I certainly mentioned it to no one except yourself." He paused as a sudden idea struck him. "But I'll tell you what might have happened. What about that other information I got this morning? Hersey's tale about the woman outside the house? I saw Mrs Holt-Lancing about it just before lunch. That may have got to Grinsmead."

"You mean that it was her being seen outside the house, not his being seen inside it, that gave the show away?"

"That's what I suggest, sir. If they knew that we had discovered that Mrs Holt-Lancing had helped on the murder, they would realise that the whole circumstances were bound to come out. I suggest she rang him up or somehow let him know, and he thought it safer not to wait for anything more."

"It might be," Godfrey admitted. "I only hope not, for if so they probably agreed that both would take the same way out. Curse it all! Such a near thing. If we'd gone out an hour earlier we'd have got him."

"I don't know, sir," said French. "If he was going to commit suicide he'd have done it the moment he heard you were there. Unless we had gone out very much earlier, it would have made no difference."

"Well, it can't be helped now."

As Godfrey thus summed up the situation, the car swung into the Frayle drive. Before the door stood another car.

"Dr Roome's," Godfrey grunted, and getting heavily out, he rang the bell. Gladys, pale-faced, opened the door. Anne at once came forward.

"Sorry to hear you've had fresh trouble, Miss Day," said Godfrey, not unkindly. "I see the doctor's here?"

"Yes, in the study." Anne led the way, then standing aside, allowed the police officers to pass into the room. Dr Roome was kneeling beside the corpse.

"Evening, doctor," Godfrey greeted him, adding for Anne's benefit, "sad affair this."

Roome slowly rose to his feet. "Yes," he answered. "It's just happened. The ladies heard the shot."

Godfrey nodded and for a moment stood looking down on the still figure. "You can do nothing, can you, doctor?" he went on. "I thought not. Then if you don't mind, don't touch him for a minute or two. You haven't moved him, have you?"

"No. I only made sure he was dead."

"Quite." Godfrey turned to the door. "Perhaps, Miss Day, you just give us an idea of what took place. Just in a word."

Anne briefly recounted the hearing of the shot, her running down, the breaking open of the door, and the tragic discovery which awaited them.

"That's all right, Miss Day; just what I wanted," Godfrey declared. "Now, I'll ask everyone to sit up just for a few minutes till I make sure there is nothing wanted tonight. Will you please arrange it? I'll not keep you longer than I can help."

Anne undertook that the members of the household should be available if called on, and disappeared. Godfrey turned to French.

"There's no doubt about what has occurred," he said. "Still, there's been so much trouble over this case that we'll not take anything for granted. Will you have a look round the room and I'll get a photograph taken of the body and then let the doctor make his examination."

French agreed, and set to work on one of his methodical examinations. His first care was to make a rough sketch of the room, marking on it the position of the body. This was attached to his final report, and is therefore reproduced here.

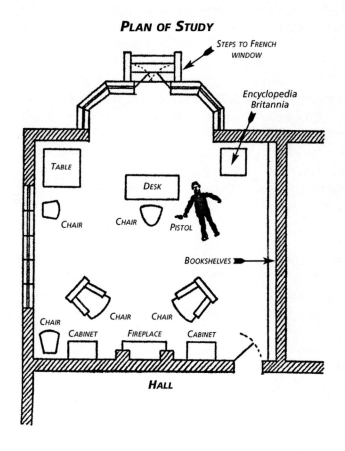

PLAN OF STUDY

Next he examined in detail the various objects in the room. He began with the door. It was a strong, well-fitting, stoutly-made door. That it had been locked from the inside was shown by the projecting bolt and the key on the inside of the door. That it had been forced open from the outside was equally clearly proved by the marks of the insertion of the bar between the door and frame, by the splintered wood, and by the keeper forced out of the jamb and still hanging on the bolt. So far there was no doubt of the truth of Anne's story. Next French moved on to the windows. Both were of the standard steel-framed, lead-lighted pattern, wide, but not very high. The bow window consisted of eight sections, the other of five. Two of the sections in the bow were carried down to form a French window, giving on the tennis ground. French examined each section in turn. All were intact and in good order, and all those which opened were securely fastened. The French window was bolted and locked, and the key was in the lock on the inside. The curtains were drawn over both windows.

It was obvious then that no one could have left the room after the shot was fired. However, to be in a position to swear to this in court, French turned his attention first to the fireplace and then to the walls and floor. A short inspection of the former showed that no one could have escaped by the chimney. The walls and floor were everywhere sound and there was no second door to the room, hidden or otherwise.

If no one had left the room after the shot was fired, it followed, of course, that Grinsmead really had committed suicide. Neither French nor Godfrey had doubted this, but here was the necessary formal proof for that hypothetical jury which is always in the mind of police officers as the final arbiter on their conclusions.

Having examined the exits of the room, French next turned his attention to its contents. He scrutinised everything with the utmost care, but nothing appeared to be out of place or to furnish a clue except the pistol.

The pistol lay within a few inches of Grinsmead's right hand. It was an automatic of a well-known make, and French believed it was Grinsmead's property. When looking through the man's papers on his first inquiry, he had seen such a pistol in his desk. He had, moreover, checked up Grinsmead's permit for it at police headquarters. Now he crossed to the desk and opened the drawer in which it had lain. As he had expected, no pistol was there.

Very carefully, so as not to obliterate fingerprints, he picked up the weapon. A glance showed him that it had been recently fired, and when he opened it up, he found that the magazine was full except for one shell. Miss Day had said that one shot had been heard, and this corresponded all right.

Laying the pistol aside to be tested for fingerprints, he went down on his hands and knees to search for the missing shell. Presently he found it. It had rolled under the set of drawers to the right of the well of the desk. This seemed to French to work in. Had Grinsmead fired at his head from where he had evidently been standing, the shell should have fallen just about where it was found.

French turned next to the deceased's desk. For the second time in a comparatively few days he ran through Grinsmead's papers. In cases like the present the suicide often left a letter: perhaps a farewell or a statement of the reasons for his action, or possibly a confession where there had been an antecedent crime. But there was nothing of the kind.

Just as he was about to report that he had completed his examination, the telephone rang. Godfrey answered it.

"Yes, yes," he said impatiently, then in a firmer tone: "speaking – oh, you have, have you? That's good, at all events. Right, I'll be back shortly. No, you needn't wait. We'll do no more till the morning."

"That Kendal, sir?" asked French.

"Yes. He's brought in Mrs Holt-Lancing all right. Very surprised and indignant and all that, but no statement. Well, I won't say she's wrong. Got anything there, French?"

"Nothing," French answered, "except what one might expect. There's the gun with one shell missing, and the used shell-case on the floor. The doors and windows were fastened on the inside and no one could have left the room after the shot was fired."

"That's all right," Godfrey returned. "The medical evidence fits in also. Grinsmead was killed by a bullet which entered the brain above the right eye. It might have been fired from a short distance away, provided this was over three inches. The direction of the wound is consistent with self-infliction. Death was instantaneous and had occurred shortly before the doctor arrived, that is to say, about the time Miss Day says the shot was heard. I've been through the pockets and there's nothing in them bearing in any way on the affair. Anything else, French, that we ought to see to now?"

"There's nothing necessary, I think, sir, because there's no doubt what happened. But to be technically complete I suppose we should take Grinsmead's fingerprints and compare them with those on the gun."

"I certainly mean to do that," Godfrey agreed. "I thought of leaving it over till tomorrow, but perhaps as we're here we may as well do it now. Will you do the gun and I'll do the body?"

A few minutes sufficed for the test. There were five prints on the gun, and without much eagerness the two men compared them with those from Grinsmead's fingers. To make a theoretically satisfactory demonstration they would have to get photographic enlargements made, but mere inspection should be enough to satisfy their own minds. As a matter of fact it amply satisfied them. There was no doubt whatever not only that the prints were the same, but that there were no prints other than Grinsmead's on the pistol.

"That about finishes us here, I think," said Godfrey. "What about that bullet, doctor? Have you got it out yet?"

"Yes, it's here," Roome returned, handing over the little cylinder. "Fits, I think?"

They tried it and found that it was the same as the others in the magazine and fitted the shell-case.

"Exhibits I, II and III," said French, as he carefully packed the pistol, bullet and case.

Godfrey looked at his watch.

"It's not twelve yet," he observed. "I don't see why we shouldn't take those blessed statements now and be done with it. They're all plain sailing and it won't take very long. What do you say, French?"

"I'd be on, sir, for getting everything done when we're here. As you say, it won't take long."

Godfrey turned again to Roome. "That's all here, doctor. The body can be removed now. Under the circumstances I don't think an autopsy'll be wanted. Of course we'll have to consult the coroner. Give me your formal statement and that'll be everything."

Dr Roome explained in technical language that the deceased had died from shock following a bullet wound in the brain, and that so far as he could see, the injury was consistent with the assumption that the deceased had himself fired the shot.

Godfrey then went into the hall and called for Anne. He presumed they would rather not make their statements in the study; was there anywhere else that would be convenient?

Anne said there was a fire in the dining-room, and there the two officers took their seats.

"We'll take you first, please, Miss Day," Godfrey decided, and Anne sat down at the table opposite them.

She told in detail of the evening, of dinner, of Grinsmead's sending for Edith, of Edith's return with the information that he was thinking of sending the children to Bournemouth for a couple of weeks, of her further conversation with Edith, of Edith's going to have her bath, of Anne's hearing the shot, of her running down, of her meeting Gladys in the hall, of her sending for Hersey to break open the door and of what they found. She made her statement pretty complete, having by this time learned what police officers wanted. Godfrey therefore had but few questions to put to her.

He next saw Edith Cheame. She corroborated Anne's story. She had been sent for by Grinsmead and had at once gone down. Grinsmead had said that the present atmosphere of the house was bad for the children, and he was thinking of sending them away for two or three weeks. He didn't much care where, but he had thought of Bournemouth or Torquay or some similar place. He wanted to know whether Edith would take them. If so, she could choose the place, subject to his approval. She would, of course, have to be entirely responsible for them.

Edith had replied that she would certainly do as he wished, and that she had no choice of places. Bournemouth was therefore provisionally settled. Grinsmead said he would have a chat with his mother on the subject and settle the date of going.

Edith had then returned upstairs, rather delighted at this unexpected prospect. She had discussed it for some time with Miss Day and had then gone to bed. But she hadn't got to bed. While in her bath she had heard the shot. She had dressed as quickly as she could and hurried down. The study door had just been burst open and she followed the others in. She had felt Grinsmead's heart, but without disturbing anything, and had then rung up the doctor and the police.

Godfrey had only one question to ask.

"Tell me, Miss Cheame, about Mr Grinsmead's frame of mind. Was it quite normal?"

"No," Edith returned, "I don't think one could say that. He seemed to me not only excited, but depressed; as if he had something on his mind. I admit that at the time the idea of suicide never crossed my mind, but now I can see that he might have been contemplating it."

"But nothing he said gave you that idea?"

"Oh, nothing whatever."

Godfrey said that was all he wanted, but as Edith was leaving he called her back.

"Miss Cheame," he said, "this is a very confidential question. This afternoon you told Inspector French about having seen Mr Grinsmead with a cord in his hand in the corridor outside your door on the night his wife died. Now tell me this: Did you repeat that statement to anyone else?"

Edith hesitated. "Only," she said, "in confidence to Miss Day."

"Oh, you told Miss Day? Anyone else?"

"No one."

"Now do you think Mr Grinsmead knew that you had seen him?"

"I am quite certain he did not."

Edith seemed very much distressed. She evidently saw what was at the back of the question.

"Anything else, French?"

225

French could think of nothing more, and Edith's place was taken by Gladys.

Gladys had not much to tell. She was just leaving the kitchen on her way to bed when she heard the shot. It had sounded from the study. She had at once run into the hall and had there met Miss Day coming downstairs. They had called Mr Grinsmead, and Miss Day had sent her for Hersey, who, she knew, happened to be in the garage. He had come and burst open the door.

Hersey corroborated this evidence. He was doing some repairs to the car when Gladys had run out for him.

Mrs Meakin was actually in bed at the time of the tragedy. She had heard the shot, but faintly, and she supposed it was a poacher outside. She had not come down and therefore could tell the inspector nothing about the affair.

Of the actual tragedy Mrs Grinsmead knew nothing, as she had been on her way from London when it happened. But Godfrey pressed her pretty hard as to her knowledge of Grinsmead's frame of mind during the previous few days. She said that the loss of his wife had certainly weighed very heavily on him, but that, apart from that, she had noticed nothing unusual, certainly nothing to lead her to suspect that he contemplated suicide.

"I shall have to ask you all to remain here until after the inquest," Godfrey concluded. "Some of you will have to give evidence, and perhaps all."

"It's what you said, French," Godfrey declared as they drove back to Ashbridge. "Hersey's statement about the woman brought in Mrs Holt-Lancing. When you spoke to her about it she saw where it was going to lead. She some-how told Grinsmead, and he saw it too. He took this way out. I don't think there's any doubt about it."

"We should be able to find out if she communicated with him."

"Yes, and I think you'd better take that on in the morning. It'll be covered by your terms of reference, so to speak?"

"Oh, that's all right, sir," French returned cheerily. "I'm here as long as you want me."

As French returned to his hotel he thought that this was turning out as unsatisfactory a case as any with which he had had to do. From the police point of view, Grinsmead's suicide had spoiled it. If Grinsmead had been arrested and Mrs Holt-Lancing had committed suicide, it wouldn't have been so bad. But for the ringleader to escape, and that a man, while the accomplice, a woman, was brought to trial, was to reverse the natural order of things. French, moreover, was not so happy as to the proof of Mrs Holt-Lancing's guilt as he had been in the case of Grinsmead. So far, indeed, he had no direct evidence connecting her with the case, except in so far as the conversation in the lane was proof of conspiracy. To get the necessary proof would, however, be his job, and it was not the kind of job he liked.

He ran over in his mind just what he thought was still required. There was first this question of whether the lady had or had not communicated with Grinsmead since she had learned that she had been seen outside Sybil's window on the night of the murder. Then there was the point about proving that it really was she whom Hersey had seen, or if this were impossible, at least of showing that she was out of her house at that hour of the night. There was the attempt to connect her with the purchase of the spring or cord. Finally, an investigation would be required in the hope of learning that she had said or done something after the crime which would be the equivalent of an admission of guilt.

In fact, French saw that there would be a good deal of rather nebulous work to be done, work of the kind he intensely disliked, work for vague objectives which were unlikely to be realised, work which was troublesome and tiresome and usually thankless. However, this was one of the drawbacks of his job and he must just make the best of it. He would leave his worries till the morning. At two o'clock he crept quietly up to bed.

16

INTERROGATION

Next day Irene Holt-Lancing was brought before the magistrates and formally charged with conspiring with the late Severus Hume Grinsmead to murder Sybil Grinsmead, a charge of murder in the second degree. Her solicitor reserved his defence, and she was remanded for a week, bail, of course, being refused.

Godfrey was looking after the arrangements for the inquest on Grinsmead, so French was free to begin at once his building up of the case against Mrs Holt-Lancing.

His first step was a visit to Grinsmead's office. There he saw the chief clerk and put his questions. He was making a report about this unhappy affair of Mr Grinsmead's suicide, and in it he had been instructed to cover the late gentleman's movements on the day of his death. He was also to prepare a list of letters, telegrams, telephone calls, or other messages the deceased had received during the day. The information, he understood, was required in the hope that by it light might be thrown on the unhappy man's motive in taking his life. Could the chief clerk let him have the required details?

The chief clerk's legal mind made him cautious, but under the influence of French's persuasive tongue his scruples vanished and he told what he knew. Grinsmead had worked in the office during the entire day from 9.30 till nearly 6 p.m., except for his usual hour and a half at lunch-time. He had gone out with his partner, Mr Bowen. They usually lunched at the Dorchester Arms Hotel, but the clerk couldn't say whether they had done so on this occasion. Shortly before six Mr Grinsmead had left for home in his car, which had been waiting for a short time. Mr Grinsmead had had, of course, numerous telephone calls and letters, but the clerk knew of none which were not on business matters. Yes, he would certainly try to check up these calls, but he doubted if he would succeed. The last post came in at half-past four, and he had himself opened all the letters which came by it, none of them being personal. There had been no telegrams.

French next interviewed the partner. Mr Bowen stated that he and the deceased had lunched together at the Dorchester Arms, afterwards chatting with other *habitués* in the smoke-room. They had walked to and from the hotel together. Bowen was positive that while out of the office Grinsmead had received neither note nor message.

From this it appeared that the only way in which Irene Holt-Lancing could have communicated with the dead man was by telephone. There remained also, of course, the possibility of an interview after six o'clock.

French called at the telephone exchange to ask them to make out a list of all the calls put through to Grinsmead's office. Then he went out once more to Frayle to see Hersey about Grinsmead's drive home.

Thinking the man might be in the garage, French passed the front door and walked round the house and along by the tennis ground towards the yard gate. This brought him past the study where last night's tragedy had taken place, and with the affair in his mind, he looked absently at the outside of the French window. Three stone steps led up to it from the path and at these also he glanced. Then suddenly he stopped, stared, and walked over to the flight.

On the steps were traces of muddy footprints. There was one on each lower step and a confused mass on the upper, as if some one had mounted and stood at the window for some moments. The traces were blurred and indistinct, and save that they were those of a man, were quite useless for identification purposes. They indicated, however, that Grinsmead had had a recent visitor.

French recalled the weather. It had rained all the previous afternoon till about six o'clock, leaving the ground soaking. Since then it had been fine and a slight wind in the evening had tended to dry away the moisture. In the evening therefore the path, on which the gravel was worn low, would be muddy, while the stone steps would be nearly dry. Anyone passing up the steps would therefore be likely to leave muddy traces, which would have since remained.

Though the fact that Grinsmead might have had a visitor on the previous evening could not have affected the method of his death, it might have affected the motive for it. French therefore determined to learn what he could about the affair.

He began by chalking on the steps such marks as he could trace, and sketching and measuring them. Then, turning back to the path, he searched it inch by inch in the hope of finding clearer prints.

But in this he failed completely. The ground had been too wet to retain such prints as might have been made. French worked back as far as the road, but without success.

However, even to know that in all probability Grinsmead had had a visitor shortly before he took his life, was not unimportant. Other inquiries might establish the un-known's identity.

French found Hersey in the garage. The man was obviously much upset. Grinsmead's tragedy meant tragedy for Hersey also, even though a minor tragedy. Hersey was out of a job, or he would be in a day or two. And with the unemployment figures standing where they were, to be out of a job was terrifying. With an anxious expression he was now lugubriously cleaning the car for Mrs Grinsmead's use at the funeral.

He was quite ready to talk to French. On the previous evening he had called with the car at Grinsmead's office at a quarter before six, in accordance with his standing instructions. In a few minutes Grinsmead had come out, and Hersey had driven him home. Mr Grinsmead had not paid any calls on the way, nor had anyone spoken to him or given him a note. They had reached Frayle at almost exactly six, and then Hersey had put the car in the garage and gone home. It was a wet afternoon and the car had got a bit dirty, so he had come back about half-past nine to clean it. In this way it happened that he had been available when required to break open the study door. He had seen no one about the house in the evening, and he had not gone to the study window to speak to Mr Grinsmead.

French next pursued his inquiries from the staff within. He learned that Grinsmead frequently used the French window, both to pass in and out himself and to admit callers. But no one knew of his having used it on the previous evening for either of these purposes.

Inquiries showed that he had not soiled any pair of shoes on the previous day. Not only, therefore, was it unlikely that he had gone out in the evening, but the marks on the steps could not have been his own.

There seemed to be nothing more to be learned at Frayle, and French walked over to try his luck at Mrs Holt-Lancing's house, The Laurels. There he saw Rose Unwin, the maid. She was packing to go to her home at Maidstone. She was evidently lonely and frightened, and seemed glad to have even French to talk to.

"Oh," said French, "so you're leaving, are you? And what will Captain Holt-Lancing do without you?"

"He can do what he jolly well likes," the girl returned, going on to explain that not for nobody would she remain on in the house after what had happened. Disgraced, she felt herself, and she wasn't going to have no more to do with none of them.

French, quickly estimating her character, sympathised tactfully. It was certainly hard lines on her, but she mustn't forget that she would be a heroine among her friends. Whatever these might say, there wasn't one of them who wouldn't give her soul to be such a famous person as Rose. She would be the most important witness at her employer's trial, and everyone would hang on her words.

As French had imagined, Rose fell before flattery. She became communicative and French pursued his advantage.

"I wanted to run over with you what your evidence would be, while the circumstances were fresh in your mind," he explained. "What about doing it now? Is the captain out?"

It appeared that Captain Holt-Lancing had gone to London. Rose graciously indicated that the present would suit her convenience.

French with skill and tact began to put his questions. First, he wanted to know Mrs Holt-Lancing's movements during the previous afternoon and evening.

It appeared that, after he, French, had left at about twelve o'clock, Mrs Holt-Lancing had remained in the drawing-room till lunch at half-past one. She had not, Rose was certain, used the telephone. In fact, she had not used the telephone during the entire day until quite late in the evening, when some one had rung her up. In the afternoon about half-past three she had gone out, though Rose did not know where. Rose imagined it was either for a walk by herself or to visit some intimate friend, because she was not dressed for a formal call. She had come back in about an hour, had had tea, and had remained in the house all the remainder of the evening until the late telephone message had come. About ten, that was. She had gone out then for about half an hour.

French saw that this late visit, whatever it was, could not affect his immediate problem. So far it did not look as if the lady had attempted to communicate with Grinsmead.

"Had Mrs Holt-Lancing any callers yesterday?" he asked.

She had had none. Rose was in all the afternoon and evening, and it would have been impossible for anyone to have come unknown to her. Nor had her mistress sent or received any letters or notes.

"You knew, of course, of the attachment between Mrs Holt-Lancing and Mr Grinsmead?"

Rose grinned. What did French take her for? Of course she had known.

"I want," French went on, "to be quite sure about whether Mr Grinsmead might not have called last night. Could he not have tapped at the drawing-room window and been let in by Mrs Holt-Lancing herself?"

Rose was certain he could not. She would have heard the door opening and shutting had anything of the kind happened. There was also a creaking board at the drawing-room door that she would have heard if anyone crossed it. "Why," she went on, "the night he did come and she let him in I heard both the doors and the creak as well."

"That's very satisfactory," said French. "Do you remember what evening Mr Grinsmead came?"

"Four or five evenings ago. Friday, I think. Yes, I remember it was the day the laundry comes, Friday."

"And what happened that night?"

French put the question as part of his routine inquiry. He did not then, nor did he for many days after, realise its importance. In fact, it was not till the end of the case that, looking back, he saw that this question represented one of the principal steps towards its elucidation.

"Lovers' quarrels," Rose declared impressively. "My word, they didn't 'alf go for one another. 'Ammer and tongs, as you might say. They didn't know I was there, or they'd have been more careful what they said. You should have heard the fur fly." She chuckled heavily.

"I knew they'd had a row," French lied easily, "but I didn't know it was on that evening." It did not do either to be too impressed or to receive information too cavalierly. "Go on and tell me about it."

She was ready enough to demonstrate, and with but little prompting the story came out.

It appeared that on the previous Friday at about five o'clock in the afternoon Mrs Holt-Lancing had rung for Rose. She had given her a note, saying that it was so urgent that it could not wait over for the post. Nor was it a matter that could be dealt with by telephone. She wanted Rose to put on her hat and take it then and there into Ashbridge. With it Mrs Holt-Lancing handed over half-a-crown, ostensibly for the girl's bus fares. Dinner that night happened to be a rather simple meal and it could wait a few minutes if Rose were delayed.

Rose accordingly put on her things and went out at the back. But she found that it was raining very much more heavily than she had believed, and she turned back for a waterproof. Then suddenly it occurred to her that she might not only save herself the journey and the wetting, but might preserve her half-crown intact. The laundry van was due in a few minutes and the vanman was one of her many admirers. He lived in Ashbridge, and she believed he could be persuaded to leave the note in her stead.

Accordingly she waited till the man appeared. She was charming to him, though pathetic about her long tramp in the rain. The scheme worked without a hitch. The vanman asked if there was an answer to the note, and when he heard there was not, asked further why he couldn't deliver it for her.

This was a new idea to Rose, and she demurred on the ground that the note had been given to her to deliver personally, and that she ought therefore to deliver it personally. However, eventually she allowed herself to be persuaded, and the vanman went off with the note.

Rose felt herself theoretically out of the house and therefore off duty. So instead of going on with some stock job, she made herself comfortable before the kitchen fire and buried herself in a shocker which she had got for a few pence at a second-hand shop in Ashbridge, and with which she was deeply enthralled. She did not intend deliberately to hide the fact that she had employed a deputy to deliver the note, but on the other hand she did not wish to advertise it. She therefore stayed quietly in the kitchen, but when a ring came to the front door, she got up from force of habit to open it.

But as she reached the door leading to the hall she heard the front door being opened and Mrs Holt-Lancing's voice raised in greeting.

"Oh, Severus, is that you at last? I thought I should never see you again! And I couldn't bear it. I felt at all costs I must see you. Come in." The door closed and there were suggestive silences broken by murmured words of endearment.

Rose listened, thrilled to her very marrow, picturing the scene and longing that she could get near enough to see as well as hear. Then Grinsmead's voice came, shorter and gruffer than in the circumstances she could have believed possible.

"But, Irene," it said, "you surely didn't ask me to come here to tell me this? Surely there's something more? Don't you realise how dangerous it is for us to be seen together?"

There were broken murmurs from Irene and the sound of more embraces. "Come in," she said, "come into the drawing-room and I'll give you tea. It's all ready here."

"Tea!" Rose heard in Grinsmead's expostulating voice. "My dear Irene – " Then the door closed.

"Lovers' quarrel! Lovers' quarrel!" Rose repeated delightedly to herself as she stood listening just outside the hall. But, beyond the murmur of voices, she could now hear nothing, and presently she retreated to the kitchen.

She now realised why she had been given the note and guessed that its urgency had been invented for the occasion. She also saw how unwise she would be to allow herself to be discovered, and she put on her hat so that if she were seen it would look as if she were just coming in.

It was a long time since Grinsmead had called, and Rose was keenly interested in his visit and what she had overheard. Here was something to tell Hersey! They had again and again discussed their employers' intrigue, but though they had assumed its existence, they had never had any real proof of it. Here now was proof overwhelming! It looked bad, that it did! With all the whispers that were going about Sybil Grinsmead's death. Very bad, it looked. Hersey wouldn't half be interested, he wouldn't! Wait till the next time they met and Rose would enjoy herself.

Lost in the pleasures of anticipation, Rose waited in the kitchen. The voices had died down in the drawing-room, but presently they rose again. More thrilled than ever, Rose crept out into the hall. Yes, they were quarrelling now all right. She couldn't distinguish the words, but Grinsmead's voice was loud and harsh and Irene's shrill and with a furious intonation. Rose, quivering with excitement, crept to the drawing-room door and put first her eye and then her ear to the keyhole. Then she heard what was said.

"Curse you!" Grinsmead cued in tones of fury, "do you want to destroy us both with your nonsense? Haven't I warned you that the police are watching us like lynxes? We play the fool and they'll take advantage of it. But you don't care. If you've no regard for yourself, you might have for me."

"Oh," screamed Irene, "how I *hate* you! Get away out of my sight, will you, and never let me see you again. I hate you, hate you, hate you! If I ever see you again, I'll kill you. I don't care if the police are watching me, I'll kill you. So look out for yourself!"

This seemed to sober Grinsmead. "Come, Irene," he said more quietly, "neither of us know what we're saying. Quarrelling like this won't help matters. Let's forget what we've said and look at the thing reasonably."

For some time the voices fell, then suddenly they rose again.

"No, I won't," Irene shouted, and Rose heard drumming as if she was thumping the table. "I hate you and I'll kill you if I ever see you again! Get away from here before it's too late. For heavens' sake get away and never let me see you again!"

"But Irene; pull yourself together! Suppose French – "

"I don't care about French or anyone else! You get out. Get out now before it's too late. And remember!"

There was the sound of a sudden movement and Rose fled precipitately to the kitchen. The drawing-room door opened. Rose, peeping, saw Grinsmead come out, snatch his coat and hat, tear open the door and vanish, banging the door as if to shake down the house. A few moments later Irene emerged from the drawing-room and went upstairs, and Rose heard her bedroom door close.

When a suitable time had elapsed, Rose opened and slammed the back door and went noisily to her room, then taking up her work at the point at which she had left it. She prepared dinner in the usual way and when she rang the gong Irene came down looking rather pale but otherwise as usual.

French did not get this information as a connected story. He obtained it by tedious questioning and by a painstaking synthesis of the scrappy and disjointed answers.

It had, he thought, a very direct bearing on the case, though not from the point of view in which he was specially interested at the moment. It might well have brought to a head Grinsmead's determination to take his own life. Grinsmead had passed through a very terrible experience. No matter how strong the motive or how callous the individual, the commission of murder must necessarily prove a hideous, nerve-racking, revolting ordeal. Grinsmead had passed through that. He had, moreover, experienced the haunting fear that the police really were on his track, and he must have seen prison and a hideous death looming before him, ever clearer and more insistent. And then suddenly he loses the reward of all this dreadful effort and misery. He loses Irene, for whose sake he has paid so heavy a price. His peace of mind has gone, his safety has gone, his reward has gone: what is there left to him? One thing is left to him – there is suicide. For the first time French realised how entirely adequate the man's motives were for the course he had taken.

Next day the inquest took place. On account of Irene's arrest on the capital charge, this new discovery of French's was not brought forward, but even without it a clear case was put to the jury.

Anne, Edith, Gladys and Hersey gave their evidence as they had already done to the police. This alone was practically conclusive as to the cause of death, but Godfrey's statement put the matter beyond doubt and enabled the jury to bring in their verdict without retiring.

Two days later Grinsmead's funeral took place. French did not attend, but he kept in touch with the remaining members of the household. Grinsmead, it appeared, had only left some £2000, all of which went to his mother and his partner in trust for his children. The trustees decided that as soon as suitable arrangements could be made for the children, Frayle was to be closed and sold at the earliest opportunity. Till then Mrs Grinsmead would remain. For the few days till the general break-up Anne and Edith would be kept on, though both had received formal notice to go.

French made it his business to see each member of the household, pointing out that they must keep in touch with the police, as they might be required as witnesses at Mrs Holt-Lancing's trial.

17

MYSTIFICATION

It was on the day after the inquest on Severus Grinsmead that French reached another milepost on the long road which he hoped was leading him to the completion of his case.

By the first post he received a letter from the Yard, enclosing another which read:

JEROME & BLUNT,
Watchmakers and Jewellers,
274b York Place, SE1.

DEAR SIRS,
In reply to your notice in current issue of *The Clock and Watchmaker*, we beg to state that the piece of clock spring referred to was purchased from us. If you care to send a representative we shall be pleased to supply him with all the information in our possession.

Yours faithfully,
for JEROME & BLUNT,
JOHN COX, *Manager*.

Two hours later French turned into a rather dingy establishment in a small street near Waterloo Station. The manager saw him at once.

"It happened," Mr Cox began, "that I attended to the customer myself. It was during the lunch hour and only one assistant was on duty. I was passing out for lunch and I saw this lady waiting. I asked her what I could do for her. She said she wanted a piece of clock spring and she gave me the dimensions. I forget what they were, but it was quite a small piece, three or four inches long, and it was to have a fairly large hole drilled at one end. I said that our men were out for lunch, but that we would prepare the spring as soon as they returned. She said she would call back, and gave her name, Galway or Galsworthy, or something like that. I left the necessary instructions, and as I heard no more of the affair, I presumed she received the spring correctly."

"Could you describe the lady, Mr Cox?"

Cox shook his head. "I'm rather afraid I cannot. In the first place it's a goodish while ago. Then I didn't see the lady too clearly. As you can see, the light in the shop is not all that might be desired, and I remember now that she stood with her back to the window."

"Tell me what you can."

"Well, she was a lady of middle height and build, elderly; her hair was white. Her face, I remember, was very pale and she wore black. She had large tortoiseshell spectacles and a rather larger hat than usual which came down over her forehead."

"Rather suggestive, all that."

"That's so, though it didn't strike me like that at the time."

"You can't remember anything about her voice?"

"I'm afraid not."

"Sorry, Mr Cox, to give you all this trouble. But could you tell me the date of the call?"

Cox also was sorry. He didn't think he could tell this either. An order would not have been made out for so small a job, and there would therefore be no record. However, he would make all inquiries.

French next asked him to find the workman who had cut the spring and to instruct him to cut another spring, as like the first as he could. When this had been done French produced what he had found in the water barrel. The two were practically identical.

"Not much doubt about that," said the manager. "Look at that, Sloan. Is that the spring you cut?"

The man said it was just the same at all events, which French took to be as satisfactory as he could have expected.

But the attempt to fix up the date of the purchase was not so successful. The most French could get was that it must have taken place from a week to a month before Sybil's death.

It seemed clear to French that the purchaser was disguised. At first sight the white hair suggested Mrs Grinsmead, but he saw that it might equally have been Irene Holt-Lancing, made-up.

At the same time he was not going to miss any chances. He took Cox down to Maidstone and let him see a parade of women in which Mrs Holt-Lancing was included, but without success. He made an excuse to bring Mrs Grinsmead into Ashbridge for Cox's inspection, but the manager was no more certain in her case. In fact Cox did not remember his customer's appearance, and it might have been either of French's suspects, or neither.

French was disappointed. The purchase of the spring had represented one of the most promising clues in the whole case, and it now looked as if he was going to get little out of it. All he finally succeeded in was to pin Cox down to dates between which the spring must have been bought, and to prove that Irene had gone twice to Town inside that period.

The question of whether Irene had or had not communicated with Grinsmead about her being seen outside Frayle on the night of Sybil's murder, also remained doubtful. French could not prove any such communication. In fact, the more deeply he went into the movements of both Grinsmead and Irene on that fatal afternoon and evening, the less probable it seemed. If everyone to whom he spoke were telling the truth, they could not have met. The posts would not have allowed of a letter having been delivered in time, there was no trace of a note having been sent by hand, nor was there any record of an express letter, a telegram or a telephone call. The only way in which French thought the information might have been conveyed was if Irene, during her walk that afternoon, had hidden a note in some prearranged place near Frayle, from which Grinsmead might have retrieved it by slipping out of the study French window. Of this, however, there was no evidence whatever.

The proof of another main plank in the case for the prosecution was also far from satisfactory: that fundamental point as to whether the woman Hersey saw outside the house really was Irene. Hersey stated that this was his belief, but he would not absolutely swear to it, and French had an uneasy suspicion that the defending counsel would have little difficulty in discrediting the evidence. And without this evidence French did not think the case for the Crown could be sustained. French had taken the usual steps to obtain corroboration of the statement. He had made inquiries among doctors, nurses, clergymen and others whose calling might have brought them out during the night. He had advertised for motorists who had passed along the roads in question about two o'clock that morning. He had tried to find out whether anyone returning from some entertainment had seen Irene. But none of these inquiries had brought in any result. The only really convincing evidence for the prosecution was that of Anne's as to the conversation in the lane, and even here French was dubious as to how far Anne would remain unshaken by cross-examination. In fact, French had to admit that the further he pushed his inquiries, the more unsatisfactory his case appeared.

French entered then upon one of those nerve-racking periods of marking time, in which he worked at his fullest pressure day after day, and for which he had absolutely nothing whatever to show. Godfrey's face grew longer and longer, and though Kendal was a thoroughly decent fellow, French could not blind himself to the occasional involuntary signs of satisfaction which the man showed.

Then an incident occurred which turned French's thoughts into an entirely different channel.

It was an incident quite unrelated to the case and French heard the details only by accident. Another suicide took place near Ashbridge and this bore a striking resemblance to that of Grinsmead. Here also the deceased had locked himself in his study and shot himself with an automatic pistol. But there were two differences in detail between the two cases. In this second one the deceased had left a note giving the motives for his act, and the pistol was found firmly grasped in his hand.

French, sitting in his temporary office, disconsolate and at a loose end, idly compared the cases. From the very first he had more or less subconsciously noted these two points in the Grinsmead case as somewhat unusual. They were, of course, by no means unique – just a bit unexpected.

With a slight feeling of guilt for indulging in irrelevant speculation, French pursued his line of thought. As he did so he saw that these peculiarities of the Grinsmead case were somewhat more striking than he had realised.

Here was a man taking his life because he realised that if he didn't, it would be taken for him by the law. So far that was a common enough situation. But Grinsmead's case did not stop there. Grinsmead's life was not alone in question. Irene Holt-Lancing shared his danger. Under these circumstances would not the average man, his own life forfeit, not have made an attempt to save his associate's? Would he not have left a confession that he, and he alone, was guilty?

French thought the great majority of men would have done so. Of course it might have been that owing to their quarrel Grinsmead wished Irene to become involved, but French could not believe this likely. The whole point was, of course, highly speculative and no firm conclusion could be drawn from it. All that French could say was that under the circumstances he would have expected a note.

He also would certainly have expected to have found Grinsmead grasping the pistol. Out of curiosity he got one or two books of reference to refresh his memory on the subject of cadaveric rigidity, which he believed was the correct title of the phenomenon in question.

In general the muscles become relaxed immediately after death. Then gradually they stiffen, and after remaining stiff for a period of indeterminate length, they finally relax. But the first period of relaxation may be absent, the body remaining stiff in the position which it occupied at the moment of death.

When was this stiffening likely to occur? French looked up "Taylor," and there he saw a good deal that confirmed his own recollection. On page 241 he read:

"Turning now to the practical aspects of the matter, experience has shown:-

1. That instantaneous stiffening is *cæteris paribus* more likely to exhibit itself when great muscular exertion has been made previous to death.
2. That it is also more likely to appear in strong and muscular subjects, whether they are or are not exerting themselves powerfully at the time of death.
3. That *sudden* death is a predisposing factor.
4. That death due to violent disturbance of the nervous system (apoplexy, shot through the head, etc.), is also a powerful element in causation. This mode of death has been experimentally shown to be capable of producing instantaneous rigidity, or cadaveric spasm."

This was all in accordance with French's own previous belief. However, it was really the point covered by paragraph 6 that he was interested in. Paragraph 6 read: "That it (instantaneous rigidity) does not invariably occur under circumstances that would seem to be most favourable, and occasionally occurs in tranquil deaths when it might not be anticipated."

That was what he thought, though he had not been quite sure. It was, he reflected bitterly, what one usually obtained from scientific or expert evidence: the building up of a strong case and then the smashing of it away by some exception or further consideration. Then he saw that he was wrong and unjust to those patient investigators by whose labours he was even then profiting. It was not a peculiarity of expert evidence; it was Nature. That was the way the world was made.

French read on: " ... It may be suggested that a weapon, although grasped by an alleged suicide to inflict the death-wound, may either drop from the hand or be found loosely in it, as a result of the relaxation of the muscles in death. This must be admitted; hence the mere fact of a weapon being found loose should not be taken as evidence of murder, unless other circumstances – such as the nature of the wound, the freedom of the hand from blood, the position of the body, etc. – concur to prove that the act was not one of suicide."

This was clear and definite. At the same time, on a mere academic balancing of the chances, French felt that the likely thing was that the pistol would have been grasped in Grinsmead's hand.

French realised that he was pursuing a will-o'-the-wisp. Owing to the closed room the fact of Grinsmead's suicide was not in question. But French was at a standstill in his work and he felt himself terribly stale on it. A change of thought, even to the realms of imagination, might prove a rest.

With the idea of setting himself an exercise in the construction of evidence, he took out Grinsmead's pistol, and placing it carefully on his desk, began to study the fingerprints. He wanted to see if he could prove from them that Grinsmead's hand had relaxed and allowed the pistol to drop. He imagined the prints should show some smudging at their edges, and he thought an investigation of this point would be an interesting exercise which might even prove useful to him in some subsequent case.

The pistol had been carefully handled by the police, so that the original fingerprints, clearly marked in white powder, remained intact. French began mentally to sort them out, so as to establish the position of the hand which had made them.

He found it not so easy as he had anticipated. By this time, however, his interest was aroused and he would not confess defeat. He therefore obtained an exactly similar pistol, of which there were two or three in the station, and tried to fit his own fingers to it in the same positions as the prints on Grinsmead's.

This, of course, should have been child's play, but to French's surprise he found it extremely difficult. If he got one or two fingers right, the others wouldn't work in.

Deliberately French cleaned his own gun of prints. Then he went through the motions of picking it up, pointing it at his head, pulling the trigger, relaxing his hand and letting it drop. Picking it up again carefully in his handkerchief, he dusted it with white powder, and compared his prints with Grinsmead's.

The result he found extremely intriguing. The prints did not agree at all. Puzzle over them as he would, he could not see how Grinsmead had held his gun.

Then another peculiar thing struck him. There were five prints, and only five, on the pistol; each finger was represented once and once only. But as French thought over it he saw that he would have expected to find a great many more prints. Even supposing that no prints made previous to that day remained, the pistol would have been lifted out of its drawer before being fired. Indeed it was almost certain that Grinsmead would have opened the magazine to make sure it was charged and that there would be no hitch in his plan. But none of these movements were accounted for. The prints seemed placed almost at random ...

French, his interest now almost breathless, sat motionless, gazing into vacancy. *What* was this discovery that he had made? What was the conclusion to which he was being led? Had Grinsmead ever grasped the gun at all? And if he hadn't? ...

Then French's sanity returned. The locked room! No one else could have fired that shot, because no one could have left the room after doing so. The print business might be puzzling, but the evidence of the room was conclusive.

He tried again. Again and again and again. But he could not make the prints work. And in spite of what his reason told him, he felt a conviction gradually creeping into his mind that the evidence of the room lied.

Could history, he wondered, be about to repeat itself. At the time it was admitted on all hands that Sybil Grinsmead had committed suicide – because of her closed room. No one could possibly have got in to turn on the gas. Yet in spite of the evidence of the room, Sybil Grinsmead's death had been proved to be one of the foulest murders on record. Was French going off his head, or was this another?

French was always glad of the opinions of other persons, though as a matter of fact he seldom allowed their views to affect his own. So much, however, hung from this particular conclusion, that he thought another opinion might be desirable.

Having hidden Grinsmead's pistol and carefully cleaned his own, he knocked at Superintendent Godfrey's door.

"I should very much like you, sir, when you have an opportunity, to try a small experiment. I think you would find it interesting. I don't want to say more about it, because I want to see if you reach the same conclusions that I have."

Godfrey looked at him keenly. "I'll be with you in ten minutes," he promised.

French went back to his room and set the stage. Godfrey came in, making no comment, but looking inquiringly at French.

"Now, sir," French began, taking up the pistol he had used. "This is one of your own pistols. It is similar to that with which Grinsmead killed himself. I want you first to make sure it is not loaded."

Godfrey did so.

"I now clean all fingerprints off it," French went on, "and place it in this drawer, which, you will notice, corresponds to that in which Grinsmead kept his pistol. Now, sir, will you pick it up and go through the motions of shooting yourself and dropping the pistol, just as Grinsmead is believed to have done. Good."

French picked up the pistol, dusted it with white powder, and blew the surplus off. "Your fingerprints, sir?"

"Well," Godfrey returned impatiently. "What of it?" For answer French lifted out Grinsmead's pistol and placed it beside the other. Then he waited in silence.

Godfrey, a slight frown on his face, stared at the weapons, his eyes passing backward and forwards from one to the other. He began to whistle softly between his teeth, a sign, French knew, of intense thought. Then slowly he turned both guns upside down and again examined them. Gradually his expression changed. The rather bored frown gave way to a puzzled look, which in its turn suggested bewilderment and finally showed incredulous amazement. At last he turned on French.

"What's all this?" he asked roughly. "What are you trying to get at?"

"I wanted, sir, to ask you what you thought of it," French answered smoothly.

"Well, what do *you* think of it?" Godfrey returned. "I tried," said French, "for over an hour to make prints like those on Grinsmead's gun, and I couldn't do it. I couldn't get my hand so spread and twisted that my fingers would reach the same places. I tried even to copy them, but it was no good. Now, sir, may I try another experiment?"

"Go ahead."

"Then, sir, will you sit down here at the desk and let your hand lie loosely on it, like this."

French once again cleaned his gun, then holding it by the muzzle in his handkerchief, he lifted Godfrey's fingers, one by one, and pressed them on the metal. Then he dusted on his powder and blew the surplus off, finally laying the pistol down beside Grinsmead's.

The result was interesting. The new prints were not by any means in the same relative positions as Grinsmead's, but they had the same curious lack of cohesion that Grinsmead's showed. French tried to fit his own fingers over them, and failed just as in the first case. Then Godfrey tried, tried again and again and again, just as had French an hour earlier.

At last he flung down the pistol, and springing to his feet, began to pace the room.

"I see what you're suggesting all right," he declared, as he walked, "but, damn it all, French, you can't be right. The locked room."

"I didn't mean to suggest anything, sir. I only point out that these fingerprints are facts just as much as the locked room."

"But – " The super jerked himself about irritably. "Confound it, it – it isn't possible. No one could have got out of that room."

"That was the argument for Mrs Grinsmead's suicide, sir."

"Are you suggesting that some one fired that pistol from outside the room with a cord and a bit of spring?"

"No, sir. I'm suggesting that we've perhaps been a bit hasty in assuming suicide."

Godfrey flung himself once more into the chair at the desk. "Clean that gun again," he said.

Just as had French some hour or more earlier, so now Godfrey began systematically to attempt to produce prints in the same places as those on Grinsmead's pistol. He was just as thorough as French had been, and he spent just as long. Finally he had to admit himself beaten. He gazed blankly at French.

"It's a true bill," he almost whispered, and an expression of something approaching awe grew on his face. "Murdered!" and then after another pause: "Good Lord!"

Once again he got up and began to pace the room. "And there," he went on bitterly, "we've made the same darned asses of ourselves that we did the first time! Reported it suicide, allowed a coroner's jury to return a verdict of suicide, agreed that it was and must be and only could be suicide. And each time to eat our words! I tell you, French, this is a knock."

"Same here, sir," French returned with tact. "It was pure chance that I noticed it."

"Huh! same sort of chance as the last time. Well, I suppose I should congratulate you and all that; it was good work." He paused and seemed to pull himself together. "Now, French, that changes our outlook on the whole affair. You'll have to start a new set of inquiries in the morning. Remember it's no good unless you can show how the thing was done."

"I see that all right, sir, and I'm afraid it'll be a job. You haven't any ideas that might give me a lead?"

"I? No. I shouldn't even have believed it, only for this demonstration of yours. No, you'll have to go ahead and do the best you can. If you start with the assumption that there was a fake somewhere, you'll probably get it."

"I'll try, sir. But there's one thing. Don't you think we should keep our suspicions absolutely secret?"

"By all means. That's the one advantage of our mistake. The murderer thinks he's all right; or she perhaps."

"She, in all probability, sir. Remember those threats to murder."

"Huh," Godfrey returned. "Don't spoil it now by jumping to conclusions. Look into the thing tomorrow and have a good think over it. I'll do the same. Then we'll have a talk. Meantime keep everything to yourself."

He left the room, and French, his mind in a whirl, returned slowly to his hotel.

18

ASSEVERATION

Next morning after breakfast French lit his pipe, and retreating to the smoking-room, settled down to consider his new plan of campaign.

He saw at once that he had to solve two quite distinct problems. The first was: How could the murderer leave the room by a door which he afterwards locked behind him, leaving the key on the inside? The second was: Assuming the murderer had thus left the room, who was he?

First as to the leaving of the room.

Exit through the walls, ceiling, floor or chimney being impossible, only the doors and windows need be considered. French took the windows first. They were of the standard pattern, with steel frames, lead lights and strong fastenings. If anyone had passed out through one of these windows it would have been absolutely impossible for him to have fastened it behind him. No cord or lever or wire could have been used, for the handle drew the window so tightly into the frame that either the cord would have prevented the fastening getting home, or else if the cord flattened sufficiently to allow this, it would have been so firmly gripped between sash and frame as to be quite immovable. The windows, therefore, were out of the question.

This left the doors. There were two; one leading into the hall, and the other giving on to the steps which led down to the tennis lawn. The latter was, of course, a French window, but for the purposes of his inquiry French thought it more convenient to consider it as a door.

Through one of these two doors, therefore, the murderer must have gone. Was there anything to indicate which? French thought so.

The locking of the door must have taken time, whatever apparatus was used. Now the murderer knew that the sound of the shot would attract the other inmates of the house. They would run down into the hall and attempt to enter the study from there. It was unlikely therefore that he would use that door. He would run a terrible risk of not getting it locked before some member of the household arrived. Further, he would have to make his escape from the hall at a time when it might be full of people.

On the other hand, the French window and tennis lawn would remain deserted. Even if some one ran round from the hall to see if the windows were open, this would not be done till the attempt to enter direct from the hall had failed. French felt that he might safely conclude that the murderer had left by the French window.

French smoked contemplatively as he sat turning the problem over in his mind. He always enjoyed these preliminary steps in an investigation, the elimination of the unfit in possibilities, as he put it to himself. This stage always suggested such enormously rapid progress. Here in a few minutes he had reduced the wide and vague question of how the murderer might have left the room to the narrow and definite one of how he could have locked the French window behind him, the key remaining in the lock on the inside. He decided that he would go out to Frayle and examine the window again, in the hope that some helpful idea might occur to him.

Leaving this problem for the time being, French turned to consider the second: Assuming the murderer had somehow left the room, who was he?

Once again French decided to work in the orthodox way, by elimination. Make a list of all concerned, reject the impossibles, and – see what was left. Was it not Sherlock Holmes who had said: "Reject the impossible, and the remainder, however unlikely, must be the truth"? No one could have admired Holmes more than did French, yet he could not agree with this dictum. When he had rejected what he knew to be impossible, there were usually a number of possibilities left. Therefore, he always said: "Reject the impossible, and – see what is left."

Well, those concerned were: Anne Day, Edith Cheame, Gladys Smith, Catherine Meakin, Joseph Hersey, Matilda Grinsmead, Irene Holt-Lancing, Randal Holt-Lancing, Some person or persons unknown.

Anne Day. – When French began to consider the possibility of Anne's guilt, he soon saw that the pros and cons were the same in her case as in that of the other members of the household. He therefore bracketed Anne, Edith, Gladys, Meakin and Hersey.

In the first place, not one of the five had an alibi. Anne said that at the time of the crime she was in her room, Edith that she was taking a bath, Gladys that she was just about to leave the kitchen to go to bed, Mrs Meakin that she was actually in bed, and Hersey that he was in the garage. But of none of these statements was there any proof.

On the other hand there were two considerations which suggested the innocence of all these five. The first was that none of them, so far as French knew, had a motive for killing Grinsmead. That was an important point, but the second was even more conclusive. It was to the interest of each that the *status quo* at Frayle should remain unaltered. Grinsmead's death would mean for each the loss of his or her job, and from what French knew of the life at Frayle, it would not be easy for them to find other jobs so congenial and so well paid. In fact, Grinsmead's death would be a serious blow to each.

Though French believed that he might dismiss these five from his mind, he recognised that his present conclusions were merely tentative and might be reversed by some further discovery. He therefore noted them as "Possible but unlikely," and went on to the next name on his list.

Mrs Grinsmead was scarcely in the same category as the previous five. She was only temporarily a member of the household and she had no financial reason to wish that Grinsmead might remain at Frayle. Moreover, she was the deceased's mother, and motives which would not obtain in the previous cases might in hers.

French had been struck with the old lady's personality. She would, he believed, take very drastic steps to accomplish her ends. Whether if her ends demanded murder she would go to that extreme, he did not know. But he almost thought, given sufficient provocation, that she would.

If the death of Sybil Grinsmead had been in question, French saw that suspicion of the old lady would not have seemed so impossible. If Mrs Grinsmead believed that Sybil was ruining Grinsmead's life, it was conceivable that she might sacrifice her daughter-in-law for her son. But what motive could she possibly have for desiring Grinsmead's death? French's inquiries had convinced him

258

that she was intensely fond of her son. Was it not absurd to suggest that she might have murdered him?

French thought so, and yet there was one case in which she might have taken this terrible step. Persons have been known to murder a loved one who was suffering terribly from an incurable disease. Suppose Mrs Grinsmead had known that her son was about to be arrested for murder and that nothing could save him from conviction and execution. Could she have killed him to save him from this fate?

French was not prepared to say. But he did not think that Mrs Grinsmead could have known either that arrest was imminent or the evidence the police held against her son.

Fortunately there was a way in which her innocence could be tested. Mrs Grinsmead had an alibi. She had been in the train travelling from Town at the time at which the murder was committed. This surely could be proved.

French went on to his next name, Irene Holt-Lancing. Here, he saw, was an entirely different proposition. There were many reasons for suspecting Mrs Holt-Lancing.

The first was a suggestion from the method of the crime. Murderers are notoriously given to repeating themselves. In this case the method of the closed room was repeated. Possibly various ways of using the closed room as a blind had been discussed between Grinsmead and Irene before Sybil's murder, and possibly again, Irene had now used one of the methods then rejected.

Secondly, there was not only motive, but proof of motive. If Rose Unwin's story were to be believed, Irene had hated Grinsmead and had several times threatened to murder him. French was aware that many a threat of this kind is lightly made, but where other circumstances point to murder such threats become important.

There was a third point, though up to now French had missed its significance. Rose had stated that Irene had been out late on the night of Grinsmead's murder. How late French had not asked, and he took a note to find this out first thing.

There was therefore a good deal of *a priori* evidence against Irene, and French put her down as his most likely suspect.

But Irene's husband could not be omitted from the list. If Randal Holt-Lancing had learned that Grinsmead had been making love to his wife, there was all the motive necessary for murder. There was, of course, nothing actually connecting Holt-Lancing with the crime. But French had not investigated the man's movements on the evening in question, and it was possible that inquiry might reveal something to incriminate him. Holt-Lancing must certainly be retained as a suspect.

The last item on the list, that of some person or persons unknown, did not give French much thought. It was obvious that until actual proof was obtained of some known person's guilt, this possibility could not be entirely dismissed.

The first thing then was an inquiry into Irene Holt-Lancing's movements on the night of the murder.

The Laurels, French knew, was closed, Captain Holt-Lancing having gone to an hotel in Town, and Rose Unwin to her home in Maidstone. French ruefully decided that another interview with Rose was indicated, and he took an early train to Maidstone. He had the girl's address and was soon at her house. By a stroke of luck she was at home.

"I forgot to ask you one or two questions, Rose," French said, as he followed her into the tiny sitting-room. "You remember when we were going through Mrs Holt-

Lancing's last day, you said she had a 'phone message in the evening and had gone out? I didn't take particulars about that, but now I see my report will not be complete without it. Will you tell me just what occurred?"

"There's not much to tell," Rose returned. "That night the telephone rang. I answered it. It was Mr Grinsmead, and he asked to speak to Mrs Holt-Lancing. He said it was very urgent and to ask her to please come to the 'phone at once. I gave the message. She kind of hesitated, then she went. They spoke just for a minute or two. Then she put on her things and went out."

French concealed his interest under a mask of boredom. "Mr Grinsmead spoke, did he? You recognised his voice?"

"No. I shouldn't be sure of his voice, not to hear over the 'phone. He gave his name; that's how I knew."

"Did you hear what Mrs Holt-Lancing answered?"

"Not me. I 'ooked it to the kitchen when she came out. I was always one to mind my own business."

"Of course, Rose," French said smoothly. "I didn't suggest that you would listen. But people sometimes hear things unintentionally."

"Well, I didn't hear anything."

"What time did the message come through?"

"Ten o'clock as near as doesn't matter. The hall clock was striking as I was answering. I remember because I couldn't hear clear on account of it."

"And then Mrs Holt-Lancing went out? What time was that?"

"Just at once. She put on her things and went out right away."

"I see. Then what was the next thing?"

"The next thing was that the captain came in and asked where she was."

"Oh, yes? Captain Holt-Lancing had been out?"

"He'd been up in Town."

"And what time do you say he got back?"

"Twenty past ten. I know because he asked so much about the time she went out that I looked at the clock."

"Did you tell him that Mr Grinsmead had rung up?" For the first time Rose looked sulky. "Well, he asked me straight. What could I tell him?"

French hastened to get the conversation back to the satisfactory level it had up to this occupied. "My dear girl," he replied, "I'm not blaming you. I think you've done splendidly all through. I'm only asking what happened. He asked you and you did tell him?"

"That's right," she answered, mollified.

"And what happened then?"

"Well, he turned and went straight out."

French could scarcely refrain from chuckling as he listened to all this. It was difficult to see why Grinsmead should have called Irene up, if it were not to arrange some kind of a meeting. And if he did so, and if Captain Holt-Lancing followed her… However, that was a matter for future consideration. He turned back to Rose.

"Very good," he said. "We've now got Mrs Holt-Lancing going out about five minutes past ten, and the captain following her at twenty past. What happened next?"

It appeared that Mrs Holt-Lancing had returned about twenty to eleven and her husband about eleven. He was not in more than four or five minutes when Kendal arrived to arrest Irene.

"You seem to remember all these hours very clearly," French went on. "Was there anything to fix them in your mind?"

"Well, the captain asked me about them. He went over them with me and said was I sure of them, and that I'd have to remember them because I might be asked about them later; just as you're doing now."

This seemed very significant information. Why should Holt-Lancing have thought that the hours of his own and his wife's movements were important? Surely his concern implied knowledge of the tragedy?

A few further questions led French to the conclusion that he had learned all that Rose Unwin could tell him. He therefore warned her to be silent about his visit, and took his leave.

The next step, he thought, should be an interview with Captain Holt-Lancing. It was now late in the afternoon, but he decided to go up to Town, if possible see the captain after dinner, and take the opportunity of spending a night in his own house.

As he sat in the train French gave himself up, not so much to considering the possibilities suggested by Rose's statement, as to making a list of the points on which he should question Captain Holt-Lancing. It was therefore with a fairly clear idea of what he wanted to know, that after dinner he presented himself at the captain's hotel. But here for the moment his luck was out. The captain was not in the hotel and it was not known when he would return.

French saw, however, that he need not lose his evening. He had also to inquire into Mrs Grinsmead's alibi, and the present was as good a time as any. According to her own story she had dined early and – wonderful old lady! – gone to a lecture at the Gwalian Hall on "Some Recent Developments in Mendelism."

French saw that it would not be easy to obtain confirmation of her statement. He began at the restaurant where she had dined, but there, in spite of a painstaking inquiry, he learned nothing whatever.

It was too late to do anything more that night, but next morning French saw the officials who had arranged the lecture. From them, to his surprise, he obtained some unexpected information.

Mrs Grinsmead, it seemed, had written from Ashbridge for a ticket. Moreover, before the lecture began she had introduced herself to the secretary and ordered from him certain pamphlets dealing with the subject under discussion. These she had paid for, saying she wished them sent to Frayle. The secretary not only identified her from a photograph, but remembered having seen her seated in the hall before the lecture began.

Unless, therefore, Mrs Grinsmead had slipped unseen from the building before the meeting came to an end, her alibi stood; she could not have reached Ashbridge earlier than she said she had. It was true that for part of the time cinematograph pictures had been shown and the room had therefore been in darkness, but the officials felt sure that no one could have left unseen by them.

It looked therefore as if Mrs Grinsmead were definitely out of the case. Not that French had ever seriously suspected her, but it was his job to make sure.

He had better luck on his call that evening on Captain Holt-Lancing. French had seen him at the inquest on Grinsmead, but he had not spoken to him. Now he began by formally showing his credentials and warning the captain that he was not bound to reply to his questions unless he liked. Then impressively he produced his note-book, opened it at a fresh page, and asked: "Full name, if you please, sir."

Holt-Lancing seemed to French the personification of his idea of the captain of an important liner. Of medium height, he was thickset in build with a squarish face, thin lips, firmly compressed, a strong jaw and blue eyes. His skin was burnt brown by sun and roughened by weather, and the corners of his eyes were wrinkled as if by endless peering into distance. A man of few words, of quick thought, of decisive action.

He did not seem in the least impressed by French's preparations, and answered his questions in a low, cultivated voice. He explained that his name was Randal Grove Holt-Lancing, that he was master of the Orient liner *Oratorio*, that he was having some special leave while a defect in his ship's port engine was being put right, and that he had been at home for some five weeks before the date of his wife's arrest.

"It is about the evening of that arrest that I particularly want to ask you," French went on. "You were in Town that day?"

"Yes, I went up in the early afternoon, did some business, dined and came down by the 8.40 from Victoria."

"That gets to Ashbridge at 10.5?"

"About that, I should say."

"And then, sir?"

"I took a taxi home."

Holt-Lancing went on to confirm the story Rose Unwin had told. He reached The Laurels at 10.20, and when he found his wife was out, he asked where she had gone. Rose told him about the message from Grinsmead, and Holt-Lancing at once assumed that Grinsmead had asked Irene to meet him. He was, of course, aware that his wife's name had been coupled with Grinsmead's in connection with the death of Sybil Grinsmead, and he thought that such a meeting – if it really were such – would be most unwise. He therefore left the house on foot with the idea of following his wife and if possible dissuading her from her purpose. But he did not overtake her, and when he returned to The Laurels she had been there for some time.

To French this statement left a good deal to be desired. He turned it over in his mind and then, in his slow persistent way, began to ask questions.

"You say, sir, you assumed Mr Grinsmead had asked your wife to meet him. Just where did you imagine this meeting might have taken place?"

"I didn't know. I imagined it might be somewhere on the road between The Laurels and Frayle."

"Then you walked in the Frayle direction?"

"Yes."

If these statements were correct, Holt-Lancing had left The Laurels about 10.20 and returned about 11.0. The distance between The Laurels and Frayle was a mile. He would therefore have had ample time to have reached Frayle. French asked if he had done so.

For answer Holt-Lancing looked appraisingly at French. Then he squared his shoulders, hitched his chair nearer to the table at which they were sitting, and answered slowly:

"See here, inspector, I see from the direction your questions are taking that you're going to get hold of the truth. I don't know what put you on to this line, which I hoped could have been kept secret. However, now you know, and it seems to me I'd better tell you the whole thing exactly as it happened. Then you won't be getting unpleasant notions in your mind about myself and perhaps my wife."

French shrugged. "I should be glad, sir, but you must remember my caution that you're not bound to answer my questions unless you like."

"And that my answers may be used against me in evidence," the captain suggested grimly.

"I didn't say so, sir, but of course there's always that possibility."

"I thought so. Well, here's the story, at all events. I can tell you the whole thing in a few words. When I didn't meet my wife I went on to Frayle, the whole way." He paused.

"Did you go in?"

"No. I intended to go in. I intended to go to the French window in the study and knock till Grinsmead let me in, that was, supposing he was there. I went as far as the window, but I didn't either knock or go in."

"Why was that?"

"Why? Because Grinsmead was dead. It happened that the window curtains were not fitting tight; there was a little space between two of them. I went up those steps outside the window and looked through. I saw Grinsmead lying on the floor with a bullet hole in his forehead, and the household standing round. I can tell you, inspector," Holt-Lancing's face was very grim, "it was the nastiest knock I ever got in my life. I couldn't tell you what I didn't think. I imagined Grinsmead might have got to know that you people were after him. I even feared a suicide pact and that my wife was in the room too. I can tell you I'll never live through anything worse."

"If you felt that way, sir, why didn't you knock and find out what was wrong – knock at the front door, I mean?"

"Well, I think you might guess better than that. If I had gone to the door it would have suggested that I feared my wife might be mixed up in it. I hurried home, thinking that if she hadn't turned up I'd go back. Thank God, she was at home. For two or three minutes I couldn't speak with the relief. She'd been back for some twenty minutes."

"And did you ask her where she had been?"

"Of course I asked her. But what she told me only made the thing a bigger puzzle. She said when Rose called her to the 'phone she heard a strange voice. It was not Grinsmead's. She asked who was speaking, and the voice said it was Mr Bowen. Bowen is Grinsmead's partner."

"Did she recognise Mr Bowen's voice?"

"She didn't know it. He said that Grinsmead had just then received serious news about Mrs Grinsmead's death. The police were likely to make a very terrible move at once. It was necessary that Grinsmead should meet my wife immediately in order to settle their course of action. He would give no details, but said that Grinsmead had asked him to urge my wife to do her part. She was to go then and there to a certain clump of trees at the side of the road near Brentwood, close to where the roads from The Laurels and Frayle join. You know the place?"

"I know the road junction, but not the clump."

"There's a clump there all right, for I've seen it since. It's about half a mile from The Laurels to the clump and about three-quarters from Frayle. Bowen explained that it would be unwise for the meeting to take place either at Frayle or The Laurels, otherwise Grinsmead would have gone across. He asked if my wife would be at the clump at ten-fifteen."

French waited without comment.

"She said yes; what else could she say? She dressed at once and hurried out. She got to the clump within a minute of the time and went round behind it, as Bowen had said. There was no one there. She waited in a fever of dread, but no one turned up. Then the question arose, how long should she wait? She was dreadfully upset, but at last she decided that if no one came in fifteen minutes it would mean that Grinsmead couldn't come, probably that he had been arrested. He was a very punctual man, Grinsmead, and she knew that if he could, he'd have been there on time.

"She waited there for the fifteen minutes, and you can imagine her feelings. At 10.30 she gave it up and came home, arriving about 10.40. Then Rose's story that I had turned up and had followed her out, scared her into fits, for she thought I might go to Frayle and be there when the trouble arose. So she was as relieved as I was when I got home and we told each other what had happened."

This story, French saw at once, hung together and might well be true. But he also saw that there was another interpretation to these facts, which appealed more strongly to himself. Suppose it was Grinsmead who had rung up Irene. Suppose he had asked her to go to Frayle on some real or trumped-up excuse. Suppose she had done so and had been admitted by the French window into the study. Suppose the captain had followed.

French halted in his reconstruction. It was not quite so easy now. From this point he saw that several different things might have taken place. Irene might have shot Grinsmead, left the room by the French window, locking it behind her in some unknown way, and at the window or on her way home met Randal, who would, of course, have turned with her. Or Randal might have found Irene with Grinsmead, and Randal might have shot Grinsmead, faking the suicide and locking the door. Or again, Randal might have turned up just as Irene shot Grinsmead, and have helped her out with it.

French saw that a good deal of thought would be necessary before a conclusion could be reached. It was, however, clear enough to him that on the information he now held, either or both of the Holt-Lancings might be guilty.

"There's one other question I must ask you, Captain Holt-Lancing," he said, "I'm afraid rather an unpleasant one. But you'll see that it is necessary. Did you know or believe that Mr Grinsmead and Mrs Holt-Lancing were more to each other than mere acquaintances?"

Holt-Lancing denied with indignation. French did not feel very sure that the feelings were genuine, but he pretended to accept the statement, and settled down to complete his notes on points of detail. Holt-Lancing answered all his questions readily, but could advance no other evidence.

French, wishing him a civil good night, took his leave.

19

FRUSTRATION

French decided that while in Town he would check the London end of Holt-Lancing's statement. Accordingly next morning he began by a visit to Messrs. Crosswell and Hergesheimer, optical instrument makers, to whom the captain had paid his last call on the afternoon in question.

French saw Mr Hergesheimer and obtained complete corroboration as to the visit. Holt-Lancing had come about certain instruments for his ship, and had remained talking to Mr Hergesheimer after the shop had closed. He had left about half-past six.

French next went to the Restaurant Trieste, where Holt-Lancing had stated he had dined. But here French had no success. No one remembered a diner of the captain's description.

It was, however, scarcely to be expected that anyone should. The Trieste is a large place and there was no reason why attention should specially have been called to him.

It seemed useless to make inquiries at Victoria. French, however, did his best there, though without result.

He therefore took the next train to Ashbridge. The train ran into the West Station, as had the 8.40 by which Holt-Lancing had presumably travelled.

He began by an interrogation of the station staff who had been on duty at 10.5 on the night in question. But except for the fact that on that night the train had arrived exactly to time, he learned nothing. No one knew Holt-Lancing, and no one had seen anyone answering his description.

French then turned his attention to the taxis parked in front of the station. He had Holt-Lancing's description of his driver, and he saw that only one man answered it.

The man proved to be the driver Holt-Lancing had employed. He remembered the affair. A man who might have been the captain had engaged him about ten o'clock. He had driven to The Laurels, which he knew, having driven a lady there on previous occasions. The gentleman had paid him and gone into the house and the taximan had returned to Ashbridge.

The driver, however, was doubtful as to the exact hour at which he had picked up his fare. He said at first it was at 10.5, on the arrival of the 8.40 train from Victoria, but on French pointing out that the matter was important, he said he had not remarked the time specially, and refused to swear to it. French tried to check the time by questioning the other drivers who had been present, but none of them had seen Holt-Lancing's man either start or return.

Though this was not absolute proof as to time, French thought he might well accept it as confirmation of the captain's story.

If then Holt-Lancing had come by the 8.40 from Victoria, he could not have been home more than a minute or two before the time he said. The train had arrived at 10.5, and he could not have left the station before 10.7 or 10.8. It would take the taxi about ten minutes to drive out to The Laurels. Therefore it was impossible for him to have arrived home before 10.15. 10.20, as Rose stated, was quite likely to be correct.

French was greatly struck by these facts. Holt-Lancing was in the taxi at 10.15. But there was ample proof that the murder took place at 10.15. Therefore Holt-Lancing was innocent.

French was invariably sceptical of alibis, and he therefore went over this argument again and again before accepting it. Finally, however, he had to admit that it was watertight.

But this conclusion was only what he had expected to reach. He had not believed Holt-Lancing to be guilty. Irene, in his opinion, was the murderess. There was ample motive in her case, and as he now began to consider the details of her evening, he saw that there was ample opportunity also.

According to Rose Unwin, Irene had been rung up at ten o'clock, and had gone out five minutes later. Say she had left at 10.5. It was about a mile from The Laurels to Frayle and Irene could scarcely have walked it in the time. But had she left at 10.0 instead of 10.5, she could have done so. That was to say, an error of five minutes in the hall clock at The Laurels would have made it possible. She had returned at 10.40, which would have allowed ample time not only to commit the murder, but to do so even if the clock were this five minutes fast.

Then there was that business of the telephone call asking her to meet Grinsmead at the clump of bushes. It was either a lie on her part to account for her absence from The Laurels, or else it was a plant of the real murderer's to fix suspicion on her. Here, however, some confirmation or otherwise should be possible. He should be able to trace the call.

What he wished for was some one who had seen Irene going to or from Frayle or the clump as the case might be. If she had been seen near Frayle it would prove her statement about the clump to have been an invention. French believed that proof of a false statement of where she had been at the time of the murder, added to the other evidence he had, should be enough to secure a conviction. On the other hand, proof of her story would, of course, clear her.

He went in and saw Superintendent Godfrey. Would the super make an investigation for him? He wanted a search for some one who might have seen Irene Holt-Lancing on any of the roads near The Laurels between 10.0 and 10.40 on the night of Grinsmead's murder.

Godfrey undertook to make inquiries, and French set off to the telephone headquarters in Ashbridge.

There he succeeded in tracing the call which Irene had received at 10.0 p.m. on the night of the crime. It had come from Frayle all right. Here, then, was a certain confirmation for Irene's story.

But as French thought over it, he saw that as confirmation it did not really amount to very much. The fact that a call was received was already testified to by Rose Unwin. Irene, further, must have known that a call could be traced. She would not, therefore, be so silly as to lie where a test of her statement was so easily obtainable.

She had stated that the caller had given the name of Bowen, Grinsmead's partner. French therefore went to the firm's office and saw Mr Bowen. But Bowen denied *in toto* having been at Frayle on the night in question, or having put through any call to Irene, or of knowing anything whatever about the affair.

From this it seemed to follow that the call must have come from Grinsmead himself. French remembered the telephone arrangements at Frayle. The main instrument was in the hall and there was an extension to the study. French's general inquiries had already elicited the fact that no one at Frayle knew of a call having been made on the night of the murder, but French was sure that Grinsmead could have made it from the study without any other member of the household being aware of it. Indeed, for the matter of that, he might easily have made it from the hall without being heard.

French wondered what Irene's motives could be in denying that the voice was Grinsmead's. He could not see what difference it would make to her story.

He spent a good deal of time considering this question. His experience was that if in a case something was done which seemed to him pointless, it usually meant that he had missed a clue. But rack his brains as he would, he could not grasp the significance of this proceeding.

French felt rather like funking the next item on his list: that intensely puzzling question of how the French window could have been closed and locked after the murderer had passed through.

He went out once again to Frayle. It had not yet been vacated, though French understood that a prospective purchaser was considering it.

French locked himself into the study and sat down to consider the possibilities. The French window was of wood, glazed to the bottom. It opened outwards in two halves. These halves closed up against the rebates in the frame and the oak sill. They fitted quite tightly, wood to wood. There was no possibility of a cord or wire being drawn between them – unless perhaps a thin piano wire with nothing at the end.

French opened the doors and examined the woodwork. If such a wire had been pulled out, a mark would show. There was none. Whatever, therefore, had been done, a wire had not been pulled out between the door and the frame.

Of the two doors, one contained the lock and was fastened by the lock bolts. The other contained the lock keeper and was made secure by two running bolts set vertically, one of which fastened into the lintel at the top of the door and the other into the sill at the bottom. In shutting the door, the first half was closed and bolted above and below, then the second half was locked to the first by the key.

There was one way, French knew, in which a door can be locked from the outside while the key remains inside. There was a tool for the purpose. It was a special kind of pincers of very hard steel by which the end of the key barrel could be grasped so tightly as to enable it to be turned. The tool was shaped like a medical forceps, and it could be inserted through the keyhole from the outside. On gripping the end of the key it could be tightened till the key would not slip in it when it was turned. This tool, however, left a little scratch on each side of the key barrel.

French took out the key and examined it with a lens. It bore no scratches. Therefore this method had not been employed.

Another plan French had read of, but not seen, was to put a piece of strong wire through the handle of the key, this wire being attached to a cord which passed down under the door. Pulling the cord was supposed to turn the key, when the wire, falling out by reason of the new position of the handle, could be withdrawn beneath the door by a further pull on the cord.

This, of course, could not have been done in the present case for the reason already stated, that there was no room between the door and frame to draw the piece of wire out.

Double doors, French remembered, could often be opened when locked, by pushing them open simultaneously. As the doors drew apart the bolt was automatically withdrawn from the keeper. But this method could not have been employed in the present instance, because one half of the door was bolted to the lintel and sill above and below.

The more French studied the affair, the more puzzled he grew. It was beginning to look as if he had assumed something which was impossible. Could anyone really have passed through that door and locked it behind him? French swore in his perplexity.

Then a fresh idea shot into his mind, or rather an idea he had already considered and abandoned, recurred to him. Admittedly it was on a slightly different point, still he accepted it eagerly. Anne Day! Could Anne Day after all be the guilty party?

Suppose Anne had reached the hall slightly earlier than she had said, so that when Gladys, the second to arrive, came on the scene Anne was already there, apparently trying to open the study door. Suppose further that instead of trying to open the door, Anne had just been closing it! Had Anne committed the murder, run out into the hall, and locked the door behind her?

French transferred his attention to this door. Here it would have been possible to pass a cord beneath it. The door had no saddle, and there was a space of over quarter of an inch between it and the floor, a space left to enable it to ride over the carpet.

But a short examination convinced French that to lock this door from the outside was also impossible. In the first place the lock was very stiff. It had evidently been but seldom used and it required a strong effort to turn the key. No wire pushed through the handle could possibly have done it. A very strong apparatus would have been necessary, which would probably have bent the key rather than turned it. Such an apparatus, moreover, would have left marks on the handle.

There were no such marks, nor were there marks on the small end of the barrel, where the forceps-like tool might have been applied. French, however, was satisfied that the lock was too stiff to have been turned by the forceps. Anyone using such a tool would have taken care to have the lock well oiled beforehand.

French sat down and wiped his forehead. Here was an unexpected dilemma. When he had once satisfied himself that Grinsmead could not have fired the pistol, he saw that some one must have left the room. He took it for granted that it would be easy to find out how this had been done. But now he was being forced to the conclusion that no one had left the room!

And yet some one must have done so.

It was a long time since French had felt so badly up against it. He was being forced to a conclusion which he knew to be false! Whimsically he wished for the skill of the White Queen in *Alice*, who sometimes believed as many as six impossible things before breakfast! Then he grew serious again, and fumbling for his pipe, slowly filled and lit it.

But My Lady Nicotine on this occasion failed him dismally. Though he spent nearly three hours pondering over the problem, he ended up no nearer a solution than when he began.

After consultation with Godfrey, French went to Maidstone prison and obtained a voluntary statement from Irene Holt-Lancing as to her movements on the night of the murder. But from this he learned nothing. She simply repeated what her husband had already told him.

The tempers of both French and Godfrey grew shorter, and even Chief Constable Oliver wore an anxious look. But their distress didn't alter the situation.

Godfrey was terribly worried about Irene. In the state of his existing knowledge he couldn't proceed against her on the charge of murdering Grinsmead. Her counsel would simply put it to the jury that as Irene couldn't have got out of the study after firing the shot, she could never have been in it. Godfrey couldn't reply to this argument, because he didn't know the answer. If he did not at once release her he would have to proceed on the original charge of complicity in the murder of Sybil. But in this also the Crown case was lamentably weak. Godfrey would have preferred to proceed on a second charge: of Grinsmead's murder.

"French, we can't stultify ourselves now and say it was suicide," he said one evening. "As a matter of fact we know it wasn't suicide. We have a good case for a second charge against the prisoner. She had one of the strongest motives extant. She had been heard threatening to murder the deceased. She vanished mysteriously at the time the crime was being committed. She told a fairy tale to account for her absence. She used a method in the murder to which she had been party in the previous crime. There is a convincing case against her; I am satisfied myself that she is guilty; but we can never prove it until we show how she could have got out of that confounded room. Curse it all, French, we must find that out somehow."

French realised all this as well as the super, but he had nothing to reply. That was the way things were and that was all there was to it.

Then at last some fresh news came in, and when he had received it Godfrey at least wished he hadn't.

A young farm labourer named Fogwill called at the station and said he had some information for the police. He had been in bed for some days with an attack of flu and had only that afternoon heard of the police circulars about a lady on the roads.

It appeared that he was engaged to the daughter of a neighbour. This girl lived along one of the roads mentioned in the circular. On the night in question they had been for a walk and Fogwill had seen her home. She lived, it appeared, within a few hundred yards of the clump of bushes mentioned. Fogwill's way home led past the clump. It happened that at the place there was a track of grass alongside the road, and Fogwill walked on this. His footsteps therefore made no noise. Just as he reached the clump, a figure crept from behind it. It was that of a woman, and there was something so stealthy about her movements that Fogwill stopped to see what would happen. But she simply regained the road and set off rapidly towards the main road, that was, in the direction of The Laurels.

There was a partial moon and Fogwill could see her fairly distinctly. He described her build and walk, and his description might have applied to Irene. He did not follow her, but waited till she was out of sight. He did not see anyone else. The time, he believed, was just half-past ten.

It was with feelings approaching dismay that French and Godfrey recognised what this evidence was going to mean to their case. Practically it cleared Irene, at least of the second charge, the charge which Godfrey had hoped to proceed on.

Irene was then innocent of the murder of Grinsmead, but was she innocent of complicity in Sybil's? There was no reason to suppose so. The evidence against her on this charge remained just as strong as before. Yet Godfrey could not see his way clear. The evidence seemed too strong to release her, yet scarcely strong enough to get a conviction.

French shared Godfrey's perplexity, though the responsibility was Godfrey's alone. The case, indeed, was becoming one of those puzzling conundrums which constitute one of the many worries of the police officer's life.

20

ILLUMINATION

The knowledge that Irene Holt-Lancing was innocent of the murder of Grinsmead admittedly solved one of French's problems, but it left the original one untouched: Who, then, was guilty?

For the *n*th time French went over his list of possibles. As he did so he gradually became more and more impressed with the strength of the *a priori* case against Randal Holt-Lancing. The man occupied the standard position of the triangle murderer. Grinsmead had taken advantage of his absence at sea to undermine his home. Many a man had paid with his life for what Grinsmead had done. Many a man in Holt-Lancing's position had turned to murder as the only way of balancing the situation. Why should Holt-Lancing not have done so too?

There was certainly here an adequate motive. Was there an equally satisfactory opportunity?

Not, French saw, if the alibi were sound. If the man was in a taxi driving to his home at the hour at which the crime took place, he must be innocent.

But was the alibi sound? Was Holt-Lancing in a taxi at the hour of the crime?

Turning the dilemma over in his mind, French went back to Maidstone and had another interview with Rose Unwin.

She had mentioned a number of hours at which certain events had taken place on the night of Grinsmead's death; from what timepiece had she taken these hours?

From the hall clock at The Laurels, Rose explained. And how had she known the clock was correct? Might it not have been quarter of an hour or more fast?

Rose said not. She knew the clock was right for two reasons. First, it was with the BBC time signal. She had a set in the kitchen and she had heard the time signal at nine o'clock that night. Besides, she had checked up her wrist watch with the time signal and it was with the clock both that night and the next day.

French then turned to his second question. She had known that her mistress and Mr Grinsmead were lovers: had Captain Holt-Lancing known it?

Here Rose was not so dogmatic. She couldn't tell whether he had or not; not for sure. But she had a strong suspicion that he did know. Why did she think so? She thought so for two reasons, and when French heard them he recognised that his journey had not been wasted.

The first reason was that Holt-Lancing and Irene had had a serious quarrel. When the captain had come home he had been extraordinarily glad to see his wife. But about a week after his arrival they had had this quarrel. Rose did not know what it was about, but she had heard them going for one another in the drawing-room. Their voices had been raised so that she had heard them in the kitchen. She had slipped into the hall in the hope of hearing more, but they had quieted down again. But their manner to one another had entirely changed from that moment. After it they had avoided one another and become cold and distant.

Rose's second reason was the captain's manner on his arrival home on the fatal night. When he went into the sitting-room and found that Irene wasn't there, he had called to Rose to know where she was. While she was replying, his manner was offhand and normal, but when she mentioned Grinsmead's name as having sent the message, he suddenly looked like thunder, seized his coat and rushed out.

French saw that here was practical proof that Holt-Lancing had not only known his wife's weakness, but had been overwhelmed with sudden fury against her betrayer. If it hadn't been for the two points, the locked door and the alibi, French would have considered it a foregone conclusion that Holt-Lancing was his man.

French felt that he had little to be proud of in the affair. He had interrogated Rose Unwin on two previous occasions, and on each he had missed getting this important information. Of course on those he had been obsessed with the belief in Irene's guilt and this had doubtless blinded him to other considerations. However, that was but little excuse for his lack of thoroughness.

Travelling back in the train to Ashbridge, French set himself once again to consider the problem. He did not place much weight on the matter of the locked door, because that difficulty obtained whoever was guilty. In spite of his failure up to the present, he believed sooner or later he would be bound to find out how that part of the affair had been worked. No, it was the alibi which settled Holt-Lancing's fate.

In attacking a problem of the kind, the first step was invariable: the separation of what was known from what was believed. French therefore began on these lines.

The known points in the alibi were: first, that Holt-Lancing was at Crosswell & Hergesheimer's in the Strand at 6.30; second, that according to the taximan, he drove from Ashbridge West Station to The Laurels at some time between 9.45 and 10.15; third, that according to the hall clock he reached The Laurels at 10.20.

The believed, but unproved points were: first, that Holt-Lancing had travelled by the 8.40 from Victoria (which was known to arrive on time at 10.5); second, that he at once took the taxi from the station. If these last points were true, he was in the taxi at 10.15, the hour of the crime.

At this point it occurred to French that perhaps he was building on a foundation of sand. Did the murder take place at 10.15? Was there an error in the clocks at Frayle?

For a moment this seemed a likely theory, then French saw that there was nothing in it. The hour of the crime had been checked, adequately checked, and by nothing more nor less than the superintendent's watch. Allowing for the few minutes which elapsed between the sound of the shot and the calling of the police – as stated by the inmates of Frayle and as necessarily true – the hour of the call just worked in.

What was not proved was that Holt-Lancing dined at the Trieste. Suppose, instead of doing so, he had taken an earlier train down? Could he not have waited about Ashbridge and driven home early enough to have committed the murder?

Suppose he had gone by the 7.25 from Victoria, reaching Ashbridge at 8.53? Suppose he had vanished, say, into a lavatory till about 9.45 and then taken his taxi? If so, he could have reached Frayle by 10.15.

This looked hopeful. Then French went a step further. Holt-Lancing could scarcely have left the station alone; to do so would have been suspicious. It would have suggested that he had not really just arrived by train. Now a train came in from Lewes at 9.49. What was to prevent Holt-Lancing mixing with the passengers from that train and so pretending he had arrived by it? A remark to the taximan might convey the suggestion that he had arrived from London.

Granted that the taximan could have made such a mistake – and from his statement it seemed possible – this would meet the facts until Holt-Lancing's arrival at The Laurels. What about the clocks there?

To carry out the fraud, the clocks would have had to be advanced from fifteen to twenty minutes. How could this have been done?

In one way, French thought, and in one way only. Suppose Irene were a party to the affair? Suppose Irene had altered the clocks between nine and ten so as to work in with the alibi her husband was preparing? Suppose after the arrest, probably during the night, Holt-Lancing had moved them back again?

French had to confess to himself that this did not seem likely. If Irene had been her husband's confederate she would never have gone off to the clump. There would have been no need. But then, there was that confounded message from Grinsmead. Curse it, that didn't seem to work in. French considered it for a long time and was finally forced to the conclusion that the assumption that Irene and her husband were conspirators did not seem tenable.

Then another idea occurred to him which seemed much more promising. Suppose Holt-Lancing had travelled down by that 7.25 from Victoria, arrived at Ashbridge at 8.53, *and gone out at once to The Laurels*? Suppose he had let himself in softly and himself altered the clocks? He could then have returned to Ashbridge and mingled with the crowd coming from the Lewes train at 9.49.

French felt that at last he was making progress. A few more steps of this kind and he would have his solution.

At the kernel of the problem remained the question: At what hour did Holt-Lancing leave Ashbridge in the taxi? If French could only settle that beyond possibility of doubt, he would be near the end of the case.

He put away his papers and walked down again to the station. His friend the taximan was there, and French called him aside.

"It's of the utmost importance that we find out what time you left the station that night," he explained. "A man's life may depend on our making no mistake. Now I want to see if we can do better than the last time and I'm going to ask you some further questions. Do your best to answer them."

French then began to make a timetable of the man's whole evening. He had had a fare about seven o'clock and he had arrived back at the station at quarter to eight. Then there had been the episode of driving Captain Holt-Lancing out to The Laurels, after which the man had returned to the station and had waited till the arrival of the last train from Town, as was his usual custom. French got nothing on these lines, but another question, asked more or less by chance, brought a startling reply. It was a repeat of a question he had put in his original examination, but whereas the driver could not then answer it, he was now able. Asked as to the conditions obtaining when Holt-Lancing engaged the taxi, he said that a number of people were leaving the station, as if a train had just arrived. But it was when French pressed him as to whether he had not recognised any of these persons, that he gave the unexpected reply. Though he had forgotten it before, he now remembered that he had seen Mr Hugh Templeton, a local stationer, among the crowd.

Here at last was something decisive. Without delay French was driven to Mr Templeton's establishment.

Templeton was an intelligent-looking man, who seemed quite clear as to his facts. He remembered the evening in question. He had been in Town and had returned to Ashbridge by the train leaving Victoria at 8.40. Moreover, he knew Captain Holt-Lancing, who had been in his shop ordering a certain pamphlet on shipping matters. He had seen the captain both at Victoria and at Ashbridge. Oh, yes, he was sure of it. He was prepared to go into the box and swear that the captain had travelled by that train.

French's theory of an earlier departure from the station had now gone west. What had been done? Something to the clocks at The Laurels, he dared swear, for he remained convinced of Holt-Lancing's guilt. But what? For the life of him he couldn't imagine.

He sat down once more at his desk, and taking out his notebook continued his work. He went on till he had visualised once again the entire happenings in the case, but no inspiration came to cheer him. He was, however, considerably annoyed to find that in spite of all his care, two points remained still not completely cleared up. Of these, the first was trifling, quite immaterial to the case, but upsetting because the mere fact that it existed proved inefficiency on his part. At this stage of the inquiry no doubt should remain as to any of the facts.

The point was in connection with Grinsmead's rolling up of the cord outside Sybil's room. Edith had seen the cord by the light of her torch, which had shone on Grinsmead's back and past him on to the wall near Sybil's door. Had this light suddenly appeared on a previously dark wall, Grinsmead must inevitably have seen it. As he did not do so, it followed that the wall must already have been illuminated by Grinsmead's own torch, which was the only other light available. Now here was the point which was not clear to French. Had Grinsmead's torch been placed on the table outside Sybil's room, and had its beam been directed on to Grinsmead's hands, it could not have shone on this wall. Its beam would rather be turned away from it. The table could not therefore on that night have been outside Sybil's door. It must have been on Edith's side of the corridor, when its beam would have shone in the desired direction. French's self-esteem was hurt because he had not seen this point at the time and had taken the position of the table for granted instead of getting Edith to confirm it.

The second of the two points, however, was more important. Here he had been guilty of a quite definite omission. He had forgotten to find out whether anything could be made of the Frayle clocks. The presumed confirmation of Godfrey's watch might be only apparent. If there had been even a slight error in the hour of Grinsmead's death, it might throw a new light on the situation. This was a matter which should be cleared up at once. French accordingly rang up Frayle to know whether if he went out then and there he could see all the inmates.

Gladys replied. She explained that Anne and Edith had that day taken the children to an aunt at Bognor Regis and that they would not be back till dinner time. French said that if convenient he would go out about nine that evening.

He turned back to the case. He *must* get further light on it. He felt at an utter deadlock, but as he looked back on all the similar situations he had faced in the past, he picked up heart. Again and again he had been up against what had seemed utterly insoluble problems, and invariably – well, perhaps not invariably, but again and again – he had found the solution. Frequently, indeed usually, it had suddenly leaped into his mind, practically complete. What had then most puzzled him was how he had even for a moment failed to see it.

He returned to the question of the locked room. On his desk he made a model of it – rows of matches for the walls, squares of matches for the tables and chairs. He looked up books containing notes of all the ways in which locks could be tampered with. He put that phase of the problem aside. He concentrated on motives; who could have had a motive for doing what? He made lists of all the people in the case and of all the possible motives for the crimes and tried to connect the two. He paced the room. He drank strong coffee...

Then suddenly a fresh idea flashed into his mind. A quite ordinary idea it seemed at first. But as he thought over it other facts occurred to him, and a suddenly rising excitement took possession of him. What was this that he had thought of? What was it? It couldn't be, no, it couldn't be – *the solution*?

He sprang to his feet and began once again to pace the room. He felt actually breathless. Was it possible that at last he had reached the truth of all these terrible happenings? That he now understood the mystery of the locked room? That he now knew what Holt-Lancing had done? For the matter of that, that he now knew what everyone in the entire case had done? That he could guess all about the message sent to Irene? That he had all the evidence he wanted about the death of Sybil? Was it possible that he had all this?

The more be thought about it the greater grew his elation. Yes, he had it! This new theory was consistent. It accounted for all the facts. There could be no doubt that it was the truth. And what was better still, absolute proof should be easy to obtain!

With difficulty French controlled his excitement. This would be something more than a *coup* for him! It would, he thought, be the best thing he had ever done. In other cases, perhaps as difficult, he had no doubt reached a solution, but here he had done better. He had reached it while the other experts on the case had failed. Godfrey had known every bit as much as he had, and Godfrey had not solved it. Surely now in the face of this, that chief inspectorship, when it was vacant...Certainly French felt he deserved it more than anyone else he knew. And Markham was getting on in years...Besides, since that business in the Channel he felt that Sir Mortimer Ellison thought a good deal more of him...

French pulled himself up with a jerk. This would never do. Too much elation usually meant that something vital had been overlooked. Even if he had got his solution, he hadn't got his proof. He was not out of the wood. Let him go on with the work that was still to be done.

Controlling his eagerness, he sat down once more and made a detailed statement of his views. Then he went in and put the result before Superintendent Godfrey.

PART 5

As Anne Day Saw It

21

NEMESIS

That same day on which French got his great idea was the day before the break-up at Frayle. Mrs Meakin had already left, and next morning the others were to follow. Mrs Grinsmead was returning to her home near Frome. Edith and Anne had that day taken the children to an aunt at Bognor Regis, and tomorrow Edith would go to see about a possible situation at Reading, while Anne would return to her old boarding-house in London. Gladys was leaving for some unknown destination. The house had not been sold, but a "party" was in negotiation about it and the agent believed he would come to terms.

Anne and Edith were having their last conversation in Anne's room after the supper which had lately taken the place of dinner. As was inevitable, their talk was tinged with sadness. A period, eventful in both their lives, was coming to an end; a period, had it not been for these awful tragedies, which would perhaps have been the happiest they had ever enjoyed; a period, because of the tragedies, which had brought them closer to one another than they would have imagined possible.

Anne had nothing in view and Edith was doubtful about the suitability of the Reading job. They had for some time been searching the advertisement columns of the daily papers, and had indeed replied to many of the notices they saw, but up to the present without satisfactory result.

The talk had touched on a variety of subjects, principally the prospects of getting suitable work, but now it turned back to the tragedies, and particularly to that last terrible evening when, as they thought, Grinsmead had shot himself.

"You know," Anne was saying as she sat waiting for the kettle to boil for their evening cup of tea, "it's strange beyond belief, the whole affair. If ever there was a clear case of suicide, you might say this was it. And yet the police keep on endlessly inquiring and inquiring and inquiring. What on earth can be in their mind?"

"Heaven knows. I suppose they must earn their keep. If there's nothing for them to do, they must invent something."

"French did not give me that idea," Anne returned. "He struck me as a man with a definite aim. No fool, he seemed, and quite straight and honest too."

Edith made a gesture of impatience. "You make me tired, Anne. If the devil were to come to you, you'd find him an honourable gentleman. Why on earth you bother to give everybody an imaginary halo beats me."

"Don't be an ass, Edith. I do nothing of the kind. French gave me the idea of working on some quite definite idea, and why shouldn't I say so? There was nothing vague about him that I could see."

"Just his job. It's his business to give people that impression."

"Nonsense, Edith. It's more than that. You don't suppose, do you," her voice sank, "that they could possibly think it was murder?"

Edith moved irritably. "Murder?" she repeated crossly. "How could it have been? What nonsense you do talk, Anne."

"You don't know that it's nonsense, Edith. We would have said that it was nonsense to suspect murder in Sybil's case, and look how it turned out."

"Sybil's case! But Sybil's case was quite different." Edith jerked herself about impatiently. "If you can't talk sense, do for goodness' sake talk about something else. I'm fed up. I'm sick to tears of the whole horrid business. What is it to us whether it was suicide or murder? We'll be quit of it tomorrow and I for one never want to hear the subject mentioned again as long as I live."

Edith's nerves had grown more and more on edge during these last few days. She must, Anne thought, have more real feeling in her than she pretended. Anne was deeply distressed for her two employers, however their lives had ended, but in spite of her hard manner, Edith seemed more distressed still. Anne liked her for it. Then she realised once more, as she had frequently realised in the past, that what Edith was upset about was herself. It was this losing of her job and the search for a new one that was weighing on her mind. Well, no wonder! As Anne thought of her own case, she shivered.

But for once Edith returned to the subject. "As you know so much about French," she said unpleasantly, "why do you think he suspects murder?"

Anne hesitated. "I don't think so," she answered, "at least not definitely. All I meant to say was that his inquiries seemed directed to some definite object. If he was satisfied that it was suicide, why should he go on making these inquiries?"

"What I say: to make work for himself. Besides, his inquiries were natural enough."

"Oh, no, Edith, they weren't. Take that last day he was here. You were in Ashbridge, but I told you about it. He spent, I suppose, three hours working at the study doors. I noticed him at the French window when I was bringing in the tennis things from the pavilion, and several times later I saw him at the door from the hall to the study."

"You never told me anything of the kind."

"I thought I had. But what could he have been doing?"

"How do I know? I'm not in his confidence. What do you think yourself, if you're so well up in it?"

"Ask me something easier, Edith. But I'll tell you what I thought: that he was trying to find out whether anyone could have got out through either of the doors."

"Do you mean that somebody walked through a locked door?" Edith asked with elaborate politeness, "or that he locked it behind him, leaving the key on the other side?"

Anne leaned forward, picked up the now boiling kettle, filled the teapot, and turned back to Edith. "As a matter of fact," she said in a lower tone, "I half imagined French thought I had been in the room. Got out through the door somehow, instead of coming downstairs as I said."

Edith seemed startled. "You never did, Anne?" she said scornfully. " 'Pon my soul, you are the limit. So he thinks you're a murderess, does he? I declare you've got an obsession about murder. It makes you a nice cheery companion, doesn't it?"

Anne felt annoyed. "What on earth's the matter with you, Edith?" she retorted. "I can't say a thing that's right. What is it?"

Edith snorted contemptuously. "You fool, there's nothing wrong. I'm about fed up; that's all. And when you began

298

about a fresh murder on the top of all that's happened, it just seemed to put the lid on everything."

"But, Edith, you're quite wrong. I never thought of murder till lately, till all these inquiries started. And what matter about it anyway?"

But Edith seemed unable to control herself. "That's a lie," she retorted. "You're trying to deceive me. Wasn't murder the very first thing you thought of when you heard the shot? 'Oh God, not another murder!' Wasn't that what you cried when you found the study door locked? You had murder in your mind from the very start. It had nothing to do with French's questions."

Anne was surprised at her vehemence. "Do be reasonable," she answered. "You know you're talking non-sense. I may have thought that before I knew the circum-stances, but directly I learned what had really happened I knew that my first idea was wrong. Besides, as I say, what does it matter? Don't let's quarrel on our last evening."

"I'm sure I don't want to quarrel," Edith returned sulkily. She paused, then went on: "I tell you, Anne, my nerves have all gone to shreds. You mustn't mind what I said. I didn't really mean it, of course. If you – "

She broke off. Anne was not paying attention. Anne was staring at her in a puzzled way.

Anne indeed was a good deal puzzled. That remark that she had made; it was really an involuntary prayer: "Oh God, not another murder!" When had she made it? She recalled to her mind the events of that tragic evening. It required no effort; every item was burnt too deeply into her memory possibly to forget it. She had heard the shot and run down. She had reached the study, followed by Gladys. They had tried the door and called on Grinsmead to open. She had sent Gladys for Hersey. Left alone, she had for a moment felt sick, almost faint. It was then that she had made this involuntary cry; while Gladys was away.

Resolutely she went over the details in her mind. Yes, she had used those words when she was alone. And she had not repeated them to anyone.

How did Edith know?

Anne shook herself. What had gone wrong with her? Edith was right. She was getting obsessions.

"How did you know what I said?" she asked curiously.

Edith moved uneasily. She did not immediately reply, then in a somewhat strained voice she answered: "You silly old ass, Anne. You told me yourself; that evening after it happened. Don't you remember?"

Anne was still slightly puzzled. "I had forgotten," she murmured.

She sat thinking. She could recall that conversation in the evening. Yes, she remembered it in every detail. And she had *not* repeated her exclamation! She was certain, positive beyond any possibility of doubt.

Then how had Edith known?

Edith, of course, couldn't have heard it. She was in her bath at the time. She didn't come down for another four or five minutes. How had she known?

Anne's surroundings slowly faded away as her mind became filled with the problem. She lost consciousness of her pleasant room with its cheery fire, of the mellow light of her shaded lamp, of the bright wallpaper, of her half-packed portmanteau. She lost consciousness even of Edith, sitting there at the other side of the fire, as she had sat on so many previous occasions. Never had Anne been so absorbed in her thoughts.

Where in the house was her remark audible? In the hall, yes. On the lower flight of stairs, yes. But both these places had been within her view at the time, and she had seen that neither Edith nor anyone else was there.

With a feeling of irrational thankfulness Anne realised that she had not been overheard. Somehow, at some time, she must have repeated the words...

Then like a physical shock another idea leaped into her mind. She was wrong about the impossibility of over-hearing her words. There was another place at which that remark would have been audible. *Inside the study door!*

With a numbing horror creeping over her, Anne continued her reconstruction of the scene. Gladys had returned with Hersey. The door had been burst open. It had swung widely back. They had run in. For a moment they had stood in a line, looking down on Grinsmead. And then Edith arrived. Anne remembered now that she had neither heard nor seen her come. On the study carpet she would not have expected to hear Edith's mules, but what about the hall tiles?

Anne realised that in her absorption she might well have failed to hear sounds in the hall. And yet...She could not rid her mind of the dreadful question, Was Edith behind the door when it was burst open?

No, no, no, it couldn't be! She shook herself. And then she looked across at Edith and suddenly, in a ghastly flash of enlightenment, she knew. More than that, she saw that Edith realised that she knew.

Anne could have screamed from sheer horror as she gazed, as if hypnotised, at Edith's expression. There sat, not the quiet, rather hard, and more than rather self-centred Edith Cheame, but a fiend, a devil in human form. For moments which seemed like an eternity they sat facing each other, while Anne felt that she was looking down into a suddenly uncovered abyss of human evil, more appalling than she could have imagined. Then Edith's eyes dropped. She swung round and flung herself face downwards into the back of her chair. Presently she began to sob, terrible slow sobs, as if at each her heart would be torn out.

Anne felt frozen. She could not move. Such horror as she had never conceived possible gripped her, both mind and body.

Presently Edith began to speak.

"Oh," she cried in a desperate, strangled voice, "it's come! It's come! I knew it must come sooner or later. And I'm almost glad! I was going mad, Anne. I had no idea what it would be like. I don't want to live. I couldn't live with this on my mind. It's a relief. It's actually a relief."

Anne did not reply. She couldn't. Edith went on.

"Of course you won't speak to me now, Anne, but you must let me speak to you. You must let me tell you. Then you can ring up French and I'll make a formal confession. I'll give them no more trouble. Let me tell you, Anne. You must! You must!" She turned and gazed imploringly at Anne.

As Anne stared at the wretched woman's twisted, anguished face, she felt a sudden pang of pity. This unhappy Edith had sinned, terribly: but she was going to pay, terribly also. She forced herself to speak.

"What do you want to say, Edith?"

But Edith seemed unable to begin. Once again the slow sobs racked her. Then suddenly confession poured from her.

"Yes," she almost panted, "it's true. You've guessed. I killed him. And I killed her. Oh, Anne, be thankful for one thing; that you've never loved! There's no hell like that. I loved Grinsmead more than my life. I thought he was fond of me. I was sure he was fond of me. But Sybil was in the way. Sybil, who hated me. I didn't hesitate. I killed her. Yes, Anne, you never guessed. It was I who did that. I killed her, thinking it would be put down to suicide. And I wasn't sorry. I wanted her dead!... And then afterwards – when I let him know how I felt – he – he spurned me. Spurned me with loathing as if I'd been a leper. Then I guessed about that – Irene Holt-Lancing. My love was turned into bitter hate. I felt I couldn't breathe the same air with him. I couldn't live if he lived. I told French I'd seen him in the corridor. I wanted him to die."

She paused, threw her hands despairingly in the air, then once more the flood of words poured uncontrollably out.

"Then he guessed. Grinsmead guessed – everything. He called me down to ask me questions. That was when I told you he was thinking of sending the children to Bournemouth. I told him I was innocent, but that I could prove who was guilty if he would let me get the evidence. I had thought it all out beforehand. I came back to you and made up that fake about the bath. Presently I went down again. I shot him. Oh, Anne, I did it, I did it! Then I locked the door. I stood behind it till you burst it open. I knew you would be looking at the body and wouldn't see where I came from. And now it's all no good! I've lost! Oh, God, I've lost!"

The words ceased as if Edith suddenly found she had no power to go on. She seemed on the verge of a collapse as she sat staring piteously at Anne. Then once more she burst into those awful sobs. "A drink," she cried faintly.

It was what Anne wanted herself. Without a word she poured out the tea – the two cups just as she would have done had things remained normal. It had grown black from standing, and she stooped again over the fireplace to get the kettle to add water. But Edith would not wait. When Anne raised herself she was pouring in the cream and she at once began swallowing down hers in great gulps.

Anne added water to her cup, but it was still bitter, and again she added water. All this water from the boiling kettle made it too hot, and she sat waiting for it to cool, while Edith continued to enlarge on her terrible tale.

Anne shrank appalled from what was to follow. She would have to ring up the police. How could she bring herself to do it?

Just then there came a knock at the door. Gladys came in. She seemed flurried and upset. She explained that Inspector French had rung up that he was coming out at nine that night and that she had completely forgotten to mention it. And now he was here and was asking for Miss Cheame.

"Yes, Miss Cheame," said a voice, and French himself appeared at the door, a uniformed constable looming in the corridor behind, "I'm sorry to say I have a very unpleasant duty to perform – "

Edith, a look of ghastly terror on her face, stared at him like a trapped animal. Then she screamed. Anne thought she would never get the sound of that scream out of her ears. Before anyone could move, Edith had swung round, seized Anne's cup of tea, and drained it at a draught.

"Stop her!" yelled French, leaping across the room. "My God, we're too late!"

Edith looked at him with a sort of despairing defiance. "Potassium cyanide. Got it for killing wasps. I've carried it for weeks." She nodded at Anne and tried to speak, but couldn't.

French swung round on Anne. "Have you drunk any, Miss Day? Hold Miss Cheame," he cried to the constable, and dashed out. A moment later Anne heard him telephoning urgently for the doctor.

Then Anne collapsed and everything merged into a confused dream. Edith disappeared. People came in and out. Someone gave her a mustard emetic. She was deadly sick. She lost consciousness. She was in bed. The doctor appeared at intervals. She was desperately ill; she was dying. She lay helpless it seemed for days and weeks. Then gradually she grew better. She was going to live.

It was not until she was convalescent that she learned the remaining details of the tragedy. When she was considered able to see him, French called to get her statement of that last dreadful conversation with Edith.

"You had a pretty narrow escape, Miss Day," he said. "Another couple of sips would have done it. There was enough poison in that cup of tea to have killed a dozen men."

"And Miss Cheame?" Anne faltered.

French shook his head. "What happened was best for the poor lady," he said gently. "We tried to save her, but the dose was too strong."

For a moment Anne remained silent. Then, "How did you find out?" she asked, and French, contrary to his usual custom, explained.

His idea was evolved from that difficulty about the lights in the corridor which he had noticed in Edith's story. He had realised on thinking the matter over, that the light-coloured wall in front of Grinsmead could not suddenly have been lit up by Edith's torch, as Grinsmead would then have noticed it, but must have been previously illuminated by Grinsmead's own torch, the only other source of light available. From this he had deduced that the table on which

Grinsmead's torch was placed must have been, not where he had usually observed it, outside Sybil's door, but on the opposite side of the corridor, beside Edith's door. That at first had seemed to meet the difficulty. But on thinking still further over it, he had seen that the light shining thus from behind Grinsmead would have left his hands in shadow. Instinctively the man would have turned round, or partially round, the better to see what he was doing. But if he had turned even a little way round, he would have noticed Edith's torch.

At first sight the matter looked like a misunderstanding, but as French considered it he found himself forced to the conclusion that Edith's statement did not clearly cover the facts.

Had Edith then lied? To French it began to look as if the whole episode might be an invention in which Edith had made a mistake in one of the details.

Reserving judgment on the point, French went on to see how such a suggestion would work in with the remainder of the case. Then suddenly another idea occurred to him. If Edith had invented the episode, how did she know about the cord?

Here at once was a fundamental point. Edith knew about the cord. Therefore one of two things followed; either her statement about Grinsmead was the exact truth and he, French, had misunderstood her about the light, *or else she herself must be guilty of Sybil's murder.*

This was an entirely new viewpoint. At first French did not take the idea seriously, but as he turned it over in his mind, suspicious details began to occur to him. Edith might well have been the purchaser of the clock spring. She was of the right height and build. Yes, and Edith – French cursed himself for not having thought of it before – Edith might have been the woman Hersey saw. Again she was the right height and build. Edith moreover would have known of the barrel as a good place to hide the spring. Yes, and Edith –

Suddenly French saw another point, a point which lit up the whole dreadful tragedy as the turning on of electric lights illumines a dark room. Edith, and only Edith, could have shot Grinsmead! She was the only person who could have done it without passing out through those locked doors!

It was at this stage that French had had his burst of optimism about the chief inspectorship, after which he settled down to put on paper his new view of the crime.

Though the case as he had himself reconstructed it proved fairly correct, a few details had to be modified as a result of the statement which Edith Cheame had made to Anne before she died. Finally it stood as follows:

Edith, unhappily for all those at Frayle, had fallen desperately in love with Grinsmead and she imagined, mistakenly as it turned out, that he loved her. She had early begun to scheme to marry him. But Sybil stood in the way, and Sybil she decided must die.

Cold-bloodedly Edith had made her plan. Her work with her father had given her the necessary knowledge to evolve it, as well as the mechanical ability to carry it out. Then she had got together her apparatus. In buying the clock spring she had made herself up as an old woman, probably only as a safeguard, but possibly that if suspicion were aroused it would fall on Mrs Grinsmead.

On the fatal evening she had lit the fire in Sybil's room and in some unknown way – the only part of her plan which never came out – had got Sybil to turn it off again. Before taking her hand at bridge she had shut the windows, fixed the pad and spring in the gas fire, turned on the gas tap with a pair of pincers, led the cord out of the room beneath the door, and left the end under the mat in the corridor. She had faked the headache to account for her leaving her room during the night, should this become known.

First it was necessary to make sure that Sybil really had been given a sleeping draught. If Sybil were to awake and smell gas it would mean the end for Edith. This Edith managed by asking Anne for a draught for herself and pumping her as to whether she had given one to Sybil. Next she must be certain that the windows had not been opened, and she slipped out and examined them with her torch, incidentally being seen by Hersey. Then she ate the food in the pantry to back up her tale of the headache. She pulled the cord out from under Sybil's door, thus allowing the gas to escape. The cord she afterwards burnt; the spring she threw into the barrel. All she had then to do was to keep quiet and to register the proper horror and surprise next morning.

So much for the murder of Sybil.

Next had come Grinsmead's repulse of Edith's advances, her sudden hatred of him and her desire to destroy him. She made up the tale about seeing him in the corridor and intended to volunteer it to French. French's interrogation, however, enabled her to get it in without running this risk.

Matters then came suddenly to a head by Grinsmead's suspicion of her guilt. On that terrible night his questions showed her that her secret was hers no longer. She saw that his immediate death was her only hope.

She had worked her plan out beforehand lest the emergency should arise. Knowing by this time of Grinsmead's relations with Irene, she decided to use Irene as a scapegoat, should suspicion be aroused. Naturally she hated Irene almost as much as she hated Grinsmead. Accordingly she sent her message making the appointment at the clump. She still lowered her already deep voice and said she was Grinsmead's partner, whose voice she hoped Irene would not know.

Next she prepared the alibi of the bath. Then putting on her dressing-gown, she went down again to Grinsmead. She had told him that she could prove the identity of the murderer if he would give her quarter of an hour to prepare her statement.

She tricked Grinsmead into leaving his desk by telling him that Sybil had been killed with an "ollophote," and when he asked what that was, suggesting that he should consult his encyclopedia. He got up to do so, thus enabling her to obtain the pistol, which, as part of her general preparation for emergencies, she had made sure was loaded. The existence of this pistol, Anne remembered, was admitted by Grinsmead at the dinner party at which burglaries had been discussed.

As Grinsmead turned back towards his desk Edith shot him. She locked the door – this was evidently what Anne had heard when coming downstairs – wiped the pistol, pressed his fingers on it, laid it at his hand, and placed herself behind the door. She knew she would be hidden between the door and the cabinet. It was then that she heard Anne's exclamation, which her overwrought nerves afterwards led her to reveal so disastrously. When the door was burst open and the others were staring spellbound at Grinsmead, she simply ran forward from behind the door. As she had foreseen, none of them noticed that she had not come through it.

The statements of Irene and Randal Holt-Lancing thus proved true in every particular. Irene had believed the message was indirectly from Grinsmead and had gone to the rendezvous. Randal, arriving home and learning that she had gone out as the result of a call from Grinsmead, was filled with bitter hate. He had followed with the intention of giving Grinsmead the best beating he had ever had in his life, but as already explained, had stopped short at the study window as the result of what he saw through the curtains.

As French later reviewed the case, he thought what a particularly miserable and sordid one it had turned out. And he, French, had not himself shone as he had hoped to do. Through his slowness to realise the truth, he had let the criminal escape the law. Altogether disastrous case.

But when he reached the Yard he revised his opinion. Sir Mortimer Ellison had him in and congratulated him on his exploits, and to this was shortly added an autograph letter in the same strain from the Chief Constable of Ashbridge.

Some weeks later the case was unexpectedly brought back to French's mind. Sent on business to Frome, he met in the main street no less a person than Anne Day. During the inquiry he had formed a high opinion of her, and it was therefore with something more than a casual interest that he learned that she had obtained a congenial job. Old Mrs Grinsmead had been a good deal broken down by the tragic death of her son, and she had implored Anne to go and live with her as her companion and friend. Anne had thankfully agreed, and the very next day, unknown to Anne, Mrs Grinsmead had sent for her solicitor and altered her will so as to include Anne among her legatees.

French's congratulations on her new home were both respectful and hearty.

Freeman Wills Crofts

The Box Office Murders

A girl employed in the box office of a London cinema falls into the power of a mysterious trio of crooks. A helpful solicitor sends her to Scotland Yard. There she tells Inspector French the story of the Purple Sickle. Her body is found floating in Southampton Water the next day. French discovers that similar murders have taken place. After gathering evidence he learns the trio's secret and runs them to ground.

The Hog's Back Mystery

The Hog's Back is a ridge in Surrey and the setting for the disappearance of several locals. A doctor vanishes, followed by a nurse with whom he was acquainted, then a third person. Inspector French deduces murder, but there are no bodies. Eventually he is able to prove his theory and show that a fourth murder has been committed.

'As pretty a piece of work as Inspector French has done...on the level of Mr Crofts' very best; which is saying something.'

E C Bentley in the *Daily Telegraph*

Freeman Wills Crofts

Inspector French's Greatest Case

We are here introduced for the first time to the famous Inspector French. A head clerk's corpse is discovered beside the empty safe of a Hatton Garden diamond merchant. There are many suspects and many false clues to be followed before French is able to solve the crime.

Man Overboard!

In the course of a ship's passage from Belfast to Liverpool a man disappears. His body is picked up by Irish fishermen. Although the coroner's verdict is suicide, murder is suspected. Inspector French co-operates with Superintendent Rainey and Sergeant M'Clung once more to determine the truth.

FREEMAN WILLS CROFTS

MYSTERY IN THE CHANNEL

The cross-channel steamer *Chichester* stops half way to France. A motionless yacht lies in her path. When a party clambers aboard they find a trail of blood and two dead men. Chief Constable Turnbull has to call on Inspector French for help in solving the mystery of the *Nymph*.

MYSTERY ON SOUTHAMPTON WATER

The Joymount Rapid Hardening Cement Manufacturing Company is in serious financial trouble. Two young company employees hatch a plot to break in to a rival works, Chayle on the Isle of Wight, to find out Chayle's secret for underselling them. But the scheme does not go according to plan. The death of the night watchman, theft and fire are the result. Inspector French is brought in to solve the mystery.

OTHER TITLES BY FREEMAN WILLS CROFTS AVAILABLE DIRECT FROM HOUSE OF STRATUS

Quantity	£	$(US)	$(CAN)	€
THE 12.30 FROM CROYDON	6.99	11.50	15.99	11.50
THE AFFAIR AT LITTLE WOKEHAM	6.99	11.50	15.99	11.50
ANTIDOTE TO VENOM	6.99	11.50	15.99	11.50
ANYTHING TO DECLARE?	6.99	11.50	15.99	11.50
THE BOX OFFICE MURDERS	6.99	11.50	15.99	11.50
THE CASK	6.99	11.50	15.99	11.50
CRIME AT GUILDFORD	6.99	11.50	15.99	11.50
DEATH OF A TRAIN	6.99	11.50	15.99	11.50
DEATH ON THE WAY	6.99	11.50	15.99	11.50
ENEMY UNSEEN	6.99	11.50	15.99	11.50
THE END OF ANDREW HARRISON	6.99	11.50	15.99	11.50
FATAL VENTURE	6.99	11.50	15.99	11.50
FEAR COMES TO CHALFONT	6.99	11.50	15.99	11.50
FOUND FLOATING	6.99	11.50	15.99	11.50
FRENCH STRIKES OIL	6.99	11.50	15.99	11.50
GOLDEN ASHES	6.99	11.50	15.99	11.50
THE GROOTE PARK MURDER	6.99	11.50	15.99	11.50
THE HOG'S BACK MYSTERY	6.99	11.50	15.99	11.50
INSPECTOR FRENCH AND THE CHEYNE MYSTERY	6.99	11.50	15.99	11.50

ALL HOUSE OF STRATUS BOOKS ARE AVAILABLE FROM GOOD BOOKSHOPS OR DIRECT FROM THE PUBLISHER:

Internet: **www.houseofstratus.com** including author interviews, reviews, features.

Email: **sales@houseofstratus.com** please quote author, title and credit card details.

OTHER TITLES BY FREEMAN WILLS CROFTS AVAILABLE DIRECT FROM HOUSE OF STRATUS

Quantity		£	$(US)	$(CAN)	€
	INSPECTOR FRENCH AND THE STARVEL TRAGEDY	6.99	11.50	15.99	11.50
	INSPECTOR FRENCH'S GREATEST CASE	6.99	11.50	15.99	11.50
	JAMES TARRANT, ADVENTURER	6.99	11.50	15.99	11.50
	A LOSING GAME	6.99	11.50	15.99	11.50
	THE LOSS OF THE JANE VOSPER	6.99	11.50	15.99	11.50
	MAN OVERBOARD!	6.99	11.50	15.99	11.50
	MANY A SLIP	6.99	11.50	15.99	11.50
	MYSTERY IN THE CHANNEL	6.99	11.50	15.99	11.50
	MURDERERS MAKE MISTAKES	6.99	11.50	15.99	11.50
	MYSTERY OF THE SLEEPING CAR EXPRESS	6.99	11.50	15.99	11.50
	MYSTERY ON SOUTHAMPTON WATER	6.99	11.50	15.99	11.50
	THE PIT-PROP SYNDICATE	6.99	11.50	15.99	11.50
	THE PONSON CASE	6.99	11.50	15.99	11.50
	THE SEA MYSTERY	6.99	11.50	15.99	11.50
	SILENCE FOR THE MURDERER	6.99	11.50	15.99	11.50
	SIR JOHN MAGILL'S LAST JOURNEY	6.99	11.50	15.99	11.50

ALL HOUSE OF STRATUS BOOKS ARE AVAILABLE FROM GOOD BOOKSHOPS OR DIRECT FROM THE PUBLISHER:

Hotline: UK ONLY: **0800 169 1780**, please quote author, title and credit card details. INTERNATIONAL: **+44 (0) 20 7494 6400**, please quote author, title, and credit card details.

Send to: **House of Stratus**
24c Old Burlington Street
London
W1X 1RL
UK

Please allow following carriage costs per ORDER
(For goods up to free carriage limits shown)

	£(Sterling)	$(US)	$(CAN)	€(Euros)
UK	1.95	3.20	4.29	3.00
Europe	2.95	4.99	6.49	5.00
North America	2.95	4.99	6.49	5.00
Rest of World	2.95	5.99	7.75	6.00
Free carriage for goods value over:	50	75	100	75

PLEASE SEND CHEQUE, POSTAL ORDER (STERLING ONLY), EUROCHEQUE, OR INTERNATIONAL MONEY ORDER (PLEASE CIRCLE METHOD OF PAYMENT YOU WISH TO USE)
MAKE PAYABLE TO: STRATUS HOLDINGS plc

Order total including postage:_____Please tick currency you wish to use and add total amount of order:

☐ £ (Sterling)   ☐ $ (US)   ☐ $ (CAN)   ☐ € (EUROS)

VISA, MASTERCARD, SWITCH, AMEX, SOLO, JCB:

☐☐☐☐☐☐☐☐☐☐☐☐☐☐☐☐☐☐☐☐☐☐☐☐

Issue number (Switch only):

☐☐☐

Start Date: **Expiry Date:**

☐☐/☐☐   ☐☐/☐☐

Signature: _____

NAME: _____

ADDRESS: _____

_____

POSTCODE: _____

Please allow 28 days for delivery.

Prices subject to change without notice.
Please tick box if you do not wish to receive any additional information. ☐

House of Stratus publishes many other titles in this genre; please check our website (**www.houseofstratus.com**) for more details